PRAISE FOR WENDY JAMES

"Australia's queen of the domestic thriller . . ."

—Angela Savage, *Books and Writing, ABC Radio*

"A master of suburban sus

The Golden Child

"James makes her thrilling mark in women's fiction with this intense and chilling American debut, offering an in-depth look at motherhood and bullying."

—*Booklist*, starred review

"*The Golden Child* by Wendy James is a next-level thriller that brims with dark surprises and unforgettable characters. Told with pitch-perfect pacing and unrelenting tension, James explores the darkest corners of the human heart in this bone-chilling must-read novel of the year. Clear your calendar—you'll want to read this one straight through."

—Heather Gudenkauf, *New York Times* bestselling author of *The Weight of Silence* and *Not a Sound*

"James invites the reader to consider a set of close relationships in all their intricacy as those involved hurtle towards an inevitable disaster. This is domestic noir at its most intelligent and sharp."

—Sue Turnbull, *Sydney Morning Herald/Melbourne Age*

The Lost Girls

"A wonderful, unputdownable story by a great Australian author."
—Liane Moriarty, *Australian Women's Weekly*

"The novel is nothing less than compelling . . . *The Lost Girls* grabs hold of you and doesn't let go—the sort of book you find yourself still reading long after you intended to put it down. In short, everything you want a novel of this kind to be."
—*Weekend Australian*

"Wendy James has again demonstrated her flair for suspenseful diversion, buttressed by her not inconsiderable literary talent."
—*Australian Book Review*

The Mistake

"*The Mistake* is a moving book that relentlessly hits the mark."
—Sue Turnbull, *Sydney Morning Herald*

"James . . . won the Ned Kelly award for first crime fiction six years ago—and she tells not just a tense and involving story, but also raises important questions about the role of the media, as the missing-baby story becomes a runaway train. *The Mistake*, credible and accomplished, also asks what happens when family members begin to doubt each other, to wonder how well they know each other."
—*The Australian*

"Compelling, well-paced, and suspenseful to the end."
—*Courier Mail*

"Within its suspenseful narrative, *The Mistake* has important things to say about how we think about motherhood, how the media views women, and how, when it comes to 'the natural relationship between mother and daughter,' few can be neutral."

—Linda Funnell, *Newtown Review of Books*

"As in the public narratives we devour with tea and toast in the morning, there is nothing to convict Jodie upon except our own judgment of her character; we relish or condemn her according to our sense of moral distance from her. We take part as armchair jurors, comfortable in our own safety, never suspecting that buried secrets of our own may one day be uncovered."

—*Canberra Times*

"An amazing book that had me hooked from start to finish . . ."

—Great Aussie Reads

"Brilliant, haunting, and disturbing, with a twist that will leave you gasping, this is both a subtle and closely observed portrayal of a family under stress, and a gripping thriller that leaves you guessing to the very end."

—Sophie Masson, author

"It's sneakily challenging, disconcerting, compelling, car-crash fascinating, and probably one of the best fictional reminders I've had in a while that public and media opinion should never be mistaken for the justice system, regardless of the ultimate outcome."

—AustCrimefiction.org

"It's hands down one of the best endings I've read in a book, possibly ever."

—*1girl2manybooks*

Where Have You Been?

"*Where Have You Been?* is a novel you'll not want to put down."
—*Australian Bookseller & Publisher*

"The narrative's power and cumulative suspense call to mind Alfred Hitchcock's *Vertigo*."
—Sara Dowse, *Sydney Morning Herald*

"Wendy James's third novel is structured like a symphony . . . Skillful structuring, fine, flexible writing, and suspense that comes to a satisfying, if not limitingly cut-and-dried conclusion, make this social-realist novel as hard to put down as any thriller."
—Katharine England, *Adelaide Advertiser*

Why She Loves Him

"Emotionally astute, vivid and eloquent, underpinned by eroticism, James's fiction traces the contours of her characters' lives as they grapple with responsibility, freedom, and love, propelled by multifarious desires. These fresh, sensuous stories are by turns witty, perceptive, and coruscating, many with a delicious wry twist."
—Felicity Plunkett, critic

"Absolutely amazing . . . There is something for everyone in this fantastic book."
—*Australian Bookseller & Publisher*

"From single-page tales to the long sequence that ends the book, James's sure hand leads us through sometimes harrowing, sometimes redemptive moments in her beautifully rounded characters' lives."

—*Who* magazine

"A penetrating picture of our life and times . . . a knockout."

—Sara Dowse, *Canberra Times*

"What quiet confidence, what an honest setting down of things as they are, nothing extenuating . . . This is a gifted storyteller and these are unusually arresting stories."

—Robert Lumsden, *Adelaide Review*

Out of the Silence

"A work of intelligence and talent informed by a deeply humane sensitivity . . . If Wendy James aspires to be our national novelist, she is on her way. In equal measures intellectual and sensual, *Out of the Silence* is a brilliantly cut literary gem sparkling from every angle."

—*Sydney Morning Herald*

AN
ACCUSATION

AN
ACCUSATION

A NOVEL

WENDY JAMES

Text copyright © 2019 by Wendy James
All rights reserved.

Originally published by HarperCollins Australia, 2019.

Published by Lake Union Publishing, Seattle

www.apub.com

Amazon, the Amazon logo, and Lake Union Publishing are trademarks of Amazon.com, Inc., or its affiliates.

ISBN-13: 9781542026253
ISBN-10: 1542026253

Cover design by Laywan Kwan

Printed in the United States of America

To my sister, Rebecca, who understands—and shares— the madness.

Ridiculous and contemptible as you are pleased to
consider this Story, it has met with extensive Credit,
and has been espoused with uncommon Ardour by
very many . . . That her Narrative is clogged with
the highest Improbabilities shall be readily admitted;
nevertheless, there are some Circumstances attending
it, that forbid my totally rejecting it,
at least for the present.

—*GENUINE AND IMPARTIAL MEMOIRS OF
ELIZABETH CANNING, CONTAINING
A COMPLETE HISTORY OF THAT
UNFORTUNATE GIRL (1754)*

PART ONE

SUZANNAH: JANUARY 2019

She's everywhere.

Google her name and you'll get over twelve million hits. The first thing you'll see is her Wikipedia entry, detailing her life before, during, and after her abduction. You can follow her on Instagram and like her favorite places to eat, her latest outfits, or whatever #Brand she's currently promoting. You can read her tweets and share her favorite articles, her random thoughts, the occasional video of cute kittens. You can scroll through the numerous images—that first, now almost iconic picture: the desolate little figure, dressed in too-big borrowed clothes, photographed just days after her escape; the pictures taken later, from magazine shoots, interviews, red-carpet appearances; the occasional candid shot taken while she's shopping, heading to the gym, dining out with her hot new boyfriend. You can see her in action on YouTube, talking about her ordeal on morning shows, afternoon shows, highbrow current affairs shows, trash TV with its shocking revelations: "Why I feared for my life and sanity." Of course, they're all careful to adhere to the letter of the law, only discussing her ordeal tangentially and never mentioning me by name. I'm guessing there'll be a role for her on *Mountain Climbing with the Stars* or *Celebrity Fondue*, and eventually, I imagine, she'll end up hosting her very own TV show—*Great Escapes with Ellie Canning*. No doubt there's a Netflix original documentary in production, ready to air the moment the case is settled.

As well as the sites devoted to her case, she's made countless guest appearances on blogs and in magazines. You can discover her favorite designers in *Chic*; her favorite recipes in *Women's Week*; her favorite books (*Jane Eyre, Lemony Snicket, Great Expectations, Harry Potter*—all underdogs, naturally) in *The Chronicle*; her favorite films in the *Global Times*. She seems to have been asked to give her opinion on everything from domestic abuse to P!nk, whom she met during her last tour (front-row seats, backstage passes, invites to the afterparty).

She's on her way to becoming the go-to girl of her generation, a kind of down-market, blonde Malala—her ordeal not as politically interesting but perhaps more relatable, and, of course, far more satisfying for those who like their trauma served up with less politics and more dirt, less high-minded ideals and more sensation.

And naturally, she's the latest feminist pinup. I watch a talk on YouTube she did a few weeks ago. She's speaking at a luncheon in the city, hosted by some big law firm that specializes in taking on high-profile cases for women, pro bono, defending them against workplace harassment, internet bullying, unfair dismissal.

It's a great gig, and I have to hand it to Honor—celebrity agent par excellence—she knows just which buttons to press, where this particular client will shine the brightest. She's the perfect victim *and* the perfect survivor; she's just what the cultural moment ordered.

"I'm here to talk," the girl tells her enraptured audience, "not just about my ordeal but the way my trauma has empowered me." She has her hair scraped back into a severe ponytail, emphasizing her long neck, the small beauty spot just below her pretty ear. If she's wearing any makeup, it's invisible. She doesn't need it anyway—her skin is pale, clear, perfect, with just the faintest sprinkling of freckles across a pert little nose. Her eyebrows are fashionably dark, heavy, her eyelashes are thick and spiky—a fringe around those big blue eyes that gaze so bravely and honestly (windows to the soul!) out into the world. She's a long way from the gaunt waif—dark shadows under her eyes, pale chapped lips, sharpened cheekbones—of her early post-release days.

The way she speaks has changed since those first appearances, too. The shrill of anxiety has gone; her voice is low and melodious and has an appealing breathiness. She looks up frequently from her notes—frowning a little, or perhaps giving a surreptitious bite of the lip to let the audience know that she's appropriately nervous, that she's not taking this attention as her due, even if she's taking it in her stride.

Her words hit the spot. She's not aggressive or dogmatic; if anything, she's disarmingly tentative. "I'm not here to make you feel bad for me," she says. "I don't want to be seen as a victim." She says a few times—indeed, this is her theme—that she has been fortunate. Bad things have happened, but mostly she has been lucky: lucky she was bright and hardworking, lucky she had such great teachers, good mentors, champions . . . She counts herself lucky even when it comes to her more recent history—*that terrible time* she can't say too much about for legal reasons—when she was taken by someone who didn't appear to want to hurt her, at least in the beginning. And of course, she was lucky that she was able—fit, determined, resourceful—to make her escape.

Her lesson is simple, and it's one we can all share, whatever our circumstances: that empowerment can come by looking for opportunities and taking them when we can. "Sometimes," she says, looking down and up simultaneously, à la Princess Diana, "sometimes you just have to wait for that opportunity to arrive. That's what I learned. You have to be prepared, always aware that there will be a moment, even if it looks like nothing can get better, nothing can change, when you can get to somewhere better—whether it's away from parents who aren't there for you, or a school, or a job, or even in the sort of extreme circumstances I was in, you just have to have faith and seize any opportunities you can . . ."

I watch her speech again and again, although not for the sisterhood feels. Even the second time round, the third, and knowing what I know, it's compelling viewing. She's so young, so lovely, so earnest. And so fucking believable.

There should be something that I can see, some sign, a flicker in those beautiful blue eyes, some moment when she falls out of character, when I can say, *Gotcha*. I'm trained, after all, to spot these moments: the random out-of-character licking of lips, idle hair twirling, random blinking, an unscripted step backward or forward, a tone that's not quite authentic. But there's nothing. Her performance is pitch-perfect.

Butter wouldn't melt in this girl's mouth, and I find myself wanting to believe every word that comes out of it.

I feel a vague lick of envy, too. If she's not telling the truth, she's missed her calling, because Ellie Canning is a much finer actress than I'll ever be.

ABDUCTED: THE ELLIE CANNING STORY

A documentary by HeldHostage Productions © 2019

EXTERIOR

Camera pans across the valley town of Enfield Wash, Mount Waltham looming in the distance.

VOICE-OVER

In the early hours of the morning of August 1, 2018, John O'Brien, a dairy farmer from the New South Wales town of Enfield Wash, discovered an unconscious teenage girl in a disused shepherd's hut on his property.

O'Brien immediately contacted the authorities, and the girl, who would subsequently identify herself as Ellie Canning, was taken to the local hospital, where she was treated for shock and hypothermia. On regaining consciousness, Canning told police she had sought shelter in the hut after wandering the countryside for a number of hours after escaping from a nearby farmhouse. Canning claimed she had been abducted by a middle-aged woman she'd met at a central Sydney café and that she had been held captive in a basement room for almost a month.

As the details of her bizarre and sinister experiences were made public, the Canning Affair, as it's known, quickly became a media sensation . . .

SUZANNAH: AUGUST 2018

"It's the pigs."

Mary twitched the kitchen curtains across to peer out into the morning. I was too busy trying to find a pair of tights without a run, or a pair of trousers that didn't need ironing, to respond. Not that there was any reasonable way to respond to this latest off-the-wall pronouncement from my mother. We didn't have any pigs.

I was running late, hair unbrushed, still wearing pajama bottoms and UGG boots, and loath to take off more than I had to until the last minute in the hideous cold. It was a Tuesday, not one of Sally's days, so I had to get everything ready for Mary before I left for work. I'd made sandwiches, cut fruit, poured some lukewarm coffee into a flask, filled a small Tupperware container with Froot Loops, turned the kitchen gas off and the convection heater on. I'd spent precious minutes of the morning forcing myself to eat dry toast and black tea between bouts of retching and now had precisely two minutes to pull it all together and get out the door, or my Year Eight drama class would be teacherless for ten minutes—a catastrophe beyond contemplation.

"The pigs, Suzie." Mary gave a couple of reasonably convincing snorts. "I wonder what they're saying I've done this time."

She pulled the curtain across and turned back to look at me, her eyes bright with mischief. "Maybe it's you they're after. What do you reckon? I always knew they'd catch up with you eventually, Miss Dudley Do-Right. Excuse me—Ms." Her cackling laughter turned into a cough.

"There's no one—" I began, but then I heard the distinct sound of feet crunching over the frosty lawn and creaking across the veranda, the quiet murmur of conversation. Three sharp knocks.

"You were saying, dear daughter?" Mary gave me a triumphant glare and tripped down the hallway, arriving a moment before me and pulling the door open.

It was the police. A woman, uniformed, in her thirties, and a man, older, suited, clearly in charge. They both had their wallets out, IDs displayed.

"Miss Wells? Suzannah Wells?" The man's words were accompanied by puffs of white cloud. The world outside was crisp and clear and covered in ice.

"It's *Miz* Wells, not Miss. What century are you from, Mr. Pig?"

The officer blinked. "Excuse me?"

I pushed past my mother. "I'm Suzannah Wells. Is there something wrong?" The sight of the police at my front door had made my nausea return. I was suddenly unbearably cold, and it wasn't just the weather.

"Ah, no." He glanced at his companion. "There's nothing wrong, not exactly. But we would like to talk to you."

His companion stamped her feet. Her nose and cheeks were pink. "It's a bit on the chilly side out here, ma'am. Do you think we might come in? It won't take long. Just some routine inquiries."

"Routine inquiries, my arse," Mary muttered behind me. "The last time a pig told me—"

"Of course. Please come through."

The officers paused in the entrance as Mary flounced off down the dark hallway, muttering. From behind, her silvery hair caught up in a loose topknot, long dressing gown trailing elegantly along the carpet, she looked like a grande dame in some Edwardian costume drama.

"Alzheimer's?" the female officer whispered, her eyes all empathy, understanding.

"Actually, it's—" I began to explain, then changed my mind, shrugged. "Yes. It's something like that."

In the kitchen the two officers introduced themselves as Detective Inspector Stratford and Senior Constable Moorhouse, then stood awkwardly until I offered them a seat and a cup of tea. They declined the tea but sat down. Constable Moorhouse took off her hat and eased out of her leather jacket. Her shirt gaped where a button was missing, and lacy white nylon underwear peeked through. Mary perched up on the kitchen counter, and although the true condition of her ancient polar-fleece dressing gown was now revealed in all its stained and threadbare glory, she still maintained an air of haughty disdain. The officers watched her warily.

"Will this take long?" I hovered, uncertain. "I should probably ring work first. I'm already running late."

"You're the drama teacher, aren't you?" Constable Moorhouse asked. "At the high school?"

"I am. And I have a Year Eight class first up—they'll need to arrange a replacement."

"Year Eight, eh? That'd be my daughter's year. I don't envy you working with that lot." She grinned, began to say something, but was interrupted by her boss.

"Probably best if you let them know—we'll be as quick as we can, but you're definitely going to be late."

I made the call quickly from the next room and arrived back in time to hear Mary regaling them, in her special-occasion American twang, with the story about the time she was arrested in New York after a weekend of debauchery at the Chelsea Hotel in the company of Lou Reed, among others.

"You're probably too young to know who I'm talking about, aren't you?" She sighed at their failure to look impressed. "And too square. I guess you listen to—"

"Mary, that's enough."

She pursed her lips primly. "Well, no one ever accused me of talking when I shouldn't. Not to the pigs, anyway. And I know you're not going to take any notice of anything I have to say, Ms. Goody Two-shoes, but if I were you, I'd be getting a lawyer."

"I'm sure a lawyer won't be necessary, Mrs. . . ."

"Oh, *I'm* a Miss. Mary Squires. You may have heard of me."

"I—er, no, I'm afraid I haven't, ma'am. But you won't need a solicitor, Ms. Wells. This really is just routine."

"Of course I don't need a lawyer." I gave the officer a conciliatory smile, glared at Mary, pulled out a chair, and sat down at the table with them. Senior Constable Moorhouse looked as if she was trying hard not to laugh; her boss frowned at her.

"So how can I help?"

Stratford cleared his throat. "I assume you've heard about the Ellie Canning case?"

My mother let out an excited squawk, and I answered quickly, hoping to forestall any further response. "The girl who was abducted? Of course."

"So you'll know that she was found not far from here?"

I nodded.

"We're currently following up some leads, trying to work out where exactly she was held. We're taking a look at some of the properties around here that fit with some of her, ah . . . some of her recollections."

"I thought she couldn't remember much? Wasn't it dark when she escaped?"

"Actually"—his face relaxed into a not-quite smile—"it seems she's remembered a few details now. They're coming back, slowly but surely."

"And what is it she's remembered?"

"I'm not at liberty to tell you that, I'm afraid. But I can say that from our initial view of the exterior of your property, it does appear to have some surface similarities to what Miss Canning recalls about the property where she was held."

12

"Oh." That was not what I expected. "What sort of similarities?"

"Again, I'm not at liberty to give you that information. Let's just say . . . the exterior has certain features consistent with Ellie's evidence."

"You mean you think she may have been held here? In this house? But that's absurd." I could control the pitch of my voice but not the sudden roiling of my stomach.

"No, we're not saying anything like that at this stage, Ms. Wells." His voice was gentle. "We're just trying to gauge her movements on the night she escaped—seeing if we can work backward to find out where she was held. It may be that she walked past or through your property at some point. We were wondering whether you'd mind us having a bit of a look around your place."

This time Mary's squawk was triumphant. "You wanna do a search? You're going to need a—what's the word? A . . . a . . ." She went blank for a moment, then became increasingly agitated. "You know what I mean, Mr. Detective—a *whatchamacallit*."

"We don't need a warrant, ma'am. As I said, this is just an—"

Mary interrupted. "I think maybe you should give ol' Chips Rafferty a call, Suzannah. Isn't that fat brother of his a lawyer?"

"Mary."

She rolled her eyes theatrically, clamped her lips together.

The detective sighed. "You're welcome to get a solicitor, of course. But in my opinion, it'll just be an unnecessary expense. And it'll certainly slow things down. As I've said, this really isn't an official search."

"Don't listen to him, Suzie. It's always official—even when they're screwing you. Actually, especially when they're screw—"

"For God's sake, Mary. Just stop."

Constable Moorhouse coughed in an attempt to smother her laughter. Her superior gave her another quelling look before turning to Mary. "I understand your concerns, Miss Squires, but yours isn't the only place we're looking at this morning. We've got a list of, what—around half a dozen other properties to view, Senior Constable?"

She looked down at her notebook. "I think it's actually nine, sir." Her voice was glum.

I made a decision. "There's no reason for us to get a solicitor. Feel free to look wherever you like. It's not like we've got anything to hide."

He gave a relieved smile. "Thank you. We won't take up too much of your time." The two officers got to their feet. "If we could have a quick look around the house first, and then we'll check the home paddocks, the sheds, and so forth. We'll probably take some photographs as we go, if you don't mind—we'll get you to sign some paperwork for that before we leave. We're happy to just wander about if you've got other things to do."

"There's not going to be any wandering, Mr. Detective." Mary's voice was fierce. "We'll be sticking to you like shit on your shoe. Isn't that right, Suzannah?"

I gave a resigned shrug. I had already missed the morning's classes, so there was no point in hurrying now. Mary slid down from her perch, her expression smug.

"So how about I take you straight down to the cellar, Officers, and show you where we kept that little bitch hidden."

ABDUCTED: THE ELLIE CANNING STORY
A documentary by HeldHostage Productions © 2019

ELLIE CANNING: TRANSCRIPT #1

I've spent a lot of my life in foster homes. I lived with my mum until I was about eight, but since then I've been in care. Most of the time that's been okay; I've been in some really good places, but they haven't always been . . . well, I won't go into details, but sometimes it wasn't all that great. My mum . . . yeah, she's got some issues with drugs and alcohol, and right now I think she's back in rehab. I haven't actually seen her for a while. Not since all this happened. We get on all right when we do see each other. I mean, she loves me and all that, but she can't really be responsible for anyone else at the moment.

We moved to Manning when I was six, and I've been there ever since. I went to Manning High until I went to boarding school in Year Ten.

My life was a bit different from a lot of kids' lives, I guess, being a foster kid, but I wouldn't say I was massively deprived or anything. Most of the time I was able to do the usual things—I played netball for a few years and had guitar lessons for a while.

I've been pretty much independent since I went to boarding school. I was still legally in care until I turned eighteen, and I always went back to my foster parents for the holidays, but I've changed carers twice in the last three years, so, you know, I didn't really know them all that well. I know there's been a lot about this in the media, about the way I fell through the gaps in the system, and the fact that nobody really had a clue where I was. But I dunno, I do tend to do my own thing, so that was probably my fault as much as anyone's.

SUZANNAH: AUGUST 2018

Of course I'd seen the news reports, had been as amazed as anyone else by the girl's story and by the little we could make out about Ellie Canning herself. It would have been a sensation even if she hadn't been picked up practically on our doorstep—only twenty or so kilometers to the south of town, and five from our place, on Wash Road. In fact, I drove past John O'Brien's shepherd's hut every time I made the trip to town.

The story was incredible—the brazen abduction, the month spent in captivity, the girl's fortunate and brave escape. From the few details that had been released about her life, it was clear Ellie Canning was someone very special: a smart girl from a difficult background, a foster child who'd won a scholarship to a prestigious boarding school. At eighteen she was still astonishingly young-looking—I would have guessed fifteen, max—and she had a winsome blonde loveliness that was apparent even in the unflattering school photo the press had been using. That such a child could be lost for almost a month with no one knowing or caring was heartbreaking.

At school the story was an endless source of conversation, of sometimes laughter-filled conjecture. There'd been no information released about the kidnappers' motives—and with no mention of either physical or sexual abuse, and apparently only women involved, speculations ranged from the sinister (enslavement, the occult) to the slightly more benign (custody issues). Since she'd been discovered locally, we'd wondered, too, about who her abductor could possibly have been and where they'd kept her. Even the native Washers agreed that there were so many new people in the area—city escapees, weekenders, Airbnbs run on local properties—it was impossible to know. Even Tania Jones, who ran the school office and whose family had lived in the Wash for generations, and who could usually be relied upon for an opinion on any local matter, wouldn't hazard a guess.

Rachel Mott, the head of the math department, told us her son had delivered groceries to a clearly drugged-out older couple up near the Woolpack Bridge a few months back. The woman had been wearing very little, just a G-string and a sheer blouse, and the couple had tried to entice him in, offering booze, a joint, dirty movies. They were both really old, her son had said, at least in their forties, and the woman seemed to fit the girl's description of one of her captors—dark hair, shortish, middle-aged. The couple hadn't been threatening at all, according to the boy. If anything, they were over-the-top friendly. Even so, Rachel had made him go to the police with his story, and he had given them the address. But it was a dead end: the place was a holiday rental and had been leased out to three or four different couples over the period of Canning's abduction.

"You know," Phil Burke, the head of phys ed, said one morning, "that description of the woman could be you, Suzannah—didn't the girl say the woman was dark-haired and short? And then there's the crazy old lady. Doesn't your mother live with you?"

"Oh, come on. There'd have to be at least a dozen women living out of town who could be described exactly the same way, surely? So many people here do live with their elderly parents." Anna Brady, our resident peacemaker, spoke before I could respond, no doubt worrying that Phil had offended me.

"My mother's definitely crazy, but she had me at sixteen, so she's not exactly old." I gave Anna a reassuring smile.

"Hmmm. But you know teenagers. They think twenty is over the hill." As usual, Phil was impervious to Anna's diplomatic efforts. "Is there anything you haven't told us, Suze? You haven't been keeping a teenage girl in your closet, have you?"

The room erupted.

"OMG. What *teacher* would do that?" Julia, the newest and youngest member of the English staff, looked appalled.

"And you do have that connection to Manning." Phil was like a dog with a bone. "Didn't you teach at some private school there?"

"Manning College. It was a few years back now. I'm surprised you remember."

"I always like to know where people taught before they washed up here in paradise." His voice had an edge of bitterness. "People don't come out here for no reason, do they? There's always something they're running from."

I'd applied for the position at Enfield Wash on spec, after a couple of years of highly unsatisfying casual teaching in Sydney. I'd been shocked when I'd got it but said yes even before visiting. Enfield Wash was a small inland town a couple of hours north of Sydney—too far from the city to be attractive to those who wanted to live close to the center, but not isolated enough to be counted as additional rungs for those climbing the education department ladder. Enfield Wash High needed a teacher who had enough experience teaching drama to run junior classes, direct a school play every few years, and take the occasional small class of students through to their final exams. Rather like mine, the school's expectations weren't terribly high.

From what I could glean on the net, Enfield Wash seemed a reasonable place to settle. The town, unlike others in the region, had somehow survived despite its small population. Perhaps because of its relative isolation, it still had a reasonably thriving commercial center, and the economic migration, youth unemployment, drugs, crime, and general disaffection that had destroyed so many other once-prosperous inland towns hadn't been quite as pronounced. It wasn't exactly a buzzing metropolis, but there were enough flourishing businesses and families to make it a viable place to live. As well as the wheat and sheep and dairy farms that had once been the town's backbone, there were wineries that attracted tourism and a growing number of city people buying up acreages. The town boasted a respectable number of cafés, a library, a bookshop, eight hotels, a twenty-four-hour manned police station, and a sense of community. It also had the Franchise, a large and very well-maintained nursing home with a waiting list that was significantly shorter than any I could find in Sydney.

Leaving Mary in the care of a respite nurse, I took a trip in early spring to scope out the town and find somewhere for us to live. I'd decided to bite the bullet and put my Bondi apartment, which I'd owned since the early nineties and had well and truly paid off, on the market. Sydney prices being what they were, I was going to be able to afford a significant upgrade and still have money to spare.

The local real estate agent, whose thirteen-year-old daughter I was likely to teach ("Total drama queen, that girl. Just like her mother.") couldn't hide his excitement when I told him what I was after—space, privacy, a garden, something old that didn't need renovating—and how much I was prepared to spend.

"Well," he'd said, after the initial thrill had subsided, "you've got two options with that sort of money." He'd driven me to the town's premier street—a wide, tree-lined avenue in an area known as Parliament Hill.

The houses were grand: late-Victorian brick mansions with manicured gardens behind high iron and sandstone fences. Most had swimming pools, and a few had tennis courts. They were elegant, welcoming, well looked after, homes where generations of children were born and raised, homes that weren't really appropriate for a single woman and her mad mother.

The agent had stopped out front of one imposing pile. "This one's been on the market for three years—takes a while to sell this sort of place. They're asking six hundred and fifty thousand, but as I said, I reckon they'd take six hundred. Maybe even five eighty. You'd still have quite a bit of change. It could do with a bit of updating, but it doesn't need too much. You could maybe refresh the bathrooms, the kitchen. Knock out a few walls and open it out."

I'd given the house no more than the briefest glance before shaking my head. "It's so beautiful, but not really what I'm after. It needs a family. Kids," I managed to say without self-consciousness.

"Yeah. True." He'd given a regretful sigh, then almost immediately brightened up. "How about out of town?"

I hadn't really considered living out of town, but why not?

"I don't want anything too big; I don't want too much to maintain. And I don't want animals or . . . *crops* or anything."

"No. I s'pose . . ." He paused and looked at me closely. "Hey, I know you. You were that girl. What was her name? Queenie? From that show, oh, what was it? *Surf* something?"

I laughed. "Gypsy. And it was *Beachlife*."

"*Beachlife*. That's it. Gypsy. Wow."

"I'm surprised you recognize me. I'd have thought you were a bit too young."

"Oh yeah, maybe. But I've got four older sisters, and they made me watch it. They had it all on video." His grin was sheepish, his cheeks slightly pink. "And you're coming here to teach? The school must be stoked to have someone like you teaching drama. An actual celebrity."

"It was such a long time ago. I'd be surprised if anyone else even remembers the show. Anyway"—I changed the subject gently—"you were going to tell me about some places out of town."

"Yeah. Right." He cleared his throat, assumed a more businesslike demeanor. "I've got just the thing. It's not quite an acre—so there's not too much to look after. There's a fair bit of lawn, I guess, but you can always get someone to come and mow it if it's too much."

He'd driven out of the town then, headed west up one hill and then down another, around what looked like a small lake but was actually the town's old reservoir, the Lock, and then out into less hilly farming country. It had been a cold, dry winter, and the paddocks were gray and not particularly appealing, but the surrounding countryside was beautiful: gently undulating land as far as the eye could see, with the peak of a heavily wooded mountain—Mount Waltham, apparently—in the distance.

"The place I'm taking you, the old Gascoyne place," the agent said, "has been subdivided. It's an old farmhouse; parts of it are more than a hundred years old, but the owner built himself a new place and is selling off a bit of land with the old homestead on it. Actually, it's a bit of a sad story."

He was clearly eager to tell me, and, curious to hear the local stories, I was happy to oblige.

"Oh?"

"Yeah. Poor bastard. He started building it when he got married. His parents were in the old place. But then his wife got cancer and the house was put on hold . . . She died, oh, a while back now. She was a lovely woman—another teacher, actually. By the time he got back to work on the new house, his parents had died, too. He probably should've stayed in the old place and sold the new one for a pile, but I guess he wanted a fresh start."

"Sounds like it."

"Yeah. He's a typical grazier, tough as old boots, maybe a bit arrogant—but I think it really stuffed him. The old place has been a bit of a nightmare to sell, to be honest. Most people who want to live out of town are after at least a couple of acres. And they don't want these old places."

"No. I like the idea of its age, but I don't know that I really need a homestead. There's only the two of us."

"Well, it's not a mansion or anything. Not like those places in town. The Gascoynes had plenty of money once, but it all went back into the land, so the house is nothing fancy. It's pretty small. And it could probably do with some renovating down the track. The garden's something special, though. And the views."

The agent was right—it wasn't anything fancy. The original house had been built in the mid-nineteenth century, but there'd been various additions and alterations since. The house was tin-roofed weatherboard, in need of a lick of paint, with a wide veranda out the front. The three small bedrooms, dining room, and dim lounge looked desperately in need of an update, but the north-facing kitchen/family room—added sometime in the 1970s—was warm and comfortable-looking. An old breezeway with a corrugated-iron roof ran from the current kitchen to the original kitchen, which was now a laundry.

A door in the hallway that I'd mistaken for a linen closet opened onto a stairway leading down to a basement. The basement had been divided into two thin-walled rooms, one with an en suite toilet. Another set of steep wooden stairs connected the basement to the laundry. The basement rooms were cool and dank and faintly whiffy.

"I think they used these for guest bedrooms at one stage, or maybe storage," the agent said. "You could make a great wine cellar down here," he added wistfully. "The temperature is perfect. But the Gascoynes weren't really a wine cellar sort of family, I guess."

The front garden, old Mrs. Gascoyne's garden, was beautiful. It was all a little wild and unkempt now, but its good bones were still in evidence. I could see the remains of old flower beds, climbing roses and jasmine, camellias, an assortment of natives. An early-blooming jacaranda scattered its blossoms across the lawn. The agent walked me from fence line to fence line and then around the perimeter of the original home paddock, which housed an enormous tin shed—a three-car garage, apparently. All up, the property was just over half an acre. The surrounding land all belonged to Chip Gascoyne—the original homestead just a small sliver in the middle.

"Chip?"

"It's Charles, I think, but he looked a lot like his old man as a kid, apparently—you know, a chip off the old block."

"So where's his new place?"

"It's across that paddock, just behind that windbreak." He pointed to a row of tall trees behind the garage. "It's actually less than half a K away as the crow flies, but you'd never know it. There's a gate in the dividing fence just behind the shed. And there's a rough kind of path between the two properties. Your only other close neighbor is Honor Fielding. She's just a bit farther up the road. Honor's that celebrity PR agent, media person? I guess you've heard of her, being in showbiz and all that?"

"Of course." I was slightly surprised. "What's she doing living out here?"

"She actually grew up in Enfield Wash, and she and her husband bought a weekender a couple of years back—five acres. They're not here that often. They come up for a few days, maybe once a month, a bit more in winter. Her dad's at the Franchise, so she comes up a bit to see him."

I looked back at the house. It was certainly no architectural marvel, but it was solid and cozy. There were views out to the mountain and across the plains, but the property was sheltered, relatively secluded. It was peaceful, a long way from the rat race, but not too far away from the comforts of civilization. It was just what we needed. I paid a deposit that day.

~

My students, too, were obsessed with the Canning case. When the story first broke, it was almost impossible to keep them focused on any other subject. I had come to my Year Eleven drama class prepared for a tedious but necessary discussion about their woefully inadequate practice journals. Instead, when I walked in a few minutes late, the class—only fifteen students, but with enough enthusiastic extroverts to make it feel like fifty—was agog with the recent news: the girl found unconscious in the shepherd's hut, her story of abduction, imprisonment, and escape. They were full of theories, too—why the woman had taken her, who they might be, whether the girl was making it all up—but then why would she? Why would anyone make up such a crazy story? The conversation was impossible to close down. Every time I tried, there was a chorus of *Oh, Miss* and someone added another unlikely fact. In the end I gave up. "Okay," I said, "I get it. I'm fascinated, too. Honestly. But I can't just let you sit here gossiping all day."

Yes, you can, came the chorus. *We won't tell. Come on, Miss.*

"But what we can do is use it," I told them, in my best inspirational-teacher voice. And I meant it. At first glance it might have looked like the tackiest of tabloid stories, but wasn't that what drama, what all art, was primarily about? To explore the full range of what it means to be human, the extraordinary moments as well as the ordinary, the extravagant, and the necessary.

So instead of the dull double period I'd planned, the class worked on three-minute improvisations in groups of two, exploring whatever elements of the story interested them.

First, though (there's always a quid pro quo for classroom fun), we discussed the story's meaning. What was the significance of this tale of abduction, imprisonment, and escape? Could they locate any universal resonances, thematic implications, mythological connections? What might it tell us about the times we lived in, contemporary culture?

As always, the class came up with more than I expected, surprising me with their insights. It was a story about moving from childhood to adulthood; a story about the perversion of adult power; a story about abuse, but without real physical harm; it was a story about courage, about heroism, about oppression and freedom.

"Does it remind you of any other stories? What about fairy tales?"

"Cinderella?"

"It's sorta like a modern Hansel and Gretel, isn't it? Only there's no Hansel."

"And no gingerbread. Or lollies."

"The basement would be, like, the cage."

"But she didn't get to push the witch into the fire before she left."

"They haven't actually found her yet. Maybe she did."

We discussed characterization. I asked them how they imagined the girl. They'd seen snippets on the news, but what sort of a girl was she, really? What sort of a girl was she before she got into this situation? Was there anything that made her particularly vulnerable? They knew bits and pieces about her: that she was a foster child, a scholarship girl at a posh boarding school, that she was probably a bit of an outsider, not a rich kid. Bright, hardworking, ambitious, most likely. And they could see from the pictures that she was pretty. But networked beings that they were, they knew other things, too, things that hadn't been reported in the media. These days there was always someone who knew someone who knew someone.

"I have a friend," one girl said, "who went to her old high school. She was a bit of a skank, apparently." Another girl said she'd heard Ellie Canning had been in trouble for drugs, that she was about to be expelled anyway. Someone else had been told she was a Jesus freak.

"And what about the two women?" I asked. "Who were they?"

So far, very little information had been released about the women who'd abducted the girl. All we knew was that there were two: one middle-aged, the other elderly. And then there was the intriguing question of motivation. What on earth was the rationale behind the kidnapping? Why did they take her? Why did they keep her?

"I really don't get it. What would two old women want with a girl our age?" asked one. "What would be the point?"

What indeed?

"Hey," said one of the boys. "You live with your mother, don't you, Miss? Somewhere out of town? How do we know it wasn't you?"

"But Miss lives miles from where she was found," someone else chipped in. "As if Miss would kidnap a girl."

"What would I want another teenage girl for," I sighed, "when I've got all of you?"

They had no trouble imagining the scenario and the characters, but a truly plausible motive eluded them.

Inevitably the subject of sex reared its head. There had been no mention of the girl having suffered any sort of sexual trauma, but what else could it be, they wondered. They knew all about the most recent high-profile abduction cases; they'd read the news, seen the movies—the ones where the girls had been held for years, given birth even, and they all knew that on some level, these cases always involved sex. But in those cases the perpetrators were men. Our scenario was quite different: this time the villain wasn't male, and the idea perplexed as much as it intrigued.

"It's totally weird, though, isn't it, Miss? I mean, women don't really do that sort of thing?"

"Don't they?"

"Maybe they're lesbians," one girl offered tentatively. "But they're both old, aren't they? *Erg.*"

"That doesn't stop them being perverts."

"Are you saying lesbians are perverts? OMG. That's like totally homophobic."

"I didn't mean—"

"Maybe she wasn't there for the women. Perhaps they'd just sort of caught her and were getting her ready for a man? Maybe she escaped before he got there?"

"Maybe they'd captured her for the white slave trade?"

"Maybe it was a brothel?"

"Okay," I said, "these are all good ideas. But I want you to try a bit harder, think a bit more deeply. What else could it possibly be? Aren't people ever abducted for other reasons?"

"Maybe they'd taken her there to do the cleaning?"

"Maybe," said Jess Mallory, one of my more promising students, a quiet, diffident girl who had a surprising intensity onstage, and who had been given the main part in the school play, "maybe the younger woman wanted a friend. Maybe she was lonely. Or maybe she wanted a daughter?"

When it came to the crunch, they all avoided making motive explicit in their improvs. Most of them portrayed the girl thrashing about, terrified, desperate to escape, and her captor either vicious and abusive or stern, cold, impervious.

Only Jess Mallory's vision departed from this. Jess's kidnapper sat by the girl's bedside, held her hand, and crooned nursery rhymes—"Three blind mice, see how they run"—with her voice high and wispy and slightly off-key. She smoothed back her captive's hair, murmured words of love, told her stories, echoes of familiar fairy tales—"Snow White," "Hansel and Gretel"—talking to her as if she were her long-lost daughter, or the ghost of the woman's own past. The captive, played by Katie Miller, one of my least enthusiastic students, lay as if catatonic, eyes open, but displaying no emotion at all. And it was this particular tableau, the entire class agreed, that was the most terrifying, the most sinister of all.

"Why?" I asked them. "What's so scary about it?"

Only Jess had an answer. "It's because the woman thinks she's doing the right thing by the girl. She actually thinks she loves her . . ."

Even Mary had been briefly intrigued by the story. Despite the fact that she spent half her day in front of the television, any real-world events generally seemed to wash over her. Occasionally she would surprise me by mentioning some random item of news—that the renovations to the local council chambers were going to cost almost a million dollars, for instance, or that a local farmer had sold a bull for a record sum. This sort of detail generally disappeared from her memory almost immediately, but she was wide-eyed about the abduction.

"She reminds me," Mary said, "of a girl I knew when I lived in Paris."

"I didn't even know you lived in Paris."

"That's because it's none of your business."

Paris was clearly a conversational red flag. I changed tack. "Who does she remind you of?"

"Who?"

"The girl who was kidnapped."

"I already told you. This slut I knew in Paris."

"Oh."

"Don't look so shocked."

"I'm not—"

"Yes, you are. I can tell. You're making that face—like someone farted."

"I'm not—"

"Anyway, we were all into it. We were *all* sluts. That was our job."

"Okay."

"That's what the backup singers were there for, really, to service the boys. And don't tell me it was any different in TV land, Miss Sanctimony."

"You were telling me about the girl? Your friend."

"Who?"

"The girl in Paris."

"Oh, her. She went by the name Colette de la . . . de la—some bullshit French name—but her real name was Betty Kane. She had tickets on herself, told everyone she was related to royalty, but that was just rubbish. She had no class. And she'd sleep with anyone, given the chance. It didn't matter if it was her best friend's boyfriend—everyone was fair game. Didn't matter if they were old or young, if they were fat or had no teeth. They just had to have a cock. Although there was a rumor that that wasn't important, either, but I think she probably spread—"

"But why does she remind you of Ellie Canning?"

"What?" Mary's interest in the present had flagged; she was wandering in the labyrinth of her past.

"You said she reminded you of the girl who was abducted. Ellie Canning. The one that's been in the news. The schoolgirl."

"Oh, *that* girl. She likes sex. You can tell by the way she runs her tongue over her lips when she talks. Betty did that, too."

"Oh."

"*And* she's a liar."

"So, how do you know that? The way she touches the side of her nose with her little finger?"

Mary rolled her eyes. "Don't be sarcastic, sweetie. It doesn't suit you. It's just that it's a bloody stupid story. It's an *unbelievable* story. Why would two women abduct a young girl? What were they going to do with her? It's so fucking ridiculous, it has to be a lie."

I called Mary Mum until I was ten, even though I rarely saw her. My grandparents insisted on it, even though Nan was, to all intents and purposes, my mother, Pop my father. Although Mary's visits to my grandparents' home were ostensibly to see me, they weren't really, and by the time I was seven or eight, I understood this. Her visits were for money, or for somewhere to stay, briefly, or sometimes, I think now, maybe as a reminder that there were people who loved her and that she had a past that was nothing like her present. None of these reminders changed the way she lived her life, though.

And the fact that her present included me, her daughter, seemed to have very little meaning for her. I wasn't a part of that benign past she wanted to recall. Her mother and her father, and their gentle, uncomplicated love for her—that was what she came back for. I wasn't a real part of her endless present either—whatever sad mess that was—the present that she couldn't seem to escape and, it seemed to me then, didn't really want to either.

She would arrive unannounced and stay just long enough to enjoy the prodigal's return: the nutritious meals, the clean sheets, the early nights, the hot showers. The desperate, aching love of her parents. And then she'd go.

There was never any warning, never any preparation. Sometimes I'd wake up in the morning and there she'd be, sprawled on my grandparents' good lounge, Nan's crocheted arm covers all awry, cushions tossed aside. To my sleepy eyes she seemed almost fairylike—ethereal and not quite earthbound, which was true, I guess. She certainly wasn't any part of our routine domestic realm.

Or I'd arrive home from school, and Mary would be perched up on the kitchen counter, grimy backpack at her feet, a cigarette in one hand, a glass of something in the other, watching Nan prepare dinner. She'd look down at me, distant but offhandedly kind, and tweak my hair, give me a wink, a lopsided not-quite smile, sing a few bars of the old song, always getting it slightly wrong. *Oh, Suzannah, oh, don't you know it's me.* And I'd smile back shyly, desperate for her attention. Always knowing that just as I began to feel the shyness dissolve, the bonds of wanting and need beginning to strengthen, she would disappear.

When she was there, we all knew to keep our distance—any sign of our wanting more would be enough to make her restless, encourage her to leave early. My grandparents had learned the hard way that Mary would put up with their love only if it was disguised. Love could be practical—my grandmother could feed her, fill the bath for her, wash and fold her clothes; she would happily take the cash my grandfather offered, the lifts here and there, but any questions, any demonstrations of affection were rejected; if they persisted, she'd go. There was never any place for me in this equation—what can a child offer their mother that isn't about love, about wanting to show as well as receive it?

The last time I saw her, until the more recent call from the hospital, I was ten. Mary had turned up, even more wrecked than usual. She was thin, her skin was bad, her mood was even more erratic. There seemed to be marks—dark smudges that might have been bruises, fading scars, faint welts—all over her: on her face, her arms, her thighs. Nan's eyes had widened when she first saw them, and she'd drawn a deep breath, a question formed and then evaporated.

After dinner, Mary showered and changed into a pair of Pop's old flannelette pajamas and then stretched out on the lounge, TV blaring, the oil heater cranked up, although it was only early April and we were still swimming at the beach on the weekends. I sat beside her, not too close, silent, my eyes glued to the screen, but every part of me quiveringly aware of her: the way she threw herself on the seat, completely relaxed, limbs deliberately spread-eagled, not the way I'd been taught to sit—primly upright, knees together and feet firmly on the ground. The way she cleared her throat unselfconsciously, the soft whistle of her breath, her restlessness, the way some part of her was always moving, a leg jiggling, her hands tapping out a rhythm. Despite the fact that she was using our everyday soap and shampoo, she smelled like no one else in the world—a mixture of cigarettes and something else, something sweet and slightly musky. Her presence made everything brighter, sharper, more alive.

She tugged her fingers through her still-damp hair, which was at least clean now, but horribly tangled.

"Do you want me to get you a brush?" I asked eventually, making it sound as offhand, as casual as I could, still not looking at her directly. Her "sure" had been equally indifferent, but I remember running to the bathroom and returning with Nan's brush—a well-loved Mason Pearson.

My mother had taken the brush and looked at it for a long moment and then handed it back, a strange smile on her lips. "How about you do it for me, oh, Suzannah?"

Mary had shifted, lying with her head hanging over the arm of the lounge as I brushed. It was a difficult job; her bleached hair was coarse and split, and the tangles were ferocious—the sort of knots that I'd ruthlessly cut out of my Barbie's head. But I persisted, kept going long after I'd brushed out every snarl, even though by then Mary was fast asleep. Sleeping, she looked as young and as pretty as she was in the photographs Nan kept in a tin, photos from when Mary was in high school, from before she had me. I sat on the chair opposite, the brush forgotten in my lap, and just watched the rise and fall of her chest, the flickering of her eyelids, the twitches of her lips, the small sighs and gasps that people make when they're sleeping. I wished so hard that she could stay like that, that she would stay there, forever. But by the next morning, she'd gone, without warning. This time there were no hastily confected excuses, no pretending not to notice her mother's distress, her father's shining eyes.

And this time she'd never come back. There'd been the odd post-card, from London, Perth, Bali, Chicago, New York—*Having a ball! Living the life! Wish you were here x*—but there was never a return address, never any phone calls, not even the promise of a visit. There were no requests, as far as I knew, for cash either. By the time I was a teenager, my grandparents barely mentioned her in front of me; it was as if they'd stopped wondering, stopped hoping, aloud at any rate—it was all too painful for everyone. They knew she was alive, which I suppose was better than not knowing.

Whether or not Mary knew—or cared—whether *they* were alive was another thing. She didn't come home for either of their funerals. When Pop died, friends of the family did their best to locate her, to send word, and I saw the desperate hope on Nan's face at the crematorium and then at the wake. But there was no one left to hope when it was Nan's own funeral a few years later. I'd wondered if perhaps Mary herself was dead, and had been surprised by my own indifference.

Oh, Suzannah,

Oh, don't you cry for me.

I'd been back in Bondi for a little over a year and had just begun looking for full-time work when I got the call from social services informing me that a Mary Squires was seriously ill at St. Vincent's. I had been listed as her next of kin, and could I come in to discuss a care plan. I went to see her, more curious than anything else. If I'd known that by the following month my mother and I would be living together for the first time since my birth, it's possible I'd have denied the connection and exited, stage left.

ABDUCTED: THE ELLIE CANNING STORY

A documentary by HeldHostage Productions © 2019

ELLIE CANNING: TRANSCRIPT #2

It was the beginning of the midyear holidays, and I'd come up to Sydney on the Friday night because I had an interview at St. Anne's College the following day. I was planning to stay with my mum, who'd been out of rehab for a few months, for the whole three weeks. It was sort of a trial visit. I'd spoken to her a few weeks before and she'd sounded really good, better than I could remember, and she really wanted me to come and stay. I wanted to see her, of course, and my foster parents thought it was a good idea, and the social worker agreed, too. I would turn eighteen while I was there, so no one was all that worried. We decided I would just play it by ear. If Mum was good, I could stay the whole time and do all my revision there. If it didn't work out, I could just go back to Manning whenever I wanted to. We had the trial exams coming up as soon as the holidays finished, so it was pretty important that I had somewhere quiet to study.

(Long pause.)

Anyway, so it didn't exactly work out with Mum. (Laughs.) Yeah. That's probably an understatement.

I don't really want to say more, but one night was enough. I wasn't going to be able to do the work I needed to do if I stayed, so I decided I'd just head home straight after the interview at St. Anne's.

SUZANNAH: AUGUST 2018

There was much eye-rolling in the staff room when it became public knowledge that Honor Fielding had taken on the girl as a client. Honor was something of a local celebrity, the classic small-town girl made good—one of Enfield Wash's best-known exports, along with an Olympic swimmer, a couple of rugby league professionals, and the drummer in a punk outfit that once appeared on *Countdown*. While newcomers weren't impressed—*Honor who?*—true locals had very definite opinions on why it was a good thing that Honor Fielding had bought a property back here, even if it was just a weekender, pleased that she was now expected to actively participate in the civic life of the town—attending openings and fundraisers, giving speeches, donating time and resources.

The other side of this local fame was the sneering that accompanied it. Of course Honor Fielding would have her finger in the Ellie Canning pie—she'd so be riding that gravy train. Of *course* she'd be up for exploiting the poor child. What percentage would she get for every interview the girl did? It was more than half, someone had heard. What a way to make a living; it was a wonder she could sleep at night. And why did she need more money anyway? Wasn't her husband some big-shot merchant banker, on multiple boards, who'd had the ear of every prime minister since Hawke? According to staff-room commentary, people like Honor were to blame for all the ills of contemporary culture—from reality TV to plunging literacy levels.

Eventually someone (the lovely Anna again) pointed out that whether or not she was being paid, Honor was in fact doing the girl a favor. Apparently (or so Anna's boyfriend, who worked as a staffer for the local National Party MP, had told her) the girl had been so bombarded with requests for interviews that she—and the police, and the hospital switchboard—didn't know what to do. The girl's foster parents—who hadn't even reported her missing, assuming she'd gone back to school after the long private-school break—had spoken to her over the phone but hadn't felt the need to visit or take her home. Ellie Canning had no one else to advise her.

The always logical Rajan Kapoor, who taught science, pointed out that it was likely that Honor would've been involved even if the girl hadn't been found locally. This was her thing, after all. She'd made her reputation agenting big names, but more quietly, if just as lucratively, she had also taken on a few "celebrity" victims—and villains—over the years. Now any interviews the girl did would be carefully managed and would be worth big bikkies. And, knowing Honor, there would probably be a book or a film in the offing.

"Honestly," said Tania, but not without a certain admiration, "that woman could work out a way to sell you the story of paint drying. So weird to think she's such a big deal. She really wasn't anything special at school."

"What was she like?"

Tania thought for a moment. "Oh, I dunno. She was pretty smart, I s'pose. Okay-looking. A bit of a nonentity."

"She's your neighbor, isn't she, Suzannah? Have you met her yet?"

"A couple of times."

"And? What do you think?"

I shrugged. "Oh, you know. She seems okay."

SUZANNAH: APRIL 2018

We'd met at a school do that the principal, Tom, had conned me into attending toward the end of my first term. It was a trivia night, a fundraiser for the school's concert band. All the town worthies would be invited, and Tom was convinced that the presence of a former soap star would be an inducement. He'd even had me sign an old publicity shot featuring a bikini-clad Gypsy for one of the minor prizes. Initially the affair was to be fancy dress, and he'd asked me to come in character, which had sent me into a bit of a panic. As Gypsy, my signature style had been "less is more"—short, low-slung skirts, midriff tops, strappy leather sandals or bare feet. This had definitely been cute and sexy when I was twenty-one, but it just wasn't going to be appealing (or even decent) at forty-six. Happily, concerned that the occasion would turn into a wild piss-up as it had for the past few years, the Parents and Citizens Association opted for semiformal dress.

Still, finding something appropriate to wear was a task, even without the *Sunset Boulevard* parallels. It had been a while since I'd had any real social life, and there was nothing vaguely glamorous in my wardrobe; even my "smart casual" selection was seriously underwhelming. In the end I settled on what could be described only as the best of an indifferent lot: a black velvet dress that I'd worn to a colleague's wedding years ago and a pair of thirties-style pumps I'd picked up for the drama costume box. I applied my usual minimal makeup and put my hair back in a schoolteacherly bun. When I offered myself up for inspection, Mary asked if I was going to a funeral. Sally—the respite nurse who came three days a week and on the occasional evening when I had to go out—gave a little snigger. "A funeral'd be more fun, if you ask me."

I wound a crimson paisley scarf around my neck, added some red lippy, let my hair down, and sighed at my reflection. It was better, but I still felt more Dolores Umbridge than Gloria Swanson. Hopefully after the first few glasses of bubbly, I would cease to care too much anyway.

I'd been seated at the main table next to Karen Ross-Smith, the mayor's wife. She had just launched into an urgent discussion of her football-mad fifteen-year-old son's likelihood of getting the marks for law in the (highly unlikely) event he chose drama in his final years when two latecomers made their entrance. The woman, tall and thin and blonde, was stylish in a way that made every other female in the room look dowdy. Her partner was the former owner of my house, Chip Gascoyne. Despite being relatively close neighbors, we'd somehow not crossed paths. But I'd googled him, curious about the house and its history, so I recognized him immediately. He'd appeared in a few local newspaper articles—detailing social events, farming news—as well as a magazine feature about the new house, which had won some big design award. In the flesh he was good-looking in an old-fashioned farmery sort of way, slightly older than I'd expected. He was an unlikely companion for the woman who accompanied him.

Karen stopped her chattering abruptly and watched, mesmerized, as the woman made her way to our table.

"Don't look so scandalized, Kaz," the woman said loudly. "We didn't come together. We just bumped into one another in the car park."

Karen blushed. "Of course not, Honor. I didn't think you—I was just thinking how lovely you look."

"Of course you were. I was only joking." The woman bent and kissed her on the cheek. "You look lovely, too." She turned to me and held out her hand. "And you must be the famous Gypsy. I'm Honor Fielding—I live across the road from you, I believe." She beckoned to the man, who was talking to someone at an adjacent table. "Chip, come and meet the woman who bought your old house. I think we need to reassure her that we're decent citizens. Kaz has been telling her stories."

The man looked over, raised his eyebrows coolly, and went back to his conversation.

Honor rolled her eyes. "He's a rude bastard. I'll introduce you later."

Karen, her color still high, left the table, excusing herself with a murmur.

Honor pulled out the empty chair on the other side of me and sat down. "You don't mind if I sit here, do you?" I shook my head. "I haven't been here for two minutes, and I've already pissed Karen off. I think that's some sort of record. She was always taking offense at school, too. And somehow I always forget that she hates being called Kaz these days." She gave a deep sigh. "I don't know why I say yes to these things—everyone's just as hung up as they were thirty years ago. It's as if I never left." She sighed again. "And tonight is going to be a debacle. I might *be* completely trivial, but I'm utter crap at trivia. I offered to make a donation, a big one, instead, but Tom can be very persuasive." She looked around the room despondently. "Oh God. This is going to be a long, long night. I don't know about you, but I need a drink."

It was a long night, requiring many drinks. It turned out that Honor wasn't utterly crap at trivia, which on this occasion revolved around sport, local history, and local sporting history. In fact, she was something of a whiz. The other members of the table, including a surprisingly competitive Karen, were equally well informed and—with negligible assistance from me—managed to win most of the major prizes, including the signed photograph.

In between questions, Honor and I conducted a whispered conversation, lurching randomly from local gossip to personal confidences in the way that drunken conversations tend to.

"So, are you over it yet?" she'd asked.

"Am I over being the only person at the table who doesn't have a clue what the hell the Green Cup is, let alone who won it in 1985? I honestly don't understand how you people remember this stuff. Or why."

"Ha. No, I meant are you over teaching drama to a bunch of kids who can't see the point. Country life. Being stuck out of town."

"Oh. All that."

"Yes." Her eyes were brimming with mischief. "It can't be your most exciting gig."

"I haven't been here long enough to be over it. And as far as gigs go, I've had worse."

"Truly?"

"I once did a margarine commercial where I had to butter a slice of bread about two hundred times before we got the take right."

I refilled our glasses, noting Karen's quickly masked look of disapproval. Honor took a long sip, moved closer, lowered her voice even further. "Just so you know: the Green Cup was a yearly sporting competition between Enfield Wash and Chester High, and 1985 was the year the students secretly added a 'hookup' tally—although I don't think that was the term we used. The Wash flogged Chester—and our girl Kaz was the overall winner. It's not something any of us will ever forget."

Back when I was acting, I'd known plenty of women like Honor in an official capacity—talent agents, publicists, producers—but for reasons I couldn't put my finger on, those relationships never seemed to go beyond the professional. Even though we were all basically engaged in the same business, there was a huge gulf between the two sides. When I first started out, I'd assumed people like Honor were bit players in the spectacle that was celebrity life. But as time went on, and I witnessed the way the wheel of fortune seemed to turn more quickly and dramatically for those in the limelight while the people like Honor not only survived, but thrived, I realized the converse was actually true. Now, at such a distance in time and place, there was a peculiar pleasure in talking to someone like Honor, someone who understood the world I'd once belonged to, who had some insight into who I'd been, if only for a short while, all those years ago.

By the end of the night, it felt as if we knew both everything and nothing about one another. And by the end of the night, I couldn't resist.

"So *is* there a story to tell? About you and Chip Gascoyne?"

"Oh." She laughed. "Only ancient history. We went out a couple of times when we were kids. Actually, I think it's possible that Chip Gascoyne has a 'story' with practically every female in the room."

"Actually, I'm pretty sure I don't have any sort of story with Karen." The subject of our gossip was standing right behind us.

I was sober enough to be embarrassed, but Honor didn't even blink. "Only because she's some sort of cousin."

"That's no impediment. So is Sarah Newman."

"Sarah? Oh my God. You didn't?"

"We did." And then to me: "I think we may have exchanged contracts, but I've been away a bit, and I don't think we've met. It's Suzannah, isn't it?" He held out his hand. "Chip Gascoyne."

"Hi. Yes, I'm Suzannah."

He clasped my hand hard, regarding me critically. "You don't look—"

I interrupted, impatient. "I know, I don't really look like I do in the photo. It's already been pointed out. What can I say? It was taken almost twenty years ago."

He laughed. "I was actually going to say that you don't look sober enough to drive. And *you're* pissed as a newt, Fielding. How about I drive you both home? Pretty sure you're going my way."

The following day I was in the kitchen garden, planting seedlings. I'd come to love the dirty work of gardening—these days it was practically my only physical activity. Where once I would have gone for a run in the early evening or visited the gym after work, being responsible for Mary had made anything more time-consuming than the occasional quick jog around the perimeter fence difficult. When we'd first moved in, I'd decided that while the front garden was too daunting for anything but mowing, I'd have a go at resurrecting the old kitchen garden. I'd also imagined that growing veggies could provide some sort of occupational therapy for Mary, get her out of the house, give her an interest, but she'd looked at me as if I were mad. *Gardening is for the elderly,* she'd said dismissively.

I'd already had some success. My initial efforts had produced more pumpkin and zucchini than two people could ever eat, and I'd been inspired to plant more. I took a taxi into town to pick up my car and, despite my hangover, called the local nursery and bought seedlings: lettuce, spinach, broccoli, beans.

No doubt there were other things someone with even a smattering of gardening knowledge would have known to do as preparation, but I was blissfully ignorant. My modus operandi involved simply pulling out everything that had previously taken root, whether weed or not, turning the soil in the established beds, then pushing the little sprouts in, patting the dirt around them, adding water.

I was digging in the bean seedlings when a deep voice asked dryly, "You do know beans need something to climb up, don't you? They're a vine."

It was Chip Gascoyne. He looked like a picture-book Aussie farmer—the tanned sinewy forearms, untucked checked shirt, riding boots, jeans, Akubra tilted back on his head.

"I thought I'd come and check that you'd survived the trivia night. And see whether you needed a lift into town to pick up your car. But it looks like you've already got that sorted."

"I didn't actually drink *that* much."

He raised his eyebrows. "So you can remember what you said to me when I dropped you off?"

I tried to remember the possible indiscretion but came up blank. "You dropped me off?" The joke was lame, but he grinned anyway. "So what embarrassing thing did I say?"

"It's okay. You only said thank you. Or maybe thanks. You did better than Honor, though."

"Oh?"

"I had to practically carry her inside. Lucky I know where she hides her front door key. You're clearly in good shape today. You could probably do with a shower, though."

I looked down—my knees and fingers were black, and there were smudges of dirt on my legs, my shirt, and no doubt on my face, too.

Chip was looking around at the garden beds. "It's good to see this all coming alive again."

"Well, I hope it all actually stays alive. I'm completely clueless, really. Do the beans really need something to grow up?"

"I think so. Though I'm not really much of a gardener either. You'll probably get a better crop than we ever did. Mum was good with flowers, but her kitchen garden wasn't ever much chop. The only thing that ever grew was pumpkin, and they weren't those sweet Kent ones you get at the supermarkets now. They were those old-man blues. Jesus Christ—every year we all prayed for Mum's pumpkins to fail. She insisted on us eating every single one, which meant we had pumpkin in some shape or form for months. And to be honest, there aren't that many shapes or forms. I think we maybe got a few weeks' reprieve."

I went to tell him about my own success with pumpkins but was interrupted by the slam of the screen and Mary's ringing tones. "Well, what have we got here? If it isn't Farmer Jones."

Mary had her hair in two long, messy braids, with a few gray feathers (from a pillow, a feather duster?) poked in the ends. She was wearing a long, floaty stretch-cotton skirt—hers—and a loose but low-cut raw cheesecloth top, a relic from my misspent youth. Her feet were bare and almost fluorescently pale, her toenails painted badly in an assortment of bright colors, the enamel covering almost as much toe as nail. She had two circles of bright red on her cheeks—my lipstick, no doubt—and her eyes were rimmed with black.

"Mary, this is Chip Gascoyne. We bought the house from him."

"I know who Chips Rafferty is. My dad always watched that movie whenever it came on—what was it? Something to do with cows and the war; I can remember that. God, it was boring." She looked over at him suspiciously. "You were younger, though. And you had those terrible sticky-out ears. I always felt embarrassed for you."

"No, he's not—"

"Well, I guess we were all a bit younger then, weren't we?" Chip had slowed down his speech, put on a country drawl. "And I eventually had my ears pinned back." He took off his hat to give her a better view.

She looked him over critically. "You're definitely older, but you're actually better-looking in the flesh."

"Well, thank you, ma'am." He offered a sweeping bow.

"I still wouldn't fuck you, though. Not if you paid me."

Mary turned and floated back inside, slamming the screen door after her.

I cringed, but Chip was grinning. "Well, that's me told. Good to know where I stand. Your mother?"

"Yep. My mother."

"She looks too young to have dementia."

"It's a long story."

He looked at me thoughtfully. "Maybe you can tell me sometime. I like long stories."

He called me that afternoon. "Have you seen much of the town?"

"I've had a bit of a drive about." We'd been here for months, and it was embarrassing to admit how little I'd explored. I'd been too busy getting the house sorted, settling into my new job, looking after Mary.

"I take it you can leave your mother for a bit?"

"I can. I just have to prepare food. Hide the matches. Make sure she's settled."

"She won't wander off?"

"I can barely get her to leave the house."

"I'll pick you up tomorrow morning, then. About eight. If we get an early start, it won't be too hot. You can tell me that story."

I should have been affronted by the fact that he'd left no space for me to disagree, but it felt good to have someone else take charge, make the decisions.

"It sounds like fun."

"It will be. Oh, and bring your togs."

"Togs?"

"Cossies. Swimmers. Bathers. Whatever you call them. There are a few spots on the river that're good for a swim."

He picked me up as promised, early on Sunday morning, in his battered but surprisingly comfortable ute. He drove us into town first. His driving was far too fast, but somehow it felt safe as well as exhilarating. He was calm, intent, didn't chat. He was so focused he didn't notice me watching. I could imagine him in a different time, with his battered Akubra, a cigarette dangling from the corner of his mouth. He wasn't quite Chips Rafferty, but there was something quintessentially Australian about him. He was nothing like most of the men I'd known and a long way from being my type.

We stopped for coffee and wood-fired sourdough croissants at a little hipster café that had recently opened in a former garage in the center of town. The café's industrial-chic aesthetic was identical to its city counterparts': the walls had been stripped back to expose the raw brick; the cement floor was polished; every beam was exposed. The baristas were tattooed and pierced and friendly. It was noisy, busy, full of life. The coffee was good, the buttery croissants even better.

Chip drove me around the streets of the town, pointing out areas of interest beyond the main tourist route. Initially there didn't seem much to distinguish it from any other Australian country town. The main street was long and wide, the buildings a hodgepodge of architectural styles, the grand nineteenth-century churches outnumbered by the even grander veranda-wrapped pubs that seemed to have been built on every corner. But Chip managed to bring Enfield Wash to life. He didn't tell me the history of the town itself, but every place he took me was rendered significant by some story or other—usually funny, and frequently involving females—from his own life. He drove past the nineteenth-century brick primary school, pointing out the classroom where Miss Von Beelan—a certifiable psychopath who'd taken a strong dislike to him on account of some argument she'd had with his mother when *they* were children—had pulled down his trousers in front of the entire class to spank him with the ruler, and to his shame, Chip hadn't been wearing underpants. The teacher had been suspended from teaching after his parents complained, but he hadn't gone back to school anyway. His parents had decided that it was time for boarding school, and he'd been sent away to Sydney the following term.

"Looking back, it might have helped my reputation if they'd let me come back for a bit," he told me, his voice dry. "The fact that I didn't come back after the Von Beelan incident made it stick in everyone's memories. I think I was known as the kid who couldn't afford undies for years. And it confirmed my old man's reputation as a lousy bastard, too."

The Anglican church, a small but imposing Gothic revival building, was the place where he'd first kissed a girl.

"I was doing confirmation classes."

"Were your parents religious?"

"Not really—I mean, we went to church for Easter and Christmas. But my mother got it into her head that being confirmed was important. I think one of her friends was related to the minister, and they were trying to increase numbers or get recruits. The Cathos were always ahead of us there."

It was all a long way from my own very suburban upbringing.

"Anyway, I was doing the confirmation classes . . . this was in fifth grade, too, just before the pants incident—"

"A big year."

"And there was this girl I fancied, Tania Brigstock. She works in the school office. Tania Jones now. You probably know her."

"I do."

"She was a couple of years older than me. A stunner. Long blonde hair, tall. She used to walk, and even run, on her toes. She was brilliant at sports—tennis, netball, swimming. Anyway, I was smitten. All the boys were smitten. She ended up married to Darren Jones—he was a jockey. You couldn't meet a nastier, more dishonest little fucker. But Tania, back in the day . . . we were all after her."

It was impossible to imagine Chip's version in the Tania I knew, although I had noticed her odd manner of walking.

"Anyway, she was a smart cookie. She knew I liked her and said if I gave her five bucks I could kiss her."

"And did you?"

"Well, I only had three bucks, so we negotiated. No tongues. I didn't even know about tongues, so that wasn't a big deal."

"Was it worth it?"

"I thought so. We did it there." He pointed to the hedge between the church and the manse. "You can actually crawl inside that hedge. There's a sort of hollow. There was back then, anyway."

"And how was it? The kissing."

"A little bit too much of a good thing. She offered to let me touch her tits for another five dollars. It took me a month to get the money together. That blew my mind."

"I can imagine. Isn't ten a bit young?"

"Way too young. I didn't go near girls for years."

I was skeptical. "Not because you were sent away to a boarding school—I'm guessing it was a boys' school?"

"Well, yeah. That's true." He laughed. "But I was definitely traumatized." We continued through the residential area, driving past the beautiful old brick homes on Parliament Hill. He pulled over in front of the grandest one. It had been built by his mother's family, the Summervilles, in the late nineteenth century and had still belonged to the family during his childhood. It was a mansion, really, some sort of art nouveau concoction—three stories, gabled and turreted, with long sash windows and generous wrought-iron balconies. I could imagine the black-and-white tiles in the foyer, the cedar paneling, the wide sweep of the staircase. We could just glimpse a tennis court, clay, lined, clearly still used.

"I didn't really think much about it when I was a kid, how big it was, how rich they were. They were just my grandparents. The money didn't mean anything. It didn't make things any better. Actually, what I remember most about that house was the fucking cold. You couldn't get warm."

He drove me down through the housing commission, a settlement of run-down fibro homes that skirted the town, then out to the new estate, big brick homes along the river. The homes were oversize, squeezed onto mean and usually treeless blocks, even though there was plenty of room to spare.

Chip turned back onto the highway, then drove down a bumpy dirt road until we reached a clearing, where a hand-printed sign nailed to a gum tree told us we had reached the Wash.

"Is a wash some kind of geographical thing?" I asked.

"It means a place that floods—or that's what they told us at school."

"And does it?"

"Not more than any other river in Australia. More likely to dry up at the moment. It was named after the place that the bloke who founded the town came from. There's no particular geographical significance as far as I know. It was just that he was from Enfield Wash, which is somewhere near London. Not all that unusual. Half the names around here have been taken from there, too. There's Turkey Brook just over the highway, the Lock, which is the reservoir at the other end of town, and then where I'm taking you now—another swimming spot called Freezywater."

"And is it?"

"Is it what?"

"Freezy water."

"Depends on how much water's coming from the dam."

The road petered out, and Chip pulled up under a tree. Ahead was a willow-tangled turn of the river. It was a pretty spot, perfect for swimming and camping. There was no real bank on our side, and the river looked deep and clear, the water running fast. There was evidence of recent campfires, despite the total fire ban, along with the usual party litter—empty bottles, chip packets, pizza boxes, a few empty condom packets.

Chip sat for a moment, gazing out. "In summer we used to float on airbeds all the way from the Lock. It'd take half the day. And then we'd walk back to my place—almost ten Ks along the road, but we'd cut through a few paddocks as well. I can't imagine anyone letting their kids do it these days. Skin cancer, drowning. Cars. Snakes. Pedophiles."

"How old were you?"

"Twelve, maybe."

"Pretty tame stuff, really."

"Oh, we progressed."

"In what way?"

"You know. Here, for instance . . . When we got older, it was the go-to place for parties. Drinks, drugs, loud music. Sex."

I pointed to the beer bottles, the condom packets. "Still is."

"Yeah. I guess it's all the same. Young love. All that bullshit."

He sounded regretful.

"Are you going to tell me more stories of your teenage conquests?"

"Nah. Not just yet." He opened the door. "Don't want you to get the wrong idea about me. I'll leave those for the second date." He grinned, tossing me my bag from the back.

"This is a date, is it?"

"Actually, this is a test of your capacity to withstand low temperatures. So why don't you get your togs on, Gypsy, and we'll go take a dip in the freezy water and see if you go purple."

HONOR: APRIL 2018

She was pleasantly surprised at how much she'd enjoyed Suzannah's company.

It wasn't usually Honor's scene, the whole female-friendship thing. She'd never really got it—not as a little girl, and not as a teenager. She'd always been part of a group, was never a loner, exactly, but had preferred to maintain a certain distance from her peers. There'd never been any of that bosom-buddy shit, no crying on anyone's shoulders, no being there for any significant female other. She'd never had any loyalty issues, simply because she'd never really had anyone to betray.

As an adult, she'd been too busy working hard to do anything more than establish alliances and allegiances, and these were always subject to change, depending on what—or who—was useful at any particular moment. She was ambitious, sure, and focused, but it wasn't actually a conscious decision; she'd just never felt the need for friendship.

A few weeks after the trivia night, she'd met up with Suzannah a second time. Honor had come alone on the Friday—Dougal was at a business dinner in Melbourne. She bumped into Suzannah at the local supermarket in the late afternoon, both of them stocking up on food for the weekend. They laughed at their similarly wholesome trolley loads. "Hope you're going to balance that with some booze."

Suzannah held up a bag bulging with bottles. "It might be the other way round, in my case."

On an impulse Honor asked if Suzannah wanted to duck into the pub for a quick drink. Honor's other arrangements for the night—the real reason for the trip—had been canceled at the last minute, and she knew she'd only be bored and slightly resentful once home.

"Oh God. I'd love to, but I have to get back." Suzannah's disappointment seemed genuine.

"I thought you didn't have kids?"

"I don't—but I've got my mother living with me, and I don't like to leave her for too long." She sounded harried.

"Your mother?" It came back to Honor now. "Oh, that's right. Dementia."

"More or less."

She gave a sympathetic grimace. "I know all about that. But at least my dad's in a home and not living with me. It must be a nightmare."

"It's not that bad. Not all the time." Honor could practically hear the gritted teeth behind the smile. "But nights can be a bit difficult."

She made a snap decision. It wasn't the sort of thing she usually did, but why not? After all, she had nothing better to do. "I'll tell you what, why don't I come over to yours? I've just got to go and look in on Dad first. And I'll bring another bottle."

"Oh, I'm not—"

"And what if I bring dinner, too? You look like you need a break. I've done nothing all day." She realized she sounded like someone's middle-aged mother: bossy, maddeningly competent, compulsively helpful.

Honor could see the other woman wavering. "Actually, that sounds fantastic."

"It won't be anything fancy, though. I'm a pretty hopeless cook. Does your mother like pasta?"

Suzannah laughed and shook her head. "God knows *what* Mary likes. Other than sugary cereal, it changes every other day, so there's no point worrying. This is really kind of you."

Honor waved a casual hand. "It's nothing. What are neighbors for?"

Suzannah's mother answered the door when Honor arrived with her hands full of groceries, a bottle of chilled bubbly tucked under one arm.

She was already half regretting her impulse. This kind of old-fashioned neighborly do-goodery wasn't really her thing, and after a disastrous late-afternoon visit to see her father, a hot bath and a couple of gins seemed far more appealing.

"Are you her?" The woman peered out from behind the screen for a long moment, her face in darkness.

"Well, I can't be sure, but I think I might be. I've brought your dinner, so I certainly hope so." Honor affected a jaunty tone.

"What are we having? Is it something I like?"

"I've brought pasta, and I thought I'd make a creamy sort of sauce to go with it. Do you like bacon? Mushrooms?"

"It's called Boscaiola." The woman gave a haughty sniff, unlocked the screen, and opened it a few inches. "I'm not an idiot, you know. And I actually lived in Italy for a number of years, *puttana*."

Honor ignored the insult. "My apologies. Do you think you could open the door properly so I can come in? I don't have any hands—"

"Suzannah didn't tell me you were an amputee." The woman gave a hoarse cackle and opened the door just enough for her guest to push through but then stayed put so Honor had to edge past her in the doorway. For a moment the two were forced together, only a few inches apart, standing practically head to head. The older woman didn't even try to hide her belligerent curiosity as she looked Honor up and down.

Honor tried to stay relaxed and cheerful under her scrutiny, but it was an effort. The other woman seemed far too young to be the mother of Suzannah, only just middle-aged herself. She was frail, all angles, her face lined, but some remnant of beauty was still evident in the wide eyes, high cheekbones, full lips. Her long, silvery mane was thick and shiny.

Eventually their eyes met in the gloom. The older woman was all hard glare, and Honor was primed for some sort of verbal attack. But even as she readied herself, the woman's expression transformed: the fierceness suddenly gone, replaced by a dull heaviness.

"Mary, what the hell are you up to?"

Honor blinked as the hall light came on, and turned to greet Suzannah.

"Oh, Honor. I'm so sorry, I didn't hear the door." Suzannah hurried up the hall and took her mother's arm gently. "It looks like you and Mary have already met."

"We have. I was just telling her that I've brought the ingredients for Boscaiola."

Mary looked up, her eyes alight again. "Did you bring the peppermint ice cream? The one with chocolate chips? And cones?"

Now she sounded as chirpy as a three-year-old, but in the light she seemed to have aged—her shoulders sagging, face lined. Even her hair had lost its luster. She could be seventy, even eighty. "Oh, Suzannah, tell her she can't come in if she hasn't brought any ice cream."

~

"Oh. My. God." Honor topped up Suzannah's glass first, then her own, generously, and raised hers in a toast. "Here's to bedtime."

Suzannah half sighed, half laughed as they clinked glasses. "Some nights are worse than others. This was a bad one."

It was an understatement. Suzannah's mother had been more demanding than any tired toddler, and it was eight o'clock before the two women were able to relax. Cooking the meal itself hadn't been too challenging: Mary had been fully occupied with the television, thank God. But then she'd complained all through the meal—the bacon was too chewy, the garlic made her sick, the pasta was slimy—until Suzannah gave up and made her a peanut butter sandwich. Happily, the peppermint ice cream had been forgotten. But then there'd been a half-hour game of Trouble, which Honor had considered the most boring game even as a child, with a clearly engineered win for Mary. Initially, the older woman had left the room for bed quite willingly, but then she

56

returned a half dozen times with various requests and complaints—she was thirsty, the bed had sand in it, the blinds were rattling, she wanted Suzannah to read her a story—but finally she was out to it. Honor had to stop herself from suggesting that Suzannah add a sleeping pill to the warm milk—maybe a few more than strictly necessary. Mary had given her a keen look before her ultimate good-night. "I like you," she said. "You're pretty."

"Thank you." Honor gave what she hoped was a friendly smile. "You're very kind."

Mary had turned her baleful gaze on her daughter. "Suzie could be pretty, too, if she lost some weight. Fat girls aren't pretty, are they?" She gave a coy smile. "No one ever wants to fuck a fat girl." She ducked her head and tripped down the hallway.

Jesus.

"I'm so sorry," Suzannah said to her now. "I really should have warned you." She took a big chug from her glass, downing half her champagne in one gulp. "But the thought of company was just too tempting."

"How do you cope with this full-time?"

"She's not always that bad, but it's an unknown with guests. Sometimes she'll behave really well—she'll seem almost normal—and then other times . . ."

"My dad's much further gone, I guess. He basically just sits there doing nothing. I don't remember him going through an in-between stage like this, though. One moment he seemed fine, and then the next, he was in care."

Suzannah shrugged. "It's different for everyone. Mary's condition is most likely alcohol and drug related. They said it could be Korsakoff's, but it doesn't really fit the pattern. She's okay during the day, at least not so bad that she has to be in a home—although I've got her on a list for the Franchise.

"Sally O'Halloran, who works there, comes out three days a week, and that's helpful. But nights can be . . . difficult. I feel like it might be because some part of her remembers that this was once her drinking time. Although she never actually asks for a drink, which is surprising. The peppermint ice cream can be a bit of a problem. I forgot it today— usually that would be a major drama."

"Ha. Yes, she asked if I had any. So it's not ordinary dementia? I thought she seemed on the young side. What is she? Seventyish?"

Suzannah snorted. "She's only in her early sixties. She had me very young."

"Wow. Sixteen or something? And she was an alcoholic. That must've made for a complicated childhood."

Suzannah shook her head, laughing. "It didn't have all that much effect on me, actually. I barely knew her growing up. My grandparents raised me. It was worse, much worse, for them. She was an only child— they were older parents—and I suspect it broke their hearts. Mary was a classic bad girl. She was always in with the wrong crowd, even when she was a kid, or that's what my nan used to say—truanting, shoplifting, 'running amok.' By the time she was fifteen, she was pregnant."

"Do you know who your father is?"

"I've got no idea. At the time she was peripherally involved in the music scene—Nan said she fancied herself a singer and sometimes did backup vocals. But I guess at that age it's more likely she was some sort of groupie. My father could've been anyone. She would never say; I suspect she never actually knew. I spent half my childhood fantasizing it was Jimmy Barnes, but I don't think the timing's right."

"And you look kinda Greek or Italian—I'm guessing that's not from Mary. And it's not from Jimmy either."

"No. My father was probably a Greek schoolboy and not a musician at all."

"So was she still involved in the music world when you were a kid?"

"Who knows? Until she moved in with me, I hadn't actually seen her since I was about ten. I didn't even know if she was alive."

"You're kidding. So why the daughterly devotion now? Is there an estate or something?"

"I wish." Suzannah filled her glass again. Took another long swig. "As to the daughterly devotion, I actually have no idea. It just happened. I got a call from St. Vincent's—she'd had some sort of turn and put me down as her next of kin. I guess I'm her only kin. I certainly wasn't looking for her—although a psych might have something to say about that. Anyway," she added briskly, "it seemed the right thing to do at the time."

"The right thing? For her or for you?"

"Ha." Suzannah's smile was rueful. "Exactly."

The conversation moved quickly on to other, more interesting subjects. Naturally, men came up, but neither Honor nor Suzannah seemed keen to expand on that particular topic. Suzannah revealed only the bare bones of her own story: she had been married and divorced, but that was years ago. There was no one at the moment, not really; she wasn't entirely up for a relationship, way too much baggage—and now there was Mary to consider. Honor had little to contribute about Dougal, who was as gratifyingly besotted with her as he had been when they first married, more than twenty years ago. And if Honor wasn't besotted in quite the same way, if from time to time she discovered other interests, she had never discussed them with anyone—and would never. And they'd had no effect on her relationship with Dougal anyway: he would always be her rock, her still center in this madly spinning world.

The conversation moved on to the town itself. Honor provided a general rundown of the place, a who's who and what's what, and told a few salacious stories that only a local could know. But Suzannah was able to tell her a few things, too—gossip she'd missed, news about people she'd forgotten. She was an acute, sometimes caustic, observer of people; her stories of her students' parents—so many of them classmates

Honor had all but forgotten (and usually for good reason)—were particularly entertaining.

"There was this one woman at my first parent-and-teacher night who asked if I was interested in coming to some sort of orgy. Or at least I think that's what it was. Right at the end of the interview, she leaned right in and whispered"—Suzannah moved her face up close to Honor's, her mouth at her ear—"'I've heard you're into alternative . . . er . . . sexual experiences.'" Suzannah's voice had deepened, developed a slightly sinister lisp. "'My hubby and I were wondering if you'd like to come along to a gathering of . . . like-minded people.'" Suzannah sat back, her face alight with laughter. "My God. And the daughter was still sitting at the table with us. When I said no, she said, 'Oh well—there's always next month,' like she was inviting me to join a book club. It was completely bizarre."

"Janet Cho, right?" Suzannah's impression had been extraordinary.

"Shit." Suzannah looked stricken. "I'm probably being indiscreet."

"Oh, don't worry about it. Janet propositioned all the teachers when we were kids, too. Teachers are her thing."

"Wow."

"It gets worse—her darling *hubby*, Antonio, is into, er, small mammals."

"No. Oh no. I can't even—" They both dissolved into laughter.

"I hope you didn't come to the country to find normal people, honey. I'm telling you, Enfield Wash is kink central."

They opened a second bottle, and the conversation moved into new territory. Like most people, Suzannah was curious about the world Honor inhabited, but hers was a curiosity born of experience, not ignorance—it had been her world, too, once; she knew the reality. Mostly she was eager to hear gossip about people she'd known. Some Honor knew; others, like Suzannah, had disappeared from the scene, leaving no trace. Honor was pleasantly surprised by the commonalities. And there was a novelty in being able to talk to someone who understood this world intimately yet didn't have an angle. There was none of the usual danger here—Suzannah wasn't trying to make contact with anyone, didn't want any favors. And there was nothing Honor wanted from Suzannah either. She could relax and simply enjoy the company.

Honor had still been a hack on a big city paper back in Suzannah's heyday and had always assumed that Suzannah had done something wrong, that her career had taken a nosedive, that she'd been left without options, forced into teaching. Celebrity worked like that for most people—took whatever they offered, chewed them up, then spat them out. Honor's job was different. She'd approached it stealthily, entered from the back door, a secret door that let her into the real powerhouse, become one of the people who ran the show. One of the people who did the chewing up and spitting out of the Suzannah Wellses of the world. But if Suzannah was telling the truth, her exit had been entirely voluntary. Her part in the show was over, and she'd simply decided she'd had enough.

It gave Honor a bit of a jolt to think that someone could actually *choose* such a life—small, peripheral, provincial, relatively meaningless—once they'd had a taste of living life at the center of things. That Suzannah had made a decision to leave, to embrace this other life, frightened her a little. And when Suzannah looked like she might be revealing more than Honor really wanted to know, Honor quickly steered the conversation back into acceptably shallow waters.

"Have you seen much of your neighbor?"

"Chip? Not really. Although he took me on a guided tour of the town one day after the trivia night—showed me the sights, drove out to the river, that sort of thing."

"What did you think?"

"Of the river?"

"Ha. No, although I want to hear about that, too. What do you think of Chip?"

"He seems okay." Suzannah's shrug was casual, her expression non-committal. "Why do you ask?"

Honor grinned. "Just a heads-up. He has a bit of a reputation around here. With the *ladies*." She stretched the word out.

"I gathered that. Anyway, there's no need to warn me. He's really not my type. He's a bit too, I don't know, a bit too sure of himself for me. And I don't think there's any interest from his side either."

"Don't be deceived," said Honor. "Chip Gascoyne is *always* interested."

"You two seem like good friends."

"I'm not sure about friends, but we've known each other forever, and now that we're neighbors, it's kind of impossible not to socialize. He and Dougal have drinks every now and then, and we have dinner occasionally."

"And you said you'd had a thing with him?"

"Very briefly, when we were still in high school. It was never going to go anywhere. I was a townie and he was a grazier's kid, a boarding school boy. And in those days that difference meant something. Maybe it still does, I don't know. There was an expectation that he would find someone appropriate—someone who would help him keep everything going for the next generation. A farmer's wife. That was never going to be me."

"I guess he was a catch back then?"

"Oh yeah. He was. Every second girl had the hots for Chip. He was good-looking, he was rich, he had impeccable manners, he was smart, he was the vice-captain of some posh school, captain of the rugby team, the cricket eleven. He only had to click his fingers and he could've had any girl."

"And did he?"

"He ended up marrying the kind of girl everyone expected him to marry—Gemma Barton. She was the female version of Chip: from an old grazing family, boarding school—you know—well bred, pretty, vacuous. Perfect breeding stock. Their fathers were great mates. Grandfathers, too, probably."

"I heard she died."

"Yeah. Actually, that was sad. It was all looking good, I guess—work had started on the new house. They'd been living in the old manager's cottage, which was pretty basic, I think. It's been knocked down since. His mum and dad were living in your place. And then Gemma got breast cancer. They shelved the build and focused on Gemma, on getting her better. She was sick for five or six years, I think, before she died. And then—*wham!* Everything else seemed to go wrong. Both his parents died, and Chip had to buy out his older brother, Hal—he's a lawyer, lives in town. So he had this big debt, and then the drought hit. He almost lost the farm. Hal helped him out, and I think he sold off some other portions of land as well. He finished building the new place a few years ago, but it took him a while to move in."

"I wonder if he's a bit sad about leaving this place. It's been in his family for what, over a hundred years? He must have some regrets."

"Maybe." Honor shrugged. "But the rest of us have never had that privilege—that history—to cling on to. I guess Chip Gascoyne has had to join the real world."

After the second bottle, Honor got up to leave. It was late, past midnight, and Suzannah suggested she stay over; it was no problem to make up a bed in the spare room, she said, or perhaps she could call a cab? But Honor insisted on driving: she would go at a snail's pace, and it was barely a K if you discounted the driveways.

As she drove carefully down the long driveway, Honor realized that she'd enjoyed herself more than she had in a long time. She liked Suzannah; she even liked the crazy mother. Suzannah was smart, curious, funny, and, despite her trying circumstances, she was far from self-pitying. And there was something about her—some residue from her years in front of the camera, an easy sort of sexiness, a confidence in her own skin that most people outside the celebrity world rarely had and that Suzannah herself probably wasn't aware of. That the sexiness was latent, and that the woman herself was so unaware of it, made it all the more potent and, to Honor—who was easily bored by anything or anyone that smacked of the commonplace—all the more appealing.

More importantly, the evening hadn't left the customary bad taste in Honor's mouth. There'd been no painstakingly disguised competition between the women; nothing was said that Honor was only just decoding now. And for once the thorny issue of children hadn't come up—Honor's lack of, whether she wanted them, and if not, why not; was it too late, did she regret it, were there problems? But Suzannah hadn't mentioned children at all, and for this she was grateful.

ABDUCTED: THE ELLIE CANNING STORY
A documentary by HeldHostage Productions © 2019

ELLIE CANNING: TRANSCRIPT #3

After my interview, I caught a bus back to Central. I had a few hours to kill, so I went to get something to eat. Somehow I left it too late, and by the time I got back, I'd just missed my train. There wasn't another until the next day and I didn't have much money left—I mean, I had some, but not enough for a hotel or anything like that, so it was a bit of a disaster. And my phone was running out of power. I decided I'd just have to hang at the station all night, which was a pain, but I thought I could try and get some sleep on a bench or something.

I wandered about the city for a bit to kill time. I went and got a snack at a café sometime around four, and a woman sat down next to me. She was old, like, in her forties, I guess, dark-haired—I thought maybe she was Italian or something. I can't remember exactly what she was wearing—it was probably, like, jeans and a jumper—but I do know she had this mad scarf with all these swirly colors. We got chatting, and I told her what had happened, and she seemed concerned and said I could use her phone if I wanted to let someone know where I was—wouldn't my parents be worried? I told her that no one was expecting me.

SUZANNAH: APRIL 2018

I walked over with a bag of late-season zucchini and squash and one oversize pumpkin, intending to drop them on his doorstep and leave, but Chip was there when I arrived. He opened the screen door as I was treading quietly across the veranda.

"G'day."

"Hi." I lifted up the bag. "I was going to drop these off. Didn't think you'd be home."

"Thoughtful of you."

I held the bag toward him. "Here. Take it. They're heavy."

He peered inside. "Glad to see you remembered how much I love pumpkin. Excellent."

"We've got more if you want them. Too many, really . . ." He wasn't listening.

"I've had a thought." He pushed his hair back. "Why don't you come for dinner? I'll do a roast. Come on—it's Saturday night. And I need to get rid of this." He pulled the pumpkin out of the bag. "I'll give it to the pigs if you don't."

"Do you have pigs?"

"No. But I do have a couple of goats that eat practically anything. Come on, Suzannah."

"I—"

He must have sensed my hesitation. "And if there's marking, it can wait. My wife was a primary school teacher, so I know all about marking. And I might be a country bumpkin, but I won't believe you if you tell me you need to wash your hair."

It was true that dinner with Chip sounded far more appealing than the previous night's spaghetti bol I was planning to heat up, the painfully drawn-out routine of putting Mary to bed, three gins on my own, and the pile of badly written essays on *Waiting for Godot* that sat waiting to be marked. But there was a problem.

"I can't leave Mary."

He looked crestfallen. "Really? But don't you leave her when you go to work?"

"I do. But nights can be . . . difficult."

"Maybe you could get a babysitter?"

I shook my head. "It's too late to organize."

"Give her a sleeping pill?"

"They make her worse."

"Damn." He brightened. "I know. How about I bring dinner over to you?"

He came just before seven, bringing the prepared meal and a bottle of wine. Mary had been fed and bathed, and he was just in time for our evening game of Trouble. She was often restless at this time of day, sometimes aggressive, and always far less tethered to reality. If she was going to forget who I was or where we were, this was when it happened.

The old children's board game distracted and focused her, and I got a strange pleasure out of it, too. I'd never really played these games as a child; once I'd moved past my earliest childhood, my grandparents were simply too preoccupied, too tired, too old. I'd had a cupboard full of games, though, and sometimes I'd take Trouble out and pretend to be two people—one me, the other some kid from a TV show or book or even school. Occasionally, I'd pretend to be Mary, although even imagining Mary engaged in such an activity was a stretch. It was bizarre to find myself playing a real game with her now, always reminding me of the improbable nature of this late-life reunion.

Chip was initially reluctant to play, but while Mary's demands might be childish, her adult perceptions only added to her cunning: if Chips Rafferty wanted to get rid of her for the evening, he would have to do as she said—viz, play Trouble. Playing with Mary was unpredictable. Some evenings she was wild; she shouted gleefully when she was winning and swore when one of her pieces was taken or if she got stuck for want of a six. She was accustomed to cheating—punching at the dice bubble manically until she landed her desired number. But tonight, with Chip there, she behaved beautifully, playing quietly and accepting her losses with reasonable grace. Still, between the two of us, we contrived to let her win quickly, and the game, which could go on for far too long, was over in half an hour.

Like a small child, Mary was desperately tired in the evening, but she would still work hard to extend her day as long as possible, demanding a hot Ovaltine, snacks, more television. But after a final crude remark—*If you two are going to fuck, make sure he wears a condom. I'm too young to be a grandmother*—she cooperated. Even so, it took a while to get her comfortable. First she demanded I straighten her blankets, pull them right up, and tuck them in firmly, then complained she was too hot, that she couldn't move and wanted them folded back down. Then she was thirsty—what did I think she was, a bloody camel? And then, naturally, she needed to pee. After the trip down the hallway, she was cold again and insisted on changing out of her summer nightdress into her favorite long pj's, a pink silk pair I'd bought for her birthday last year that she called her Chanel pajamas. As always at times like this, I felt the rage and resentment begin to bubble up, along with a childish desire to pinch her or push her or say something vicious, and as always I took deep breaths and held my tongue.

Chip's meal was simple but good: slow-cooked lamb, squash, roast potatoes, zucchini. He'd baked one small slice of pumpkin especially for me. Neither of us had dressed up for the occasion, though I'd made a bit of an effort with makeup, and he was clean-shaven, his hair tamed.

Chip insisted on serving the meal, and I leaned against the bench and watched, sipping champagne, as he carved the meat, piled the plates with veggies, poured the gravy. He was clearly practiced in the kitchen. We sat up at the breakfast bar to eat, and the conversation, slightly awkward at first, gradually became less stilted as the champagne took effect.

He told me stories about the house, about his family, their long history in the area. The first Gascoyne had come to Australia as a convict—a fact that had been hushed up by the succeeding generations. I told him about school: gossip from the staff room, a few stories of bad behavior from the students. He seemed to know most of the staff and almost all the kids, had something to say about their various backgrounds, sometimes surprising, frequently counterintuitive. No wonder Demi Barnes was a shit of a kid: her father, Gary, had been the same, and her mother—Jenny Downey before they married—was wild, too; he was pretty sure she'd had an affair with one of the math teachers when they were kids. And Connor McFarlane's lawyer dad was a violent alcoholic who should've been locked up and the key thrown away.

I laughed when he told me of his own most recent adventure: a visit to Italy and Germany, where he had attempted, and ultimately failed, to make deals with continental wool buyers. He'd been a classic innocent abroad, bumbling through encounters with rich and sophisticated, and frequently snobby, Europeans.

"There's something I need to tell you. A confession." He sounded serious.

I didn't know quite how to respond, so I kept it light. "I hope it's nothing illegal." Was it drugs? A second wife? A fatal disease? A criminal record? Somehow it already mattered.

"It's a bit embarrassing to admit, but I've never ever seen that show."

"What show?"

He was having trouble keeping a straight face. "That soapie you were in. *Surfworld* or whatever it was. I've never seen it."

"*Beachlife*. Really? Not even one episode?"

"Not one. We didn't—we could only get the ABC out here then. And Channel Seven when the wind was blowing from the south."

"Seriously?"

"Seriously."

"So you never saw the episode when Jason and I got married? I thought everybody under the age of thirty saw that."

"No, I . . . hold on—wasn't that the other show? The one with Kylie in it?"

"Ah—so you're not a complete philistine. You watched *Neighbours*?"

"I told you—we occasionally got Seven. But I only watched it once or twice. I promise. And it was total rubbish."

"Hmmm. Well, I'm just sorry you never got to see me in my prime."

"Pity. But you're not that bad now, you know."

"Not that bad?"

"Actually, I've just ordered the full box set off Amazon."

"I didn't even know there was such a thing. You didn't really?"

"No. But maybe I will." He thought for a moment. "Or maybe you could act out all the most important moments for me." I choked on my wine. "It'd save some time. Not to mention money."

Dinner eaten, the champagne drunk, we opened a bottle of red and moved into the lounge room, sitting in front of the fire I'd lit earlier in the evening, which, I was pleased to see, had somehow managed not only to stay alight but to warm the room, which had cooled down quickly even though it was still only autumn. The conversation became quieter, more personal. Chip told me about his marriage, the death of his wife, his sadness at not having children. "What about you?" he asked. "You were married, weren't you? No kids?"

I answered the first half of the question.

"I was married. We split up fifteen years ago."

"And there's been no one since?"

"No. I mean, I've been out with a few people, but I guess I wasn't . . . ready. You know how it is."

He knew.

"So who was he? Your husband? Is he someone I should have heard of?" Chip looked embarrassed. "I probably should have googled all this—but I've never bothered to get the internet set up at the new place. And anyway—it's a bit dodgy, isn't it? Doing searches on your neighbors."

"You wouldn't know him. He was a builder. Steve." I was relieved that he didn't know much about me, somewhat hypocritically, considering my own research efforts.

"Right." He looked surprised. "A civilian? Isn't that a bit unusual in your line of work?"

"Maybe. But I met him after I got out of acting. I'd landed my first full-time teaching job. It was in Collaroy, which is an impossible commute from Bondi, so I rented out my place and moved there. My landlord sent him over to fix some windows."

"And he never left."

"Something like that." I laughed. "Actually, I moved into his far bigger, far fancier place."

"And didn't live happily ever after."

"Not exactly."

"What happened? Was the celebrity thing too much for him?"

"It wasn't that. Any fame I had was pretty much over by that time, anyway. We lived this totally conventional life. I was teaching; Steve was building. We went to the pub on Friday nights, dinner at his parents' on Sunday nights. We had friends over for barbies, renovated. It was wall-to-wall picket fences." I could hear the wistfulness in my voice.

"So what? Was it you? Did you miss all the excitement?"

"God, no. I'd been happy to get out. I'd had enough."

"Enough of what?"

"Of acting, partly. But mostly it was the whole scene. Being a celebrity."

"Isn't that something most people dream about?"

"Most people don't experience it. It's not what they imagine."

"Most people don't give it up without a fight, so it must have some . . . consolations."

This was something that I'd spent a lot of time considering, so the answer came easily.

"It wasn't bad at all. It was the opposite, if anything. And it was highly addictive. It was like the public me pretty quickly began to feel like the only me—and eventually that began to feel pretty scary."

"Why scary?"

"I think you lose your sense of being like everyone else. You don't have the same limits. It's hard to describe. Anyway, I decided that I wanted out of it before it . . . consumed me."

"Was it to do with your mother?"

I laughed, but his question was surprisingly perceptive. "Aren't most things? But yes, I suppose she was a sort of . . . cautionary tale. I guess her life might have been exciting on one level—but on every other it was completely fucked. And I really didn't want to go there. I realized what I really wanted was what other people had—marriage, family, a job I enjoyed, enough money to have a decent life. I got some of them. And I still don't regret getting out. Most of the time, anyway."

"Only most of the time?"

"Well, sometimes I miss the food. They always fed us really well on set. I never had to cook."

"Actually, there's another thing I don't get. What's with all this dutiful-daughter stuff? Are you some kind of saint?"

"A saint?" This time my laughter had a brittle edge. "I don't think so. Half the time I want to kill her."

"Then why take her on?"

"I really don't know. She's on the list for the Franchise, but that could take years. Living with her was never meant to be a long-term thing."

"So, why don't you find her a place elsewhere? It doesn't have to be close to you, does it? It's not like you owe her anything."

I didn't have a rational answer to that. "I honestly don't know, Chip. Sometimes I think I might be a bit mad."

He looked thoughtful. "Have you checked your palms lately?"

"Checked my palms? Why?"

"For stigmata. Or hair. Maybe both."

I turned the conversation back to Chip, asked if he'd had other relationships since his wife died. He'd had a few flings, he told me, and his late wife's younger sister had tried to set him up with a few of her friends, but nothing ever worked out. "Kate thinks that I'm still mourning Gemma, and it's true, I do miss her, but it's not that. Or not just that," he said. "The truth is, I just don't have the energy to do it all again. I'm sure a shrink would say it's fear of loss, and maybe that's part of it, too—but I think maybe I'm lazy. What about you?"

"Am I lazy? Or do I think you're lazy?"

"No. I mean what's your relationship to . . . relationships? I know you said before that you weren't ready, but . . . I thought maybe . . ." He faltered, suddenly awkward.

The wine had loosened up more than my tongue. "What I think is that we're two lonely people with nothing left to lose, and that you should probably stay the night."

He didn't disagree.

ABDUCTED: THE ELLIE CANNING STORY
A documentary by HeldHostage Productions © 2019

ELLIE CANNING: TRANSCRIPT #4

She asked where I lived, and when I told her Manning, she laughed and said, what a crazy coincidence, she was actually heading up that way herself.

So when she offered me a lift, I agreed. Okay, in retrospect it was dumb—what sort of an idiot accepts a lift with a stranger? But she seemed so genuine and kind, and so concerned about me spending the night at the station by myself . . .

She said I should wait and finish what I was eating, and she'd get her car and come back for me in half an hour—she wanted to get a few things for the trip first.

She picked me up and we drove for a while and chatted about things, school mostly, what subjects I was doing and that sort of thing. We'd been driving for an hour or so when she offered me a thermos of hot chocolate, told me to drink as much as I wanted, that it would warm me up.

The next thing I remember was waking up in that room, tied to the bed.

HONOR: MAY 2018

The two women met whenever Honor was in town for the weekend and didn't have other plans. Usually she went to Suzannah's, but there had been drinks at the pub and the occasional meal out when Sally was available to stay with Mary. Dougal had even been persuaded to come with Honor to Suzannah's on one of his increasingly rare weekends away with her. He had enjoyed the company, though he'd been bemused by Mary, who had insisted on calling him Hannibal throughout the evening and made frequent allusions to eating human remains. (Dougal was round-faced and balding, but that was his only resemblance to Anthony Hopkins.) And he'd been pleased to see Honor making new connections, he'd said. When she'd laughed, pointing out that making connections wasn't something she had a problem with, surely, he'd looked at her curiously for a moment.

"You're right, of course," he'd said. "But you know I worry about you, Honor. You don't really have many friends, do you? Suzannah seems a bit more real than most of the people you know. And she doesn't want anything from you." He'd given her shoulders a friendly squeeze, removing any unintended sting from his words.

She enjoyed the informal meals at Suzannah's place the most. They could both relax, let their guard down, and talk without worrying about being overheard. It was completely unexpected, Suzannah confided, the way being a teacher in a small town was a bit like being in show business—you really couldn't say or do anything in public. There was always likely to be someone listening in, taking notes. They talked mainly about their current lives, but they gradually learned about one another's pasts, too. Honor had told Suzannah bits and pieces about her happy-enough country upbringing, her hard-fought-for career, her marriage . . . had even mentioned the once-heartbreaking fact of her infertility. She, in turn, had managed to build up a picture of the other woman's history—Suzannah's entry into and exit from the limelight, her motherless childhood, the sad failure of her marriage. There were certain things that Suzannah hadn't mentioned, too, that Honor had read about online, but her desire to keep parts of her life private was something Honor respected, and understood.

Honor had also come to enjoy Mary's company—not when she was sitting blankly in front of the television, barely conscious of the world around her, but when she was in one of her manic, refractory moods or telling outrageous stories about her misspent youth. Honor was never sure whether she should believe Mary's anecdotes about all the famous people she'd worked (and frequently slept) with in the music industry. Suzannah was no help; her mother's life was a complete mystery.

"She really could have been anywhere, doing anything. Mary tells a lot of stories and drops a lot of big names, but I don't know how much of it is true. She says she lived in New York and Rome and Paris, but she could have been living in the next suburb for all I know. She doesn't have anything from her past—no photos, not even a passport. I've done online searches, looked in rock histories, but never come up with anything. Maybe she didn't use her real name. But who knows," she added, "maybe some of what she says is true. Maybe she was bigger than we know. Then again, maybe it's all bullshit."

"It'd be interesting to find out, don't you think?" Honor said. "Maybe I can make some inquiries for you. I know a few people who were around back then—they might know something."

Suzannah dismissed the idea. "I'm not sure that I really want to know, to tell you the truth. I kinda like the mystery."

One late-autumn evening, Honor and Suzannah were sitting out on the veranda, drinking gin and tonic, as the sun sank slowly behind Mount Waltham, bathing the surrounding landscape in golden light. Mary, who had rather rudely rejected the lasagna that Honor provided, was inside watching back-to-back episodes of *SpongeBob*. They had been trading tales about a notoriously handsy film executive, long dead, they'd both had dealings with when they were startled by a faint rustling in the trees to the east of the farmhouse. They heard the crunch of footsteps across the gravel driveway before a figure moved out of the shadows and resolved into a familiar male form.

Honor spoke first. "Chip Gascoyne. What're you doing here?"

"Saw the lights on, thought I'd drop in." His voice was as laconic as ever. If he was surprised to see Honor, he didn't show it.

He loped up the veranda steps and walked toward them. "I hope I'm not interrupting anything." He held out a bottle of red.

Suzannah jumped up. "Not at all. We were just having an after-dinner drink. I'll get some more glasses." She seemed awkward, her speech slightly stilted. "Take a seat."

Chip sat down in a vacant chair and yawned.

"Big day?" Honor asked.

"Not really. Just long." He yawned again and stretched his legs out in front of him.

Honor broke the silence. "I didn't realize you and Suzannah knew each other that well."

"We don't. I just felt like some company, thought it might be time to do the neighborly thing. Wasn't even sure there'd be anyone home." He added casually, "Didn't know you were coming out this weekend."

"I left a message—"

Suzannah walked back out onto the veranda, carrying three wineglasses.

"I was just telling Chip that I wasn't planning to be here; it was all very last minute. I had a call from the Franchise this morning. They were worried about Dad—thought he'd had a stroke." Honor sighed. "But it was a false alarm. Just the aftereffects of some nasty virus, apparently."

"Ah. Well, I guess that's good news. And how're things in the big smoke?"

The night was pleasant, the conversation among the three of them comfortable, lighthearted. Mary made a brief appearance, requesting that Chips Rafferty show her his spurs. She demanded more ice cream and then disappeared inside again.

Around ten, Honor called it a night. "I have to be back in Sydney early, so I'd better go get some beauty sleep." She offered Chip a lift home.

"Thanks, Hon. It's not that I don't trust your driving, although I don't"—he smiled up at her—"but I might just wander back the way I came." He picked up the wine bottle, tilting it toward the light. "And I'm not quite ready yet. There's at least another glass; this is a good red, pity to waste it."

Suzannah walked Honor to her car. As soon as they were out of earshot, Honor clutched Suzannah's arm. "You should be very careful with Chip," she whispered, shocked by her own bluntness. "He's a player. You'll only get hurt."

"You don't need to worry about me." Suzannah sounded amused. "I'm not exactly an innocent."

Honor considered her for a long moment. "Okay. As long as you know what you're getting yourself into." She realized she sounded like a drunken maiden aunt but couldn't help herself. "Just don't say you weren't warned."

SUZANNAH: MAY 2018

Honor wasn't the only one to warn me off Chip. Tania from the school office, whose unerring instinct for gossip was evenly matched by her compulsion to stick her nose in other people's business, told me in no uncertain terms, and in the hearing of a couple of smirking colleagues and several round-eyed Year Seven girls, that Chip Gascoyne had a bit of a reputation and I should watch myself around him. This was right back at the beginning of first term, before I'd even met him, and I dismissed it with a laugh. She looked at me sternly. "You haven't met him yet. I've known him all my life. He's not a bad bloke, as blokes go. And he may have been a model husband when poor Gemma was alive, but now . . ." She slammed her fist down on the stapler.

Mary, too, in one of her odd moments of (usually malicious) insight, had told me that I was an idiot to think a bloke like Chip would want a woman like me. "Why would he go for you? I mean, you're not that bad for your age, but he could get someone a fair bit younger." She had given me a critical once-over. "He might want kids, and you're a bit past all that, aren't you? A bit long in the tooth?"

"I'm not actually that old, you know." I couldn't resist. "Not as old as you, anyway."

She ignored my adolescent jibe and continued, "Anyway, he'll probably be the last fuck you'll ever get, so you may as well make the most of it."

I'd confessed to an old friend from my early teaching days, Laura, that I'd met someone.

"Is it serious?"

"I don't think so. No."

"You mean *he's* not serious."

"No. It's mutual. We're having fun. He's someone to talk to, but that's it. I don't want serious at this stage. Everything's too complicated. I've got to sort out Mary first."

She'd sighed. "There's never going to be a stage where it's simple, Suze. Not at your age. You've got baggage. And he's going to have baggage, too."

"He does. But it's not . . . well, it's not like mine."

"Well, duh." She gave an exasperated sigh. "You need to protect yourself, Suze. And you know I don't just mean use condoms." We both laughed. "And if he's not serious, you need to be extra careful. You really don't want to get burned."

I didn't want to get burned, but I didn't want to run away from something that was proving to be far more pleasurable and far less complicated than I'd ever imagined. After that first dinner, Chip had begun calling in, uninvited but never unwelcome, once, twice, sometimes three times a week. If it was late, past Mary's bedtime, he'd bring a bottle of wine to share; if Mary was still likely to be awake, he'd bring a tub of her favorite ice cream. Sometimes he'd even arrive in time to join in our nightly Trouble game. It was clear Mary enjoyed his company almost as much as I did. She'd swing between outrageous flirting and affecting a painful Victorian coyness, all giggles and sweetness, sometimes even to the point of letting him come close to (but never actually) winning. Occasionally she'd beg him to read to her—"You do it much better than Dame Judi here. She sounds like she's got a peg on her nose"—and mostly he'd oblige.

Most nights, once Mary was asleep, we'd be up late drinking and talking, and almost always Chip would end up staying over. Somehow, regardless of our virtuous intentions—the good sleep I desperately needed, his early-morning start—he never seemed to make it home. Because if our conversations were good, and they were, the sex was even better.

ABDUCTED: THE ELLIE CANNING STORY
A documentary by HeldHostage Productions © 2019

ELLIE CANNING: TRANSCRIPT #5

When I first woke up, I actually thought I was in hospital, that I must have been in an accident.

It was just like one of those scenes from a movie. You know, where the heroine's just out of surgery, and all she can see are bright lights and blurry figures leaning over her, with all the sound muffled as if it's coming from far away. It took me ages to work out what was going on, where I was, what was happening to me. There was just, like, this blurry figure, and a voice murmuring, or maybe singing, and then it would go dark again.

Sometime later—I really don't know whether it was hours or days—I woke up a bit more, though I still felt pretty foggy and disoriented. I tried to get out of bed, but there was some sort of restraint around my waist—like, not tight or anything, but my movements were completely restricted. But I was so out of it that it didn't really bother me. I just lay back down and drifted off again.

When I was conscious enough to look around me, I saw that the room was sort of like a hospital room, only dingier. There was hardly any furniture—just the bed I was lying on, which had this old metal headboard; there was a bedside cabinet, a chair beside the bed. There was a sliding door on one wall, and the main door, one of those old timber-paneled doors, on the wall across from me. It was kept closed. There were no windows; the only light was from a bare bulb dangling from a black cord. Oh, and there were these two paintings on the wall opposite me.

It seemed like days before I actually saw anyone for real. I had vague memories of someone being there, but there never seemed to be anyone around when I was awake. I have no idea how I was being fed, or if I was being fed, but I had no consciousness of hunger, only sometimes my throat would be sore, and I would be very thirsty.

I could never work out how much time was passing. It was like time had become something sort of meaningless, you know. Even when I thought I was awake, I was kind of, like, floating. I spent days just gazing at the pattern on my quilt. There were these tiny flowers all over it, and if I squeezed my eyes half-shut, they turned into fireworks. I used to play that childhood game, open-shut them, open-shut them, watching the colors burst and fade and burst and fade.

HONOR: AUGUST 2018

Honor took Ellie Canning on as a client just a few days after the story broke. She'd driven by the hospital earlier, seen the crowd outside, and she knew that this story was only going to get more intense and that her services—or the services of somebody like her—would be desperately needed.

She'd known the officer in charge, Hugh Stratford, since childhood. They had moved in very different social circles even then, but he'd been very helpful when her father reversed into a bakery in Enfield Wash's main street a few years earlier, and as was her practice, Honor had cultivated the connection. She could hear him sigh when her call was put through, initially irritated by the interruption, but he still gave her the information she needed.

Yes, he'd told her reluctantly, the girl was still in hospital, and yes, she was up to talking to visitors, and yes, Honor was right—she probably could do with some help dealing with the media. Right now they couldn't move without treading on the bastards, and the station and the hospital were being inundated with calls—it was almost impossible to get a line in. It would be helpful if they could direct them elsewhere. And as for the girl herself, the situation was stressing her out. It was all a bit much after everything else that had happened. Anyway, yeah, he'd tell the nursing unit manager, another old schoolmate, that Honor would be coming in to talk to her.

"Are there any clues yet about where she might have been? Or why they took her?"

"Oh, come off it, Honor. Of course we've got some ideas, but I'm hardly likely to tell you, am I?"

She laughed. It had been worth a try. "It's mad, though, isn't it? The town's full of rumors. I heard that Jane Wetherby and her mum have been questioned. Although that's ridiculous. Jane's legally blind."

"I can't comment, Honor." He sounded huffy.

"Okay. Sorry. I'll be at the hospital in an hour or so. Will that work?"

"Yeah. That's fine. Actually, Honor," he added, "the girl could probably do with some more, ah, *personal* advice, too. She's a state ward, and the foster parents aren't much use, to be honest. They live up north—Manning—and we can't get either of them to come down. They've got a bunch of other kids to look after and reckon it's impossible to get away. I guess they don't want the publicity; they'll be up shit creek because they didn't even notice she'd gone missing. She hasn't got anyone else. No aunts or uncles or grandparents. There's the school, but she doesn't want them involved, so it's not their responsibility either. She's just turned eighteen, but the department has sent some bloody girl, a social worker, to cover their arses. She's barely older and hasn't got a clue how to handle something as explosive as this. I mean, who does?"

Honor couldn't resist. "Well, you know, I *have* had a teeny bit of experience in these things."

"Yeah, okay. I get it. Anyway, the girl could probably do with a little female TLC right now. And some sensible advice. We don't know what to do with her, where to send her. She can't go back into any sort of state care at this stage, even if she wanted to, but she doesn't have any resources. It's a bit of a nightmare, to be frank. Maybe you can help her out?"

"I'll see what I can do."

"And maybe"—his voice was hesitant—"you could persuade her to agree to a full sexual assault exam?"

"Surely that's been done?"

"Well"—he sounded slightly embarrassed—"she's had blood tests, but she's really adamant that she doesn't need a doctor to look at her. She insists that they didn't touch her, that she'd know if they did."

"I suppose she would."

"Maybe. But apparently the woman—" He stopped abruptly. "Anyway, it's just something that needs to be done. For her own good as well as ours."

"I'll see what I can do. But surely if she says she's sure nothing happened, then nothing's happened?"

"She was unconscious half the time. She might not even know."

"I'll do what I can."

"I'll make sure they're expecting you. And Honor—"

"What?"

"Maybe you could bring a few things for her. Bathroom stuff. She's still in the hospital nightie . . . You know what it's like."

Honor said hello to the officer stationed outside the girl's hospital room. The woman stood and held out her hand. "G'day, Honor," she said. "Been a long time." She gave a sympathetic smile when it became clear Honor didn't recognize her. "Jenny Irvine. Moorhouse now. You used to babysit me and my sisters when we were little. I've probably changed a bit."

"Oh my God. Jenny! It's lovely to see you." Honor's pleasure was feigned, but her surprise was genuine—there was no way she would ever have recognized Jenny Irvine. She'd been the cutest kid—elfin, dark-eyed, sweet-natured—but there was no sign of her in this sloppy, tired-looking woman. She looked ten years older than Honor when she must have been ten years younger.

"You're here to see Ellie, are you?"

"Hugh Stratford said she could do with some help."

"Yeah. The poor darlin'."

"How's she doing?"

"It's hard to tell. Every now and then she sort of fades out, but most of the time she seems pretty calm, despite everything. Maybe it's the residual effect of the drugs."

"Do the doctors know what they gave her?"

"Well, it looks like she was given benzos of some sort. It's possible she was given Rohypnol as well, but that's out of your system fairly quickly."

"No permanent damage?"

"No. Nothing physical. I probably shouldn't be saying this, but you know she won't let them do a rape exam?"

Honor shrugged. "I suppose it just seems like too much right now. I guess she knows what she's doing."

"I don't know that she does, actually."

"What do you mean?"

"Well, there's got to be some serious psychological stuff going on. You know she's a state ward? Her life's already been hard enough. She's the last person who needs this sort of shit."

"Maybe that's made her more . . . What's the latest buzzword? Resilient? Gritty?"

Honor moved closer to the door as she spoke and peered through the window. The girl was sitting in her hospital bed watching a sitcom on the television. She looked small, young, and somehow even more vulnerable than in the school photographs that had been published in the newspapers and on the net. She was wearing a hospital gown, the ties loose on her back, and Honor could see the curve of her spine, her pale skin.

Jenny sighed. "Maybe. But she needs someone."

Suddenly the girl turned her head and gazed at them through the glass, her face unreadable, unsmiling. Honor smiled, gave her a tentative wave. "Well, I guess she's got me for now, hasn't she?"

She met up with Suzannah at the RSL for a quick drink late that afternoon—they'd made the engagement weeks ago. Honor told her that she'd seen the girl in the hospital, that she'd be handling all her publicity.

Suzannah was curious. "So how is she? It's just completely mind-boggling, what happened to her. I can't imagine it's easy to . . . process."

Honor took a moment to answer. "She's surprisingly okay. I mean, she's a bit out of it, but she's not huddled up crying or anything. I don't know exactly how these things work—maybe the trauma will catch up with her later?"

"What's she like?"

Honor took a long sip of her wine. "I like her. She seems a bit lost, to be honest. A bit dazed. Scared, maybe. But she seems smart, too. She's listening to the police, the doctors; she's mostly happy to do what she's told. But she digs her heels in when she doesn't want to do some-thing. And she's being pretty sensible about the press interest. Most people want it to go away, and others are pains in the arse, wanting to tell the press everything."

"And has she told you anything? I mean, the reason she was taken? No one seems to be saying, but it's the thing everyone wants to know."

Honor laughed. "We haven't got that far yet. I think the police are probably keeping a lot of info from the public. It's pretty wild, though, when you think about it."

"If there'd been a man involved, it would be so much easier to under-stand. I don't think I've ever heard of anything like this happening."

"Not that anyone can remember."

"I guess the media is going mad?"

"Totally. I've had calls from five morning shows asking if they can talk to her when she's out of hospital. And three women's magazines, two of them willing to pay a decent amount for an exclusive. And then there's all the web-based stuff. It's going to be huge."

Suzannah sipped her drink, thoughtful. "This'll change her life for-ever, won't it?"

"Oh yes." Honor had to work hard to keep the excitement out of her voice. "I feel like it might change a few lives."

~

It wasn't until she had observed the girl herself (clearly traumatized, disoriented, and yet so undemanding) and witnessed the way everyone in her orbit—the nurses, the doctors, the motherly police officer Moorhouse—instinctively rallied around her that Honor really understood just how big this could get. In media terms, Ellie was a natural.

It had happened only once or twice in Honor's career. Usually she was employed to push, to make a small story bigger, to help the undeserving but desperate make their way into the public consciousness. She knew the choreography of this particular dance by heart: when to move forward, when to pull back, how to keep the public hungry for more. But occasionally the dance wasn't even necessary; occasionally a story—and a person—had a rhythm that was entirely its own. Sometimes a story came along that wasn't, strictly speaking, "of the moment"—instead it created the moment.

Caution was required, of course. Stories like Ellie's could be like an out-of-control wildfire—if the wind suddenly changed, everyone could end up burned.

ABDUCTED: THE ELLIE CANNING STORY

A documentary by HeldHostage Productions © 2019

ELLIE CANNING: TRANSCRIPT #6

I would stare at the two paintings in the room for hours. One was of sailing boats in bright-blue water. There were these red dots in the background that sort of looked like blood.

The other one was really freaky. It was this huge picture of a naked woman, really pregnant, lying on a couch. I remember her nipples. They were, like, huge and dark—bigger than any nipples I'd ever seen. Her stomach looked like it was about to burst. There was this man's head leering over her shoulder.

I gazed at the painting for hours, thinking about who the people in the picture were, what they were doing, wondering what was going to happen next. Some days I would imagine the woman dying, her stomach exploding, the man left holding the baby.

I knew every line, every color, every shape. I could probably draw it by memory now.

Sometimes the two paintings would merge in my dreams—the woman would be in the yacht sailing away, only she was me. And sometimes there'd be a baby, too.

SUZANNAH: AUGUST 2018

The police search was, as they'd told us, brief. They had a quick look around the house, Moorhouse taking countless photographs of every room on her iPhone, including the two rooms down in the basement, one still crammed with odds and ends of furniture left behind by Chip—a couple of old iron bed frames, mattresses, two big wardrobes, all of which I was planning to dispose of—and the other crowded with still-to-be-emptied moving cartons. Mary led the way enthusiastically into the smaller room, opening the door, flicking on the light, a bulb that dangled unshaded in the center of the room. It had been painted a mustardy color God knew how many years ago, and the walls were grimy, the ceiling speckled. It smelled faintly of cat piss.

"And this"—she gave a gracious wave of her hand—"is where we keep all the girls we kidnap, Officers."

Stratford and Moorhouse ignored her, surveying the room silently.

"We haven't been here that long." I felt like an explanation was required for the room's depressing condition.

Moorhouse gave me an understanding smile. "We've been in our place for two years, and there are still boxes I haven't unpacked. Really, sometimes I think I should just grit my teeth and throw them away. I can't even remember what's in half of them now."

Stratford had a quick look around from the doorway, then followed Mary into the bigger room next door. Moorhouse edged around the maze of boxes and crates and looked through a box stacked with old paintings I hadn't yet got around to hanging. She pulled up a framed print of Margaret Preston's *Sydney Heads* that I'd bought when Steve and I first set up house together.

"Oh, I love this," she enthused, lining it up against the wall. "I've been thinking about taking up painting. This looks like something I could manage. I might just take a snap."

"It's not actually a painting, it's a woodblock print."

Moorhouse looked at me blankly and took the photo. She rifled through the carton and pulled out another—a long, framed poster of one of Alice Neel's pregnant women that I'd picked up years ago. Under the dim light, the green tones looked even sicklier than usual.

Moorhouse gazed at it for a long moment. "Wow. That's kinda grotesque. She actually looks like she's about to burst. I might get a photo of that one, too." Her phone flashed. "Excellent." She gave me a bright smile.

Back upstairs, the two officers took a quick look through the living areas and bedrooms—not even blinking at the chaos in Mary's room—and then headed back outside. Mary changed her mind about accompanying us when she saw the frost still glistening on the lawn, and the three of us trudged across to the car shed. When I pulled up the central door, Stratford gave an appreciative nod.

"This is a good size," he said, looking into the cavernous space from the doorway. "Three cars, eh? I'd love one like this, but the wife won't be in it. I've got a boat," he added by way of explanation.

"All this space is wasted on us, I'm afraid. We've only got one car, and most of the time I can't actually be bothered driving it in. Though it's a bit of a mistake in this weather, isn't it?"

He looked over at my little Mazda, its red paint shrouded in heavy frost, and grimaced. "So you've only got the one? Your mother, she doesn't have a car?"

"I don't think she's ever had a license, actually. I don't remember seeing her drive. But even if she did, they'd have taken it away now."

They both looked at me sympathetically this time.

"She doesn't seem *that bad*," Moorhouse said. "Just . . . a bit eccentric?"

"It varies. Today's a good day. So far. It tends to get worse at night, or when she's tired."

"Is she okay on her own—or do you have to get someone in to help with her?"

I explained that Sally came in three days a week, that when Mary was at home alone, I checked in on her by phone. It wasn't ideal, but so far it was working.

"And lately Chip's been calling in, too, when he can."

"Chip Gascoyne?" Her surprise was obvious.

"Yes. We're friends. And he's good with Mary." It was too complicated to go into details.

"This was the Gascoynes' place, wasn't it? Must've been a bit of a wrench for him, splitting the property like that. Selling up."

"Oh, you couldn't really call it selling up. It's just the old homestead, and not even an acre of land. I've only got the home paddock. Chip's land actually starts right there." I indicated the fence that ran along the perimeter of the shed. "Anyway, I'm sure he's happy enough in his new place."

"That's it, isn't it?" The inspector gestured across the paddocks. There was a dense windbreak of pines between the two properties, but it was still possible to make out Chip's chimney and a small section of his roof. I nodded.

"It won some architecture prize," Moorhouse piped up helpfully. "I saw the pictures in some magazine a few years ago. It looks awesome."

"Yes. It's perfect, really—not as big as the old place, but very comfy. Everything's new. And it's warm." A gust of icy-cold wind whipped around us, as if to illustrate my point.

Stratford laughed. "And that's something you really appreciate at this time of year."

"Anyway, I think we've seen enough here. We've got quite a busy day ahead of us. How many more did you say, Constable?" He stamped his feet, looking glum at the prospect.

ABDUCTED: THE ELLIE CANNING STORY

A documentary by HeldHostage Productions © 2019

ELLIE CANNING: TRANSCRIPT #7

One day I woke up and there was a woman sitting beside me in a chair, holding my hand. I can remember just lying there, gazing at her, saying nothing, wondering who she was and where she'd come from. It took me a while to understand that she was real. That she wasn't just a part of the weird dream world I'd been in for so long. Sometimes I thought she might have been the woman from the painting. She looked similar—dark hair and dark eyes—but she was older, and she wasn't pregnant. After a while I decided she must be a nurse, although she wasn't wearing a uniform or anything, just ordinary clothes—jeans and a shirt, a cardigan. She did seem sort of familiar, but it was ages before I remembered who she was, and how I'd met her.

That first day she sat beside me and stroked my hand. She smiled and said hello. I tried to speak, to ask her where I was, what had happened, but my lips wouldn't form the words.

Eventually she asked me if I wanted something to eat. There was a bowl of soup, some pieces of buttered bread. The soup didn't smell like hospital food, or even school food—it smelled spicy and delicious. Suddenly I realized I was starving.

She helped me sit up, arranging the pillows behind me. I was too weak to feed myself, so she fed me, spoon by spoon, wiping my face with a napkin when I dribbled. It was the tastiest soup I've ever had. After the soup she gave me a drink of something sweet—juice or cordial—from one of those baby cups with a lid.

After I'd eaten I started to fall asleep again, but the woman shook me gently and told me I should go to the loo first. She helped me up, and I was surprised to find that my legs were still working. She led me across the room and opened the door. There was a little toilet with one of those heavy black lids like in public toilets. The room smelled of eucalyptus, which was better than the bedroom itself, which was kind of rank.

She handed me this pair of disgusting granny undies and told me to put them on and give her mine. I was scared that she was going to make me pee in front of her, but she closed the door and told me to let her know when I was done.

Anyway, when I was done, she helped me across the room again and back into the bed. She put my dirty undies into a bag, then straightened the bedcovers and tucked me in. She sat back down on the chair beside me and stroked my hair while I drifted off.

HONOR: AUGUST 2018

Honor was with Ellie in the temporary accommodation the police had arranged for them at the Luxury Inn when Stratford called to say he and Moorhouse were heading over, that they needed Ellie to look at some pictures. Honor had been trying to work—she had other clients who needed her attention—but it had been difficult. Incoming calls from outlets trying to talk to Ellie were so constant that she'd had to hand all her other clients over to her assistant. There would have to be some serious rescheduling when she was back in Sydney, but now was not the time.

The girl had spent the afternoon lying on the lumpy double bed, eating cheese puffs and watching *Geordie Shore* on an endless loop. She hadn't been the best company, was anxious and demanding, and Honor had had to work hard to stay patient. The constant noise from the television was doing her head in, but they'd finally reached a compromise—Honor paid the receptionist a ludicrous amount of money to go out and buy Ellie a pair of headphones.

The receptionist—Elaine someone or other—was another middle-aged dowd who claimed to have been an old friend of Honor's at school. "My parents ran this place back then," she'd said with a fat smile, as if inheriting this dump were something to be proud of. These multiplying numbers of former "acquaintances" were doing her head in, too. Since buying the weekender, most of her visits into town had been brief, and, apart from a few unavoidable celebrity guest–type appearances at local functions, her encounters with locals had been mercifully limited. But since the news got out that she'd taken Ellie on as a client, things had changed. So many people she'd forgotten, or would really rather not remember, had been keen to renew her acquaintance, welcome her back into the fold, so to speak. It was as if she were wearing a neon **Prodigal Daughter** sign on her back.

"I remember when you were just a wee thing," one very old lady, apparently an old friend of her grandmother, had said, baring startlingly white teeth. "You were such a quiet little thing. Like a little mouse. I never imagined you'd grow up to be such a bigwig."

There'd been others, too—friends of her parents, the woman who'd run the corner store, a couple of old schoolteachers, parents of classmates—who had come up to speak to her on one pretext or another but who had all really wanted to talk about that poor sweet girl.

She'd been taken aback by the interest—Ellie wasn't a local, after all. But as the editor of the local paper had pointed out, Ellie Canning was the biggest story since local underworld identity Billy Cominos was shot point-blank in the Paradise Café back in the 1960s. Now *that* had been a scandal, sure, but one tinged with tragedy. Billy had, despite his undoubted criminal tendencies, always been a good bloke.

But this story was different. This time the town could enjoy the proximity of the crime without being personally involved.

There were no sides to be taken, no judgments to be made. The perpetrators, everyone was certain, would be out-of-towners, because there was literally no one that anybody could think of, no one who counted, no one who belonged, who fit Ellie's description of her captors. Washers simply didn't *do* this sort of thing.

Honor knew the police had been conducting searches of all the properties that matched Ellie's description from the few details she could recall of the exterior of the place where she'd been held—a milk pail–shaped mailbox, a long driveway, a cattle grid, a low-hanging front veranda. All these features were utterly commonplace; no doubt there were dozens of local properties that fit the bill. She hadn't imagined they'd come up with anything solid this early on in the investigation.

Honor did a quick clean of the room while Ellie showered and brushed her teeth, making herself presentable just moments before the two detectives arrived. Hugh maintained his professional distance, but Jenny Moorhouse gave her a friendly grin.

"How's the babysitting going, Honor?"

She rolled her eyes, gave the requisite heartfelt sigh. "Teenagers. I only just got her out of bed, to be honest. She's basically been doing nothing but eating junk food and watching reality TV shows all afternoon. It's driving me up the wall. I feel like I should be encouraging her to do something more wholesome, but I'm not sure what."

"Teenagers are such a joy. Or so I've heard. Mine aren't quite there yet, but I'm happy to wait." She added, her expression more serious, "It's good what you're doing, though. It's shit that a decent kid like Ellie is going through something like this and has to cope with it all on her own."

"She hasn't said much, but yeah. It's a tough old world for some. Don't worry about me. I'm getting business out of it, don't forget." Hugh filled them in on the investigation's progress. They'd been to a number of farmhouses that morning, all within a ten-kilometer radius of where Ellie had been found. Even though, Stratford explained, that was probably far in excess of the distance she was capable of walking, taking into account the state she'd been in when she was taken to hospital, the drugs she'd been given. But as the doctors said, the human body was capable of amazing things when put to the test.

"And," he pointed out, "we can't be sure that Ellie's memory of that time is intact. It's still possible there are things she can't account for. We can't, for instance, rule out the possibility that she was given a lift at some point after her escape and we've been looking in the wrong area."

What they'd expected was that it would be almost impossible to find any conclusive evidence of just who the perpetrators were. The most likely scenario was that they had been visitors to the area, perhaps even using aliases, and that they'd cleared out as soon as Ellie made her escape. They hadn't had great hopes about finding the place she'd been kept either. It was really a needle-in-a-haystack situation, going on the information Ellie had given them. Even within their defined radius, the number of homes in the area, which included a large number of holiday rentals, made it challenging, to say the least.

But as it turned out, Hugh went on, his expression almost cheerful, the first few days of the investigation had been far more productive than expected.

"We don't want to get your hopes up, Ellie, but we do have some possibilities. We've brought along some photographs for you to look at. Places with some of the features you've described."

Ellie, sitting cross-legged on the bed, listened intently, her hands clasped nervously in her lap, eyes wide, expectant.

"So have you actually worked out where she was kept? Who did it?"

Hugh took his time answering. "There's no way we can be sure about anything until we have confirmation from Ellie. So if it's okay, love, Jenny will show you some photos." He spoke soothingly, obviously sensing Ellie's discomfort.

Jenny took an iPad out of her bag. "Can I sit beside you?"

Ellie nodded, and Jenny sat down on the bed, wriggling over awkwardly with the tablet. "Just say no if you don't recognize anything, yes if you do. It might take a while. There are quite a few."

"I'm just scared I won't remember right." Ellie sounded very young.

"Just do your best." Stratford's voice was kindly, encouraging.

Honor watched Ellie as Moorhouse swiped through the images.

"No. No. No." Initially the girl shook her head at each picture, her face impassive, but then something in her expression changed, a degree of uncertainty creeping in. "I'm not sure—there's something about this one." She hesitated. "I think it's the trees. There's something familiar . . . Oh God, I really don't know. It was so dark. And I was so out of it."

"That's okay, sweetheart." Moorhouse was calmly reassuring. "There's plenty more." She swiped the screen again.

"No." Again. "No." And again. "No."

A new image. Ellie paused. Looked more closely. Took a shaky breath.

"Yes. Yes. I do recognize this one. Definitely. It's a bit different, but I recognize the light. And that horrible paint color."

She looked up, smiling triumphantly at Honor and Stratford. Then her eyes filled with tears. Honor felt her own shoulders sagging with relief.

"This is the room," Ellie whispered. "This is where they kept me."

The two officers exchanged a rapid glance. Considering what Ellie's identification meant, it seemed to Honor that they were incredibly calm.

Moorhouse held up the iPad again, her expression somber. "I'm going to show you a photograph now of the owners of this house, Ellie. I'd like to know whether you recognize them."

Ellie's eyes widened, her hand moving involuntarily to her cheek.

"Oh my God. That's her. That's the woman." She shook her head as if she couldn't quite believe it, enlarged the image. "It's so weird," she said wonderingly. "She looks so . . . normal."

Moorhouse's jaw clenched; she flicked to the next picture. "And what about this one?"

Ellie gave a short laugh. "Yes. That's the other one—the mad old lady. Her mother." She shook her head, slid her finger across the screen, swiping back and forth between the two images.

The two officers looked at one another again.

"Are you certain, Ellie? It's very important that we get this right. You've accused these women of an extremely serious crime. They could both go to prison for a very long time. You need to be one hundred percent certain."

"Can I know who they are?" Ellie asked. "Are they, like, known criminals or anything? Have they done this sort of thing before?"

Moorhouse looked up at Stratford, who nodded.

"That's the thing. They haven't. They really don't fit any sort of . . . regular profile for this sort of thing," he explained.

Honor couldn't help herself. "I can't imagine there is a regular profile for any of this. There's nothing *regular* about it, surely?"

"No, you're right. But this has come as a bit of a surprise, if I'm honest."

"Who is it?" Honor tried not to sound too interested.

"You understand that anything we say here is in complete confidence, Honor? It can't be mentioned outside this room until our investigations have been completed. There's a lot of work to be done before we can lay charges, and we need to ensure there are no stuff-ups. We don't want to lose this one on technicalities."

"Of course I understand!" She didn't even try to hide her impatience. "And I'll make sure Ellie understands, too."

"Okay. If I have your assurance." He nodded at Moorhouse again, and she turned the screen so that Honor could see the image.

"This might come as a bit of a shock. I believe she's a friend of yours."

Honor moved closer, and the image on the screen resolved. The figure was familiar, as was the background. She looked at Moorhouse, then at Stratford. She laughed but again felt herself closer to tears. "You're not serious?"

The policewoman gave an uncomfortable shrug.

Honor turned to Ellie. "You really recognize her? You're sure this is the woman who abducted you?"

ABDUCTED: THE ELLIE CANNING STORY
A documentary by HeldHostage Productions © 2019

ELLIE CANNING: TRANSCRIPT #8

When I look back now, it's, like, so crazy that I really didn't think about trying to escape at first. I really should have freaked out, but I didn't. It's hard to explain. Maybe it was because the woman was so calm and so kind. There wasn't anything frightening about her. Nothing at all. And I couldn't remember meeting her, the car trip. Whatever it was that she gave me did something really strange to my memory. I'd remember bits and pieces sometimes—like pieces of a puzzle that I couldn't quite put together.

To be honest, most of the time I actually enjoyed being there. Being with her. She was really motherly . . . in a way that my own mum never had been. And none of my foster parents either. She would do my hair. Sing to me. Read me books. I was always warm and comfortable—oh, and clean. There was this little bucket bath thing she'd set up in the toilet room every couple of days. She gave me this really sweet body soap, and I'd just, like, wash all the important bits so I didn't feel grotty. And then she'd give me a fresh pair of pj's.

And the food was really good. Like, almost gourmet compared to what I was used to. And there was always dessert.

Every now and then I'd be conscious enough to get a bit bored. Once I spent a couple of hours scratching my initials into the wall behind my bed with a teaspoon just for something to do. And every now and then I got really peed off about being left alone all day and started shouting—hoping that someone would come down and talk to me. I could hear them walking about upstairs, but no one ever came.

Mostly I was sort of content. It was like I was a little kid again, only it was a different sort of childhood to the one I'd actually had. And it was kind of amazing to have no responsibilities all of a sudden. Life had been pretty stressful. I'd been working really hard all year—with the exams coming up and trying to get the scholarship for college. Being stuck in that room was like this mad holiday.

After a while everything about my old life—the Abbey, my mum, exams, teachers, my foster parents, all my plans for university, going to St. Anne's next year . . . all of it began to feel like a dream. And the bed and the room and the woman and the days I spent lying there doing nothing and no one ever expecting anything from me—this felt like the real world. Like the only world I'd ever known.

SUZANNAH: AUGUST 2018

The police came back in the afternoon.

Despite my late arrival, I had managed to get away from school reasonably early. I called into the supermarket to get dinner things and then headed straight home.

It wasn't quite four when I arrived, but the day had turned gloomy, and it was already beginning to get dark.

I'd left the convection heater on in the family room, but for some reason Mary was watching the television in the freezing-cold lounge room. She didn't respond when I greeted her, the manic energy of the morning gone, but just stared blankly at the screen. She was wearing an old cotton shift of mine—a beach dress, short and sleeveless—and her skin was covered in goose bumps, her body shaking. I moved her back to the warmer room, brought her a rug and wrestled her into a woolly cardigan, pulled socks up over her ice-cube feet, and turned the convection heater up to full blast. I asked her if she wanted tea, something to eat. There was no response, but I made her a cup of tea anyway, sweet and milky, sliced bread for toast. She ate only a little but slurped down the lukewarm liquid and eventually perked up enough to begin whining about being tired, cold, needing a bath.

Mary's bath had become another nightly ritual since winter hit. It seemed to soothe her, and in this weather, it was almost the only thing that would warm her perpetually cold body. I ran the water for her, added a generous squirt of some musky body wash, and helped her climb in. Her body, once strong and shapely, was all bones and angles, her stomach concave, hip bones jutting, breasts shrunk into two small drooping sacks. She gripped my forearm with a clawed hand and climbed carefully into the bath, then sank down into the water. She lay low in the bubbly water, eyes and nose just above the waterline, relaxed, her hair in an untidy pile on her head. After a long, relieved sigh, she closed her eyes.

"You won't fall asleep?" I asked the same question every night. I'd had a tempering valve fitted to the bathroom taps, so I didn't have to worry about her scalding herself.

"Don't be so silly." She waved me away dismissively. I could have been a servant, a nurse, someone she'd hired, certainly someone she considered entirely insignificant. I guessed that wasn't so far from the truth. I left her there, the door partially opened. She'd call out when the water cooled down or she wanted to get out.

While she soaked, I made myself a cup of ginger tea and a piece of Vegemite toast, trying to beat the nausea that had made its evening return.

This time I heard the car—or was it cars?—pull up, the march of feet across the gravel. Mary was still in the bath, so for once I managed to get to the door before her. The same two police officers were standing on the veranda. There were no friendly smiles this evening, and they hadn't come alone. A small crowd milled about outside, awaiting instructions, some officers wearing those white suits that made them look like they were about to handle radioactive material.

"Ms. Wells." Stratford held out a document, his face grim.

"What's wrong? Why are you back?" I took the official-looking paper, glanced down, but it was impossible to read in the gloom.

"This is a warrant to conduct a full search of your premises."

I could hear Mary padding up the hall, her damp feet sticking to the worn carpet. She was singing, her voice low and sweet, some song I didn't recognize. I heard the sharply indrawn breath and saw the startled glances of the officers but didn't turn around. She came up behind me, rested her sharp chin on my shoulder, her hair dripping on my shoulder, down my back.

"Oh, hello there, big boy. Are you a friend of Suzannah's? I'm her mother."

He swallowed. "Evening, Mrs.—Miss Squires."

Mary pressed in behind me damply; I tried to shrug her off. "A warrant? But I don't understand. You've already looked around. You said that everything was fine. What have you come back for?"

He ignored my question, but his voice was gentle. "I think this might be a good time to contact that solicitor, Ms. Wells." He looked behind me briefly, cleared his throat. I turned at last. Mary was stark naked as well as dripping wet. "And you should probably get some clothes on your mother—I think it's going to be a cold night."

I rang Chip, who laughed. "A police search? What's going on? Did you murder Mary and hide the body?"

"It's serious, Chip. It's about that girl, the one who was abducted. Ellie Canning. They came this morning and had a look around—they said they were just checking out all the houses in the area . . . and now they've come back with a search warrant. They—he, the detective, Stratford—"

"Stratford? I don't think I know him."

"What does it matter? Anyway, he said I should probably get a solicitor."

"He told you to get a solicitor?" Chip shifted gears immediately, his voice suddenly brisk, businesslike. "Right. I'll ring Hal. And I'll be over in five. Tell them to wait until I get there." He disconnected.

I passed on Chip's message, but Stratford just gave an infuriatingly serene smile.

"I'm sorry, Ms. Wells, but there's no actual legal requirement that I wait. You can have a solicitor here, as I said, to advise you, but he won't actually have any jurisdiction over us." He didn't sound at all apologetic. "I've got a dozen officers being paid overtime, so if you don't mind"—he motioned to his team, who crowded into the lounge room—"we'll get started."

I did mind, but there was no way to stop them. Moorhouse, who had already helped Mary get dressed, offered to keep her occupied in the kitchen while the search was underway, and I was grateful for this one small act of mercy.

Chip arrived, still in his work clothes, his shirt untucked, his hair full of dust. He tried hard to look stern, to assert some authority, but it was clear that he was as clueless as me.

"I think before you start that you'd better give us some idea of what you're looking for, Inspector. Suzannah says it's something to do with that girl, Ellie Canning. The one who was kidnapped."

Stratford shook his head. "I'm afraid I can't give you any details at this stage, sir," he said in his impeccably polite way.

"Why not?"

"I understand Hal's on his way. I'm sure he'll explain."

"You know my brother?"

"I work with him a fair bit."

"Right." Chip nodded, then turned to me with what I assumed was meant to be a reassuring smile. "I guess we just wait, then."

The detective coughed. "Actually, I'm not altogether clear on what your involvement is here, Mr. Gascoyne. I know this is your old home, but . . . ?"

"Ms. Wells, I mean, Suzannah and I are . . . we're getting married." Chip said the words steadily but avoided looking at me.

"Is that right? Ms. Wells didn't mention that." The look he gave me was faintly quizzical.

I swallowed, looked down at my feet. "We haven't—it isn't def—"

"We're having a baby." Chip's statement sounded more like a proclamation.

"Right." For a moment I thought the detective was going to offer up congratulations, but none were forthcoming. "Well, you're quite welcome to watch that there's nothing out of order as we conduct the search, Mr. Gascoyne. We'd like to do this as quickly as possible, and I'm sure you'd all like us out of your hair."

~

I'd told Chip my news a few weeks before, had rugged up and tramped across the misty paddocks late in the evening, as soon as I was sure Mary was sound asleep. He hadn't been expecting me, but there had been genuine pleasure in his voice when he answered the door.

"Can't keep away, eh?"

"I'm pregnant." I'd blurted it out, right there in the doorway.

"What?" He'd made a move to usher me in, but then he stood motionless, as if rooted to the spot.

"I'm pregnant." I said it again, my face deliberately expressionless.

"Jesus." His eyes were wide, his voice barely audible. "Holy shit. Are you sure?"

I'd kept the stick in a pocket of my purse for a couple of days, waiting for courage, for just the right moment, and now I held it out for him to see—both lines were a distinct blue. Chip looked at it for a long moment, and then at me, and smiled. It wasn't his usual smile, full of charm, certainty, confidence, but something more tentative, as if he wasn't quite sure how he would be received. He cleared his throat.

"So—this is good news for you, I'm thinking? You do want it?" He looked hopeful, and suddenly younger.

"Yes. I really want it, Chip. That's definite. I'm not going to get many more chances. But I need to know what you want. How we're going to make it work."

"I guess we've got a bit to talk about, then." He smiled again, and for the first time I relaxed. He reached for my hand. "I think we can make this work, Suze. Don't you?"

It was more than a question—it was almost a plea. He squeezed my fingers.

I returned the pressure.

"So, you . . . you want to do this? Have this baby? Together?" I felt dazed, almost delirious, from the joy—or maybe it was just hormones.

"I can't believe you even have to ask. I know it's all happened pretty fast, but I've kinda been hoping we'd be doing a lot of things together. This is just the icing on the cake." He held my fingers to his lips. "Speaking of ice, your hands are freezing." He tightened his grip, pulled me inside. "I've got the kettle on. You look like you could do with a cuppa."

There had been so many things I was going to say, that needed to be said. I'd had it all planned—even written a list—before I arrived. I'd decided what I'd say if he looked terrified, which was, I thought, the most likely scenario. After all, Chip was almost fifty, and while he may have wanted children once, things had probably changed.

I was ready to tell him that I was prepared to leave, if he'd prefer it. I would sell up, move elsewhere, maybe back to the city. It would be easier to find a place for Mary there, and I wouldn't have to work full-time. I had enough money put away after the sale of the apartment to get me through a few years of part-time teaching. Whatever happened, I was going to have this baby. Even if he wanted nothing to do with it. With us.

But if Chip chose to share in the parenting, that would be okay, too, even if it was going to be a whole lot more complicated. After all, we barely knew each other; our relationship, if we could even call it that, had barely begun. We were, to put it crudely, only fuck buddies. But we could take it slowly. We could go on as we were for a few more months, at least while I was still working. We didn't need to tell anyone, change anything. I was happy for him to be a part of this baby's—*our* baby's—life, if that was what he wanted. He was welcome to come to scans, clinic appointments, parenting classes, antenatal classes—but I didn't need him to. I didn't need anything.

We were older parents, *old* parents, which meant we would do things very differently. We would be able to avoid the disorienting passion of lovers and of younger, more idealistic parents, forge a more civilized connection. I'd thought it all through logically, conscientiously. I was going to be grown-up about this.

I didn't allow myself to acknowledge what I was beginning to feel about Chip, how much I enjoyed his company, how much I wanted this—whatever it was between us—to keep going, to become something real, something more than a casual affair. I didn't let myself imagine raising this child together, as a couple. I didn't dare go there.

In all our wide-ranging nighttime conversations, we'd avoided almost any discussion of the two things that probably mattered the most right now—children and the future—and I hadn't for a moment considered that Chip's reaction to my news would be this. That he would be desperately, tenderly excited—that he would want this baby just as much as I did.

He pulled me to him the moment I walked through the door, held me tight for a moment, then stood back and looked at me, his eyes glistening.

"Let me look," he said, unbuttoning my shirt.

"I'm only six weeks," I protested. "There's nothing to see."

He ignored me, continued to unbutton the shirt, then ran his hand across my stomach. "Oh God, Suze. A baby. I can't believe it." He knelt down and laid his head against my stomach, pressed his ear against my middle, listening. I stroked his hair gently, all sensation, no thought.

"I didn't think it would happen. That I'd actually ever meet anyone that I wanted to spend the rest of my life with." He spoke quietly, not looking up. "And then you came, and I was . . . *smitten*. Like a, like I was a kid again." His laughter was warm across my belly. "I was trying to take it slow; I didn't want to terrify you with how badly I wanted you. And that's all I was thinking of—just you. But now this. A baby. Our baby. It's something I never thought would happen. It's like . . . it is a bloody miracle."

And then all the words I had planned, every single one, evaporated. I may as well have been a teenager again myself, with no thought but for the now, for the moment, full of lust, desperate for connection, and not a pregnant fortysomething woman with a mad mother to look after and an unplanned baby on the way.

~

By the time Hal finally arrived, the search was well underway. I'd met him briefly once before and been surprised by the differences between the two brothers. Physically, Hal was a complete contrast to Chip—bespectacled, balding, a big man running to overweight, dressed formally. Though he was the younger by a few years, he looked older, with a slight stoop and a permanent frown creasing his forehead. Chip was more compact, wore a uniform of jeans and boots, his shirt untucked and unironed, his graying hair messy and slightly too long. Hal's voice was nothing like Chip's lazy drawl; it was clipped, precise. Hal's personality was lower key, too; he radiated good sense, calm decision. His composure in the face of the police presence was reassuring. My panic began to recede, and after a warning glare from his brother, Chip became noticeably less hostile.

The officers had already searched two of the bedrooms and were about to begin on the third. They'd looked through our wardrobes, our chests of drawers, under carpets, gone through desks, and though there was something shameful about having your messy underwear exposed to strangers and recorded on film, they had been surprisingly careful about it. There were none of the spilled-out drawers or messes of fingerprint dust that I'd seen in crime shows.

Hal insisted on checking over Stratford's documentation, but there was nothing he could dispute; everything was completely in order.

He looked at me apologetically. "Sorry about this, but Inspector Stratford is right. There's really nothing I can do to stop them."

"But the whole thing's ridiculous. How can she have anything to do with that girl's abduction? Someone's fucked up big-time." Chip glared at his younger brother as if it were all his fault.

"I don't know, mate. But the cops have managed to convince a judge that there's a good reason. They don't just hand out search warrants for nothing. Did something happen when they came this morning, Suzannah?"

"No. There was nothing, really. They called in and had a quick look around. Inside and then around the yard. They told me they were looking at a few properties around the place. We weren't the only ones."

"They must have found something."

"But what? There's nothing to find."

"I don't know." Hal looked thoughtful. "The police work in mysterious ways. Anyway, you look all in, Suzannah. Why don't you go and wait with your mother? Chip and I can watch the rest of the search." He addressed the detective, who had just joined us. "If that's okay with you, Inspector?"

Stratford nodded his assent, and I moved back to the warm kitchen, grateful to be released.

By the time they finished, it was almost midnight. I was sitting on the lounge, pretending to watch television. Mary was sprawled out beside me, snoring loudly. Constable Moorhouse was at the kitchen table, drinking her fourth cup of instant coffee and doing a crossword. She'd played three games of Trouble with Mary, losing them all, and between them, she and Mary had demolished an entire pack of Tim Tams.

"It does terrible things to your waistline, shift work," Moorhouse said shamefacedly.

I'd drifted in and out of sleep myself, slightly queasy, my head pounding. I heard the heavy tread of footsteps across the veranda, and then Chip and Hal came back into the kitchen, followed by the inspector. He was carrying several small ziplock bags and the two framed pictures that Moorhouse had photographed earlier in the day.

"I'll get you to sign for these, if you don't mind, Ms. Wells."

I looked over at Hal, who nodded his approval. "What am I signing for?"

"We'll be taking away some items for verification. We've also taken swabs from a number of surfaces." He held up a plastic bag. "The first item is a plastic cup, taken from the basement bedroom."

The cup was a familiar one—an old infant's sippy cup that had been stored in one of the boxes. I felt a sharp pang at the sight of it.

"But that was . . . I'd really rather you didn't take that."

"You'll get it back," said Stratford. "And there's this. Also taken from the basement room."

He held up a second bag that contained a pair of lacy black-and-red underpants, brief, and far too small to be mine. I'd never seen them before.

"And this." It was the Neel print.

"What on earth do you want that for?"

He held up the smaller Preston print. "And this one, too."

"I don't understand. What are you taking them for? How are they evidence?"

I looked at Moorhouse, who was frowning steadfastly down at her puzzle.

"We'll make sure they're looked after, Ms. Wells. Don't worry."

"I'm not worried, I—"

"There's just one more thing," he interrupted, holding up another clear bag, this one containing a cheap plastic brush. "Now, if you could just sign here, we'll get these processed as quickly as we can."

"That girl can't have been here," Chip said quietly as I signed the forms.

The officer raised his eyebrows.

"If she'd been here, I'd have known." His voice was louder, more certain.

"And how would you know, Mr. Gascoyne?"

"I told you, we're engaged. I've practically been living here for the past couple of months. If that girl had been here, I'd have seen her, wouldn't I?"

The detective looked at him dubiously. "Is that right? It doesn't look like Ms. Wells is sharing a bedroom."

Chip didn't hesitate. "I still keep all my stuff at home."

"I'm surprised you didn't speak up earlier."

"It's only just occurred to me."

"And you're completely sure about the timing?"

"Chip." Hal put a hand on his brother's shoulder, shaking his head. "You should probably leave it for now, mate, sort it out when things are a bit clearer."

"You really should think about this overnight, Mr. Gascoyne. If you're certain, you can come down to the station tomorrow morning, and we can take a statement."

Chip said nothing, but Hal gave a short nod.

"We'll be in touch again shortly, Ms. Wells. Now, we'll let you get to bed."

I was desperate for sleep, the headache worse, my stomach churning, and every part of my body aching, but first there was Mary to deal with. Tonight, even though I had to wake her to get her to bed, she was perfectly docile and let me lead her to the bedroom and tuck her in.

She grabbed my hand as I turned to go. "Mummy?" she whispered.

"No, it's me, Mary. It's Suzannah."

"But I want my mummy." The eight-year-old child she once was looked at me with frightened eyes. "When's she coming back?"

I smoothed back her hair, kissed her gently on the forehead. "She won't be long," I said.

"Where's she gone?"

"I don't know. But I'm sure it isn't far."

"Maybe I'll see her in my dreams," Mary said sleepily, her eyelids fluttering.

I turned out the bedside light. "Maybe you will."

Chip and Hal were in the kitchen. Chip had found a bottle of red, poured them each a glass, and the brothers were leaning against the countertop talking, their voices low and intent, their expressions grim. I watched them for a moment. Though the two men couldn't have been more different, they shared a sort of ease in the world, and with other people, that I envied. But right now there was no trace of Chip's habitual good humor; he seemed angry, the tension apparent in his rigid jaw, the vein pulsing near his temple. I was suddenly aware of how little I knew him, how little he knew me. And yet he was here, now. We were in whatever happened next together, linked forever by this unexpected life within me. I wasn't sure whether to be comforted or frightened by this fact. Right then, I was simply exhausted.

They paused in their conversation when I entered the room. Chip attempted a reassuring smile, held out the bottle. "You're probably not meant to, but you look like you could do with one of these."

I shook my head, tried to smile back. "I don't think that's going to help at this point. I might just have a hot chocolate. So what was that all about? Do they seriously think I have something to do with what happened to that girl?"

I addressed my question to Hal, who took a moment to answer.

"A search warrant is always serious. They have to get permission from a magistrate, which means they must have some sort of corroborating evidence from the girl. Did you get any sense when they came this morning that they thought anything was out of order?"

"Not really. They took pictures of all sorts of things, and of us, but I assumed it was just for elimination."

"Surely that's illegal?" said Chip.

"No. Not if Suzannah said it was okay," said Hal. "I assume you signed something? And you hadn't been singled out, had you? They were just checking possibilities."

"Yeah. They said they had a heap of places to visit. I imagined they were probably checking all the properties around here."

"That's probably true, too. But there must have been something here that she recognized. That's why they came back with the warrant. And isn't the girl saying there were two women? One younger, one older? On the surface, it seems . . . possible, I suppose." Hal looked at me steadily. "Do you want to engage me as your solicitor?"

"Do I really need one? That seems a bit drastic. Surely this will all be cleared up? It won't go to . . . court or anything?"

Hal looked worried. "They've obviously got something. More than something. They must have serious evidence. As I said, judges don't give out warrants without good cause."

"But this is insane. As if I'd—"

He held up his hand. "I'd rather wait until we hear what the police have to say before you tell me anything more."

"Jesus Christ, you're a wanker, Hal." Chip rolled his eyes. "It's not like Suzannah's some bloody druggo." He reached an arm around my shoulders, gave me a steadying squeeze. "You don't really have to bung on all this lawyer crap, you know."

For the first time, Hal looked faintly amused. "If I'm going to be her lawyer, I have to, ah, behave like a lawyer."

"Yeah. Well, this is bullshit. I'll tell them tomorrow that I've been living here for the last couple of months."

"Chip, no. You can't," I said. "I'm really grateful for the offer. But you weren't here *all* the time. Not really." I smiled to take away the sting, but he glared at me.

119

"How're they going to know that?"

"You'd better make sure of the dates before you go making any statements." Hal kept his voice light, but he was serious.

"What do you mean?"

"They're not going to take your word for it. You need to make sure you weren't elsewhere at some crucial time."

"I wasn't."

His brother sighed. "You can't lie, Chip. You'll get caught. This is bloody serious. I don't suppose you have a convenient alibi, Suzannah?"

"Alibi?" The word came out as a frightened squeak. "What do you mean, an alibi?"

"I don't suppose you went away for a holiday? If you can prove you were away during the period in question, it would help."

"No. We've had no holidays. I'm pretty much always here with Mary when I'm not at work. Oh, I took a day trip to Sydney to see a play at the beginning of the school holidays."

"Have you had people over to stay?"

"Well, there's Chip. But there's been no one else." I could feel myself blush, but Hal didn't seem to notice.

"People for dinner?" He sounded apologetic. "Other than Chip, I mean."

"There's Honor Fielding. She's been over a couple of times for dinner. I'm not sure about the exact dates, though."

"Does anyone else come to the house regularly? A gardener? A cleaner?"

"Yes! There's a woman who comes in three days a week, to watch Mary. Sally O'Halloran. The nursing home recommended her. And I've used her as a babysitter, too, when I've gone out at night. And a couple of times on the weekend."

Hal brightened. "She might be useful." I gave him her contact numbers.

"So, is there anyone else? No old friends have called in on their way through? No other family?"

The nonexistence of my social and family life was suddenly crushingly obvious. "We haven't been here that long."

Chip cut in, his tone decisive. "You honestly don't have to worry, Suze—I can be your alibi. I'll just say I was here that whole time. That girl couldn't have been here. No one's going to say otherwise."

Hal shook his head, exasperated now. "How many times do I have to tell you that you can't say that? You'd be up for perjury at the very least. And look—even if you were here, it doesn't necessarily follow that the girl couldn't have been here, too. Wasn't she kept drugged in the basement? Suze could have kept her hidden from you."

"I can say I've been down there. That there was no girl."

I took his hand. "Hal's right. You can't lie. You could actually go to jail. And what good would that do?" My voice shook.

"I know it doesn't sound like a big deal, Chip," his brother added. "But you don't want to start lying to the cops. And, mate, I don't know how it hasn't occurred to you, but there is another scenario. An even more serious one."

"What sort of scenario?" Chip looked puzzled, but I knew what his brother was about to say.

"They could suggest you were in on it."

"That never even occurred to me," he said.

"So you're better out of it. But I'm sure there are other things you can do if you want to help. Maybe you could . . ." Hal paused and looked around the kitchen as if searching for chores for his brother to do.

Chip's expression brightened almost instantly. "How about I do actually move in now? That way I can protect you."

I had to try not to laugh. "Protect me? How?"

"Oh, come on, Suzannah." Chip grabbed my hand. Hal cleared his throat and walked out of earshot. "I know it's a bit old-fashioned, but I want to do all the things blokes normally do for the woman who's having their baby."

It was old-fashioned—also endearing. "What sort of things?"

"It's probably not much, but I could . . ." He paused, scratched his head. "Bring you tea. Or make sure you don't have to . . . climb ladders. Make sure you eat properly. Send you to bed at a decent hour. Make sure you have a bucket handy."

"But I don't need—"

He interrupted. "And I can help entertain Mary. You know she likes me."

He had a point.

"Okay. Whatever. You can stay."

"No. Not *you can stay*. It should be, I *want* you to stay, Chip, my darling."

"Okay. Yes, I do."

"No. I need you to say it."

"I want you to stay, Chip, my darling." I somehow managed to keep a straight face.

He moved closer, whispered, "I want you to stay, Chip, my darling, because I want to fuck you silly every night of the week—"

"Chip. Come on."

"You need to take this seriously. You can think of it as a sort of nontraditional betrothal. Repeat after me: I want you to stay, Chip, my darling . . ."

". . . because I want to fuck you—oh, this is ridiculous. You know I don't want to fuck you silly every night of the week. I don't want to fuck you at all. I just want to sleep. And when I don't want to sleep, I want to throw up. This baby . . ."

"What baby? Are you having a baby?"

None of us had seen Mary standing quietly in the doorway. "What the hell are *you* going to do with a baby, oh, Suzannah? That sounds like a very bad idea. You killed the last one, didn't you?"

Chip waited until Hal had gone and Mary was safely back in bed before asking, "What was Mary talking about? That stuff about you killing a baby?"

"Oh. That." I'd been dreading this moment. I had known it would be this that Chip would want to talk about, that it would cast an even darker shadow over all the crazy stuff that had gone on this evening.

"Is there something you haven't told me? Something you maybe *should* have told me?" It was hard to read his expression, whether he was angry, upset, concerned, curious.

I gave him the facts—bare, blunt, and with no unnecessary details. It was still the only way I could discuss it.

"Stephen and I—we had a child. A daughter. Stella. She died when she was nine months old. Sixteen years ago."

"What happened?"

"SIDS. Cot death." It never seemed to get any easier.

"I'm sorry." He looked as if he wanted to say more but didn't. I was the one who finally broke the silence.

"I'm sorry that you found out about it that way. I didn't even realize Mary knew. The story was in a few papers, mostly gossip magazines, when it happened. I was surprised it was mentioned at all. I was pretty much a has-been by then. She must have taken more of an interest in me than I knew."

"But why didn't you tell me about it before? Something so huge?"

"I'm sorry. It's just, it's hard to talk about. And I didn't want it to change things."

"Change things?"

"Between us."

It was impossible to explain how your child's death changed the way other people, especially other parents, related to you, the way they avoided contact—as if tragedy were contagious.

Impossible to explain how eventually I had stopped telling people, had tried hard not to be Suzannah-whose-baby-died-poor-thing, to pretend that I was someone else. Here, in Enfield Wash, nobody knew that part of my history. I might have been an ex-celebrity, but to most I was just a hardworking teacher, a dutiful daughter—a simple, almost two-dimensional character with all her baggage on display. I knew that this role play would never work entirely, that it couldn't, but some days the transformation felt possible. Fake it till you make it, as the psychologists advised.

"But we're having a child together," said Chip. "I'd have thought you'd want me to know." He looked downcast, uncertain, vulnerable. "I'm not just anyone."

"I know you're not. And I was going to tell you. I was working up to it. Truly. But then . . . then I was pregnant. And suddenly there was an us. I didn't want to spoil things."

He was beside me then, his arms around me.

"I know it all seems unlikely. You and me, I mean. A sexy soapie star and a rough-as-bags farmer who's barely left the paddock? Seriously, we must have rocks in our heads. Who'd have thunk it?"

Suddenly we were both laughing.

"But I reckon"—he took a breath—"I reckon we can make this thing work, don't you?"

I answered as honestly as I could. "I actually don't know. Everything's so . . . up in the air." It was a massive understatement. "But I really, really want it to."

He nodded. "Well, I guess maybe it's as good as it's going to get right now. But no more secrets. I don't care what happened in your past. You can tell me everything, Suze. You can tell me anything."

ABDUCTED: THE ELLIE CANNING STORY

A documentary by HeldHostage Productions © 2019

ELLIE CANNING: TRANSCRIPT #9

And then there was the other woman. She was the younger one's mother, I found out later. She came in some days, but not all the time. She was always dressed in this crazy stuff.

Nothing ever matched. At first I thought she was ancient—with all that silver hair—but then I worked out she wasn't, like, in her nineties or anything. But she was still old.

The other woman, the younger one, she was never hostile, but this one was. I mean, she never touched me or anything, but sometimes she'd sort of hiss at me. And the stuff she said. OMG. It was mad. Like, once she came in and shouted that I needed to leave him alone, that he was hers, not mine, and I better watch out, she wasn't going to let a little slut like me screw up her life . . . And this other time she came and told me that her voice was better than mine, that I was singing flat or off-key or something, and that I'd only got the job because I was fucking the drummer. It would have been funny if it wasn't so scary.

It was almost scarier when she wasn't nuts. A couple of times she came in and sat beside me and held my hand, and sang to me. All this old stuff from the eighties. And a few times she came in and wanted me to play Trouble with her—you know, that dumb game with the clicker in the middle? Mostly when we played I just drifted off and that was fine, but then she'd lose it completely when I took one of her pieces. I tried not to, but it wasn't that easy to let her win. You know—it's one of those games where it's just dumb luck. Anyway, a couple of times she upended the whole thing and left. Oh, and sometimes she brought me these bowls of Froot Loops to eat.

Just dry Froot Loops. I had to pretend to like them, but they were always a bit stale, and it was hard not to gag.

The two women never came in together. In fact I got the feeling that the older one wasn't really meant to be there.

She would only come in during the daytime. Maybe when the other woman was away? And I never mentioned the mother to the other one. I don't know why, but it seemed important to keep it a secret.

SUZANNAH: AUGUST 2018

"Suzannah Wells, you are under arrest for the abduction and imprisonment of Eleesha Britney Canning. You are not obliged to say anything unless you wish, as anything you say will be given in evidence . . ."

It was like one of those nightmares, where on some level you're fully aware that you're caught in a dream and that what's happening is completely ludicrous, but you can't work out how to stop it, how to wake yourself up.

Parts of it were bizarrely familiar: the phrase itself—"you are under arrest"; the modulations of the detective's voice; the way the world wobbled around me, contracting, expanding, contracting again as I tried to make some sense of what was happening. All this, every word, every action, felt as if I were inside a living cliché. Those moments were just as I would have imagined them, had I been playing the scene in a film, acting the part of a woman unfairly accused.

But other moments were closer to high farce. There I was, trying hard to appear calm but worrying about packing an overnight bag, as if I were going on a holiday, before being bowled over by a wave of nausea and running off to vomit.

There was the panicked discussion about what to do about Mary, the two brothers arguing about whether Chip should come with me to the station or stay home with her, to give me one less thing to worry about. Then there was Mary herself, who decided that Hal was actually an old boyfriend from her LA days and that he owed her forty dollars for some gear he stole and was only appeased when Chip promised her an ice cream cone. ("Sprinkles, too?")

The police observed all this patiently and politely and then informed us that although they weren't arresting her, they did want Mary to come in for questioning. Then Hal was arguing angrily about the legality of interviewing someone who was so obviously psychologically impaired.

And then we were back to the crime-show clichés again: the slow walk across the icy gravel to the police car (unhandcuffed, thank God); Constable Moorhouse standing too close, her gloved fingers clamped on my elbow, her hand pressing gently on the top of my head as she guided me into the back seat, leaning over me, buckling me in as carefully as she would a small child.

There was the recorded interview in the dingy room, the revelatory production of all the impossible, crazily damning evidence. Hal sitting beside me, interjecting periodically. This scene felt entirely scripted, even more so when I realized there was a camera, that a transcript of the conversation would be typed up and that eventually the entire performance would be made available, part of the public record, evidence to be presented in court.

Like all theater, it was an ensemble effort, but individual performances varied. Inspector Stratford's delivery was rather wooden, as if he'd learned his lines but hadn't been able to inject any feeling.

My own act left a great deal to be desired. My emotional range was limited—there was very little nuance in my approach. If I'd had more time to prepare, perhaps there'd have been greater tonal variation, but as it was, I was invariably shrill, barely managing to keep the panic under control. The one saving grace was that later, I would only have to read through the transcript and not watch a rerun, for without a doubt, this was the worst performance of my career.

Only Hal's execution was halfway decent. He gave a fabulous impression of a quick-witted if somewhat cynical defense lawyer, and his dramatic timing was spot-on: he never hesitated, didn't overdo the emotion; there were even moments of sly humor.

"Before you go any further," he began, his expression severe, his voice perhaps a little too loud, forceful without being aggressive, "I'd like to make it clear that my client, Ms. Wells, denies all the charges that have been made against her, and that, furthermore, she finds these allegations ludicrous."

"Thank you, Mr. Gascoyne." Stratford's manner was deliberately calm. "Your comments have been noted. Now, Ms. Wells, you have told us that you've never met the victim?"

Hal interrupted before I had an opportunity to speak.

"As far as she knows, Inspector. As we've already pointed out, Ellie Canning grew up in an area close to where Ms. Wells herself lived only a few years ago, so it's entirely possible that Ms. Wells has had some kind of contact with Miss Canning previously, without any recollection of having done so."

"Thank you, Mr. Gascoyne. If I can continue? Ms. Wells, you have told us that you've never met Miss Canning, and that the first time you heard anything of her situation was through news reports approximately a week ago?"

I glanced at Hal. He nodded. "That's—" I faltered, cleared my throat. "Yes, that's right. I can't be a hundred percent, but as far as I know, I've never met her. Her name wasn't at all familiar."

"So you're certain she's never, to your knowledge, been in your house, or on your Wash Road property during the time you've lived there?"

"No. I mean, I don't know for certain. It's possible she could have been on my property at some point without my knowing about it, I guess."

"But you yourself have no knowledge of her having been there?"

"No, of course I don't."

Stratford paused for a moment, looked through his papers. "Did you make a trip to Sydney on Saturday, July 7, Ms. Wells?"

I thought back. "If that was the first day of the school holidays, then yes."

"Can I ask what the purpose of that visit was?"

"I went down for the matinee of a play I've been wanting to see. I was meant to meet up with an old teaching friend, Laura Huber. It's a tradition. We've been going to the theater at the end of each school term for years, and we'd decided to keep doing it even though I'd moved. We met up after first term, in the April holidays, but this time she was sick and couldn't go. I'd paid for the tickets, and I was really looking forward to it, so I decided to go down anyway. I'm sure I still have the tickets in an email if you want to see them."

"What did you do after the show?"

"What do you mean?"

"Did you go elsewhere? Meet anyone? Or go straight home?"

"I . . . I went to DJs and had a quick look round. I think I got some chocolates at Haigh's. And I grabbed a cup of coffee. By then it was already pretty late, so I got going."

"What time was that?"

"How is this relevant?"

"Can you answer the question, please?"

"It was . . . around four o'clock. Four thirty, maybe."

"And what time did you get back?"

"I don't know. It was probably around seven. Just before."

"And you went straight to your home—you didn't call in anywhere else first?"

"No. Sally O'Halloran was here looking after Mary. She needed to go home."

"And what happened when you arrived?"

"I paid Sally, and she left."

"Was it dark when Miss O'Halloran left?"

"Yes."

"And where did you park your car?"

"Where did I park? I don't rem—oh, probably over near the garage. Sally would have pulled up right outside the house. She's always running late . . ."

"So she wouldn't have had any reason to go past your car when she left?"

"What has my car got to do with anything?" I looked at Hal, confused.

Hal folded his arms. "Come on, Inspector. Get to the point." Stratford ignored him. He gestured to a uniformed officer, who brought over one of the pictures they'd taken the day before and held it up in front of me.

Stratford spoke directly to the camera. "For the record, I am now showing Ms. Wells a painting taken from a basement room of her home." He turned back to me.

"This painting was taken from your downstairs storeroom during our search yesterday, Ms. Wells. It has been identified by Ellie Canning as identical to one hanging in the bedroom in which she was held. The painting shows the figure of a heavily pregnant woman lying on a lounge. Is there anything you wish to tell me about this?"

Was there anything I wished to tell him? I looked at Hal, who nodded.

"I'm not sure. I mean, I'm not sure what you want me to tell you. It's not a painting, actually, just an old poster print that I had framed."

"It's quite an unusual painting, Ms. Wells. It's certainly not one I've seen before."

"But that doesn't mean . . . I'm sure there are heaps of them around. It's pretty well known."

He nodded to the officer, who leaned the painting against the wall. Stratford picked up a plastic bag from a pile on the chair beside him.

"I am now going to show you Exhibit B, which is a pair of red-and-black lace underpants. These were also seized during the search of your premises last night." Stratford held the bag up delicately. "What can you tell me about these?"

"I can't tell you anything. I've never seen them before. I have no idea why they would be there. They're not Mary's either. Maybe they were left by someone else?"

"And who might that someone else be? Do you have any ideas about this, Ms. Wells?"

Hal sighed. "She's said she doesn't recognize them, Stratford. Can you make your point?"

"Miss Canning claims that these items resemble undergarments belonging to her and says that they were taken from her by the woman who abducted her, along with other items of her clothing. Do you have any response to this, Ms. Wells?"

I shook my head. What was there to say?

"If you could actually speak for the purposes of the recording, Ms. Wells. I asked if you have any response to this?"

"No. No, I have no response."

"I am now going to show you further items of clothing: these are Exhibits C and D." He took a pale-pink silk shirt with black edging, and matching long pants, from another bag.

"Can you tell me anything about these items, Ms. Wells? For the record I am showing Ms. Wells a pair of pink pajamas, size twelve."

Those I recognized. "Oh. Yes! They're Mary's favorite pajamas. She calls them her Chanel pajamas, because they look like—"

Hal was glaring at me. I paused, took a breath. "Did you take these, too? Were they in the downstairs room? I haven't been able to find them for weeks, but I don't know why they'd be down in the basement."

"These are the clothes that Ellie Canning was wearing when she was found."

"She was wearing them? Mary's pajamas. But how could she—"

"That doesn't mean anything, Inspector," Hal said. "Clothes are mass-produced."

Stratford ignored him, again asking me if I would like to say anything.

I still didn't know what he wanted me to say. The pajamas did look exactly like Mary's, and they were the same size. But if they were hers, I had no idea how the girl had come to be wearing them.

"Perhaps someone stole them from my washing line," I offered. "Or maybe they got muddled up in a charity-shop bag?" I couldn't remember the last time I'd taken a bag to a charity store, but it seemed worth suggesting.

Stratford held up a black plastic hairbrush. "This hairbrush is Exhibit E. Does this belong to you, Ms. Wells?"

"I can't be sure, but if it's the one you took last night, I suppose so. It certainly looks like one of mine."

"I am now going to show you Exhibit F." He picked up a folder. "This document outlines the results of a DNA test from hair that was taken from this hairbrush." He slid the folder across the table. "I'll give you a moment to read over it."

I tried to make sense of the printed matter, but the writing blurred before my eyes. Who knew what it said? I gave up, passed it over to Hal, and waited expectantly.

"As you can see, some of the hair on this brush matches the DNA of hair taken from Ellie Canning. You'll see that DNA taken from Exhibit B—the underwear—also matches that of Miss Canning. Can you think of any reason why that might be so, Ms. Wells?"

I didn't understand any of this. It made no sense at all. I shook my head. My voice was barely a squeak. "No."

"I am now going to show you an infant's drinking cup, which was taken from your basement room. Does this cup belong to you, Ms. Wells?"

"Yes. But as I said when you took it, I don't even understand where you found it. It was packed away."

"If you look at the report, you'll see that Ellie Canning's DNA was also found on the lid of this cup. We also found benzodiazepine residue inside the cup. Is there anything you'd like to tell me about these facts, Ms. Wells?"

"But that's impossible. That was my daughter's cup. And I certainly never gave her any sort of drug in it."

Stratford's back stiffened. His eyes narrowed. "Your daughter? You haven't mentioned that you have a daughter. She doesn't live with you?"

"No."

"Where is she?"

"She . . ." I took a breath, started again. "She died when she was a baby. Almost sixteen years ago."

"I see." He paused for a long moment, as if considering this new information. "And can you tell me about the circumstances of your daughter's death?"

Hal interrupted, his voice harsh, "I really don't see how that's in any way relevant to the Canning girl's allegations, and as you can see, it's distressing to my client."

"It's not up to you to decide what's relevant, Mr. Gascoyne. You know that as well as I do. I'm sorry it's distressing, Ms. Wells, but I need to ask, how did your daughter die?"

"It was cot death." I didn't elaborate.

"And your daughter's father? Where is he now?"

"Stephen. We . . . split not long after her death. He's remarried and was living somewhere in Western Australia, last I heard."

"And your daughter would be how old now?"

"She'd be sixteen."

"So a similar age to Ellie Canning?"

"Oh, come on!" Hal's outrage seemed genuine. "What's that got to do with it? Are you suggesting that my client kidnapped Canning to somehow replace her daughter? That's absurd."

"Ms. Wells, have you ever attempted to get pregnant since the sad loss of your daughter?"

"What? This is a completely outrageous question. Suzannah, you don't have to answer that."

"No, it's okay, Hal." I held up a hand, suddenly calm. I didn't understand why he was asking, but there was nothing to hide. "No, I haven't tried to get pregnant since my daughter died. I haven't really had any long-term relationships since that time. And I wasn't planning to now. I'd never even thought it was possible. But why do you want to know?"

After the interview, the paperwork, the fingerprinting, the giving up of personal effects, I was led into a holding cell to await the afternoon bail hearing. An egg and lettuce sandwich was provided for lunch, along with a cup of watery lukewarm instant coffee (which I had imagined might be marginally better than the watery lukewarm tea-bag tea on offer). In the late afternoon, I was conducted to court by Stratford and another officer. The courthouse was across the road from the station, but the journey for offenders was underground and involved a long walk down a dim subterranean corridor. I wore handcuffs this time, and they were heavy and uncomfortable, chafing against my wrists. I was taken not to the court itself, but into a small, brightly lit office somewhere in the depths of the court complex, where Hal was already waiting, along with the magistrate and a man who was introduced as the prosecutor. The prosecutor was the father of one of the girls in my senior drama class, and we'd had several friendly conversations, but there was no indication that he recalled this or that we'd ever met before. The business of whether I was to be released on bail was briskly conducted by the four men without any input from me.

Despite being at the center of it all, I was somehow entirely peripheral. The magistrate—thin, bearded, impassive—gave me a brief once-over before agreeing with Hal that I hardly appeared to be any sort of a flight risk—a pregnant, middle-aged schoolteacher with an elderly mother to take care of—regardless of my alleged crimes.

The magistrate made his decision quickly—bail was set at $10,000, and a committal would be scheduled at a later date. I was conducted (no handcuffs this time) back along the corridor to the station and, after another hour or so of bureaucratic wrangling, released into the real world.

It was all so utterly strange, so far beyond my experience, that there was no possible way to orient myself. I felt as if I had fallen into some crazy experimental film, where I was the only actor without a script, the only player who had no idea what was going to happen next.

ABDUCTED: THE ELLIE CANNING STORY
A documentary by HeldHostage Productions © 2019

ELLIE CANNING: TRANSCRIPT #10

Footage of approach to Suzannah Wells's property, down long driveway. Zoom in on homestead. Segue to silent footage of a young, bikini-clad Wells flirting with a group of bronzed surf life-savers in Beachlife.

VOICE-OVER

Following an investigation by local police, Canning identified local drama teacher Suzannah Wells, forty-six, as her captor. Wells is a former actor, best known for playing Gypsy in the long-running Australian soapie *Beachlife*. The police search for Canning's abductor was narrowed down after Canning identified Wells's property, along with several items from her basement bedroom. A wealth of DNA evidence was also found in Wells's farmhouse.

Wells was arrested on August 8. Her mother, Mary Squires, who suffers from dementia, was interviewed but not arrested. Wells, who was pregnant at the time of her arrest, was released on bail.

It was only after Wells's arrest that the alleged motivation behind the abduction was made public.

ELLIE CANNING

It was the old lady who told me about the surrogacy plan. Well, she didn't exactly tell me, but she was always going on about this big secret she had, and how she was never going to tell me, but that I'd find out eventually, and it would be, like, this huge surprise. I never took much notice of what she was saying because she seemed so mad half the time—like, nothing she ever said really made sense. And then one day she told me that her daughter had found the perfect specimen, a man whose baby she wanted, and I would be getting my lovely surprise soon, just as soon as she could get him into bed with her and get her hands on his stuff. It took me a while to figure out what she was talking about. I mean, his stuff? But then I started listening to her properly, and it sounded as if she was actually talking about me having a baby for the other woman.

It was only that once, and when I asked her again, she just changed the subject.

But later, some of the things the other woman said made me wonder.

She'd ask me the strangest things, like, did I have anything wrong with me down there? Were my periods regular? Were there any illnesses in my family, anything hereditary? And she was so strict about the food she gave me—there wasn't anything unhealthy. She told me there were vitamins in the water she gave me in the sippy cup, but when I asked her what the vitamins were, she wouldn't tell me—just something to keep you healthy, she said, and help you sleep. And then there was the thing with the undies. She'd give me a clean pair every day, even if it wasn't one of the days that I had my bath. She'd put the used ones in this plastic bag, always separate to the other dirty clothes. I dunno what that was all about, but maybe she was checking them out? Oh, it's too gross to think about, but can't you track cycles and all that?

So after she said that, I began to freak out and start thinking that I needed to get out of there. But it was only sometimes, when I was properly awake. Mostly I just kept drifting, like before. It was like I didn't even have the energy to worry properly. And for some reason it didn't ever occur to me to wonder how she was actually going to get me pregnant, and, even more frightening, what she was planning to do with me after . . .

PART TWO

ABDUCTED: THE ELLIE CANNING STORY

A documentary by HeldHostage Productions © 2019

VOICE-OVER

Canning's media appearances were managed by Australian celebrity agent Honor Fielding. Fielding, who grew up in Enfield Wash, was visiting the town at the time of Canning's escape. Initially invited by the local police to help deal with what rapidly became overwhelming media interest in the abduction, Fielding subsequently became Canning's unofficial guardian. Fielding's canny management of her young charge's appearances in the media helped propel Canning to celebrity.

HONOR FIELDING: INTERVIEW TRANSCRIPT

A few days after her escape, I was called in to help Ellie cope with all the attention. The media had already descended on the town, and the local police as well as the hospital staff were besieged by reporters shouting questions, requesting interviews, taking photos. Like everyone else, I was utterly fascinated by Ellie's story, so when the local police got in touch, I was eager to offer my assistance. Once I'd actually met her, I was so impressed with Ellie—she was so smart, so gutsy—I was determined to do anything, everything, I could to help her.

At the time Ellie and I first met, all that was known for certain was that she had been abducted and held in a farmhouse by two women, somewhere west of the town of Enfield Wash. At this stage the police hadn't released information about why she'd been abducted; they'd decided to keep that quiet, and most people in the town, and elsewhere, were utterly mystified, not only about who the perpetrators might be but why they'd done it. I guess we're all familiar with men abducting girls, and sometimes women might be accomplices . . . but Ellie's story was completely different—she'd been abducted by two women. Well, I guess most of us had never heard of such a thing.

I don't think anyone—I certainly didn't—ever entertained the thought, even briefly, that Suzannah Wells and her mother might have been Ellie's abductors. Even though, in hindsight, they so clearly fitted the bill. So when the police and Ellie identified Suzannah and her mother, it was completely gobsmacking. It was just bizarre; you can't imagine how crazy it seemed. Because I knew Suzannah—I guess I would have said she was my friend—and there was nothing even remotely sinister about her. She might have been a minor celebrity years ago, but she seemed so ordinary. A schoolteacher, for God's sake! And Mary—she was certainly eccentric, but harmless. It seemed impossible that the Suzannah Wells I'd met could be involved in such a disturbing crime.

I was actually there when Ellie identified Suzannah, and at first I didn't want to believe it. I couldn't believe it. Surely Ellie was confused? Perhaps she'd been brainwashed? Maybe she was crazy. Perhaps she was some sort of sadist who was simply making things up for her own peculiar pleasure?

But by then I'd spent some time with her, and I knew if anything in the world was true, if anybody in the world was telling the truth, it was Ellie.

SUZANNAH: AUGUST 2018

"They want to come now? It's almost dinnertime," Chip spluttered over his drink.

I had managed to stay composed during the call, but now my voice shook. "They'll be here in half an hour. And they're bringing her. Bringing the girl. Apparently she's remembered something new, and they want her to show them."

"Bring her here? What the fuck?"

"I didn't think farmers swore." Mary looked over from her afternoon cartoons, briefly curious. "Maybe there's hope for you yet, Mr. Rafferty."

She went back to her program. For once I was glad of her propensity to focus on some tangential element and completely miss the point of the discussion.

Chip looked at me. "I'll call Hal. I'm sure there'll be some way to stop them."

"Yes, do. But Stratford says they have another warrant. I don't think there'll be anything he can do."

Chip took out his phone and made the call.

"He says that if they've got new evidence, they're within their rights. It's irregular, but her, ah, amnesia complicates things, apparently. He'll be here soon, and he's suggested we leave. There's no reason for you to be here, is there?"

"They said not. In fact they said it would be better if I wasn't here."

"So why don't we go and leave them to it? Hal can hold the fort."

I considered it; the urge to run was strong. But there was another urge, even more powerful. The fear was mixed with curiosity, along with something else, more hard-edged. "No, it's okay. I want to be here. I think I actually want to meet her. I really want her to see us—to have her look me in the eye and realize that she's made a terrible mistake."

That day, my first as a bonded felon, had begun badly.

Chip had left the house early, was gone before I even woke up. There was no work. I'd called Tom the previous afternoon, on Hal's advice, to tell him what had happened, what to expect, before he heard the news from someone else. He'd been shocked, disbelieving, but the regulations were clear: I was suspended until further notice. Stratford had made a statement on the evening news. He'd kept it brief and simple—"A suspect has been charged and released on bail in relation to the Canning case"—his expression bland, voice devoid of emotion. He hadn't mentioned my name, but it was only a matter of time before everyone knew.

The press had been a presence in town since the day Ellie Canning was found in that shepherd's hut. I'd seen the chaos of cameras and mics outside the hospital and then at the police station in the days after the story broke, and the town was still as busy as I'd only ever seen it on race day: the local motels at capacity, the main street hectic with traffic, the pubs and cafés crowded. Despite this, news of my impending arrest hadn't been leaked—and there'd been no crowd waiting to take happy snaps when Hal and I left the police station in the late afternoon.

After breakfast, with my morning sickness temporarily subdued, and desperate for something to occupy my mind and body, I took Mary for a walk down our long driveway. Mary was never keen to go outside—she was never keen to go anywhere. The doctors had explained that it was a condition similar to agoraphobia, not so much about new people, but unfamiliar spaces. She was happy enough for others to enter her space, although sometimes even that could upset her, but take her somewhere unfamiliar, and she was disoriented and fearful. I tried, once a week or so, to get her out into the garden, to get her to feel the sunshine, to breathe fresh air, to move her body, but it was a challenge. Today, after the usual arguments and demands—it's practically snowing, her coat has missing buttons, her boots will get muddy, she needs a hat, a scarf, the sun is too glary and her sunglasses are all scratched—I managed to drag her outside after lunch by promising her ice cream for afternoon tea. Such blatant bribery would be classified as bad parenting, but the jury was out when it came to daughtering. It was too late to train Mary in good dietary habits, anyway.

Like a child, Mary was always more enthusiastic if there was some kind of purpose to our walk, so I told her we were going to check the mail. I had a post office box in town, so there wasn't likely to be any, but this wasn't the sort of information that Mary retained. Today Mary had her own ideas about the mail.

"I'm actually expecting a letter from Serge," she confided as we set out.

"Who's Serge?"

"What do you mean, who's Serge? Everyone knows Serge. Do you live under a rock?" Her smile was full of pity. Despite the mismatched clothes, the grimy woolen beanie that almost obscured her face, her hair hanging beneath in rats' tails, in Mary's eyes, I was the one whose connection to the real world was limited. And with everything that was happening, who could say she was wrong?

Mary reached the mailbox first and pulled out a rolled-up newspaper. I was surprised. I didn't have a subscription to any of the big papers, and the free local paper never seemed to make it out this far. My fingers trembled as I unrolled the paper—the *Enfield Wash Clarion*—and took in the front-page headline, Mary peering over my shoulder:

ENFIELD WASH DRAMA TEACHER AND FORMER SOAP
STAR CHARGED OVER CANNING ABDUCTION

There was a photo accompanying the story, a fuzzy close-up of my face that must have been taken from a distance without my knowledge just as I was leaving the station yesterday. My expression was grim: my mouth a thin line, face puffy, eyes dark slits. I tried to roll the paper back up quickly, but Mary had seen enough.

"Ooh. That's nasty. Didn't get your best side, did they?" she hooted. "Maybe you should sue."

Once we were back inside, I took the newspaper into my bedroom to read away from Mary's prying eyes. It was a perfectly straightforward article, with nothing speculative or salacious about it. And there was no mention of the forced-surrogacy claim, for which I was grateful.

> Suzannah Wells, 46, a drama teacher at Enfield Wash High, was yesterday charged in connection with the abduction and imprisonment of Ellie Canning. The 18-year-old schoolgirl made international headlines early last week after her daring escape from the Enfield Wash property where she had been held captive. Wells, who is rumored to be pregnant, has been released on bail, with a committal date pending. Detective Inspector Hugh Stratford, who is leading the police investigation, says that while the evidence against Ms. Wells is compelling, the case is an unusual one, and the investigation is still ongoing. It is understood that Ms. Wells's mother, who suffers from dementia, has also been questioned in relation to the abduction.
>
> Wells was a well-known actress during the 1990s, when she played Gypsy in the popular soapie *Beachlife*.

Even though I'd had a brief glimpse, the accompanying photograph shocked me. It wasn't just unflattering—I looked haggard, a good ten years older, and hard, mean, vicious. I looked like someone who was capable of kidnapping, capable of anything. What made it worse was the contrast with the adjacent picture of Ellie Canning, one that I hadn't noticed when I first opened the paper. It wasn't the school photo that had been used for all the previous publicity, but a candid shot, perhaps cropped from something larger. The background was slightly out of focus, the backlighting creating a halo effect around her hair. Her smile was incandescent; she radiated joy, beauty, innocence. It was a face designed to launch not ships but the online outrage army. What sort of monster would threaten to harm such a glorious being?

~

The police car pulled up with a spray of dust and gravel, and I watched from the kitchen window as the three of them marched across the yard: Stratford in front, followed by Moorhouse and the girl. From this distance she looked much slighter than I'd imagined. She was wearing a gray sweatshirt with the hood pulled up, faded jeans, new-looking canvas sneakers. She was slightly hunched over, her eyes on the ground as she walked, her steps small and precise, perhaps reluctant.

Hal flung the door open before they knocked, and there was a brief whispered conversation in the hallway before he ushered them into the kitchen. Chip and Mary were sitting on the lounge. Mary, seemingly oblivious to the newcomers, focused on the muted television, while Chip, his arms crossed, glared at them. I forced myself to stay in the kitchen, pretending to make coffee, trying to look busy and calm, alert but not alarmed.

The officers' greeting was perfunctory; they were no longer pretending to be anything more than polite. Part of me expected it—after all, to them I was just another criminal, out on bail. But I was shocked by their unfriendliness, the way Stratford's gray eyes slid past mine, Moorhouse's stiff nod, the way neither officer smiled.

"We've brought Miss Canning in," Stratford said, as if I might somehow have missed this. He gestured for the girl to come forward.

She clutched at Moorhouse's shirtsleeve and shuffled into the room, the hood still obscuring her face.

Moorhouse pulled her sleeve back gently. "Ellie. It's okay, darling." Her voice was low, tender. "You can let go. I'm not going anywhere. I really need you to look up now. No one's going to hurt you."

The girl pushed back her hood and raised her eyes.

Up close she was tiny, just over five foot, and looked frail and underfed and far younger than her eighteen years. She wasn't quite as radiant as she appeared in her photographs—the loveliness was still there, but she looked tired, unhealthy, undernourished. Her skin was pale, and a few pimples clustered at the side of her mouth. She'd pulled back her dark-blonde hair into a loose, low ponytail, and the greasy tendrils of hair pushed back behind slightly sticking-out ears made her look urchin-like and even younger. Only her eyes had any color; they were a startling blue, dark and opaque. The look she gave me was startling, too. I'd expected her to be anxious, perhaps afraid, at the very least tentative. But her gaze was direct, considering, maybe even critical.

"This is Suzannah Wells, Ellie." Stratford was watching the girl intently.

"Yes." Her voice was low and curiously flat.

"And her mother, Mary Squires, sitting over there on the lounge."

"I know."

"*Slut.*" Mary was still facing the television, but the word rang out, hard and clear. "I told you to keep away from him, you little bitch." Mary turned and fixed Ellie with a gorgon stare.

"Mary." I started toward her, but Stratford gestured for me to stay put.

"I told you what I'd do to you if you went near him, didn't I?"

For the first time, the girl looked discomposed. She moved closer to Moorhouse.

"Oh, don't pretend to be so innocent. We all know what you really want."

Chip had moved along the sofa and taken Mary's hand, murmuring soothing words in an attempt to distract her, but she took no notice, her angry attention all on the girl.

"Everyone knows what you did, you little cow. Everyone knows the lies you've been telling about me. Don't think you're going to get away with it." Mary's glare transformed into a triumphant smile. "You know what karma is, don't you?"

The hissed words resonated in the quiet room. The girl was clearly stunned but couldn't take her eyes off Mary.

"It's coming for you. You know that, don't you? Your pig buddies won't be able to protect you then." Mary smiled, her sharp canines showing, eyes glittering, then turned back to the television. "Oh no." She crossed her arms, pouted at the screen. "It's over already." Her voice was a high-pitched whine. "Can't we have another episode, Mr. Chips?"

Hal and I traipsed behind the police as they moved through the house. It wasn't a search this time—they just went briefly, almost apologetically, from room to room, guiding the girl to each doorway, asking if she recognized anything. The girl herself seemed reluctant. She dragged her feet, looked around blankly, answered monosyllabically, if at all, but mostly shrugged, shook her head. Every now and then she wrapped her arms around her body as if she was cold. I watched her closely. I couldn't pull my eyes away, but at no point did she ever turn and look at me. I could have been invisible.

Once again I led them down the stairs to the basement rooms.

Moorhouse took her into the larger room first and flicked the switch. Hal and I stood to one side, both of us watching for her reaction. She stared blankly into the room and shook her head.

Hal looked at me and raised his eyebrows, but neither of us spoke. We followed them silently to the second basement room.

The girl stood in the center of the dreary room and turned around slowly, looking from wall to window, and then slowly the other way. "I remember this. The awful color." She pointed a shaking finger at the internal door. "That's the toilet over there."

Stratford marched across and pushed the door back, revealing the small tiled room—the toilet, as described.

"There was a bed when I was here." The girl spoke so softly that it was hard to hear her. "Against this wall. You can see where it was." She pointed to some rusty indentations in the old carpet; there had clearly been a bed there at some stage. "And that painting, the one with the woman, it was hanging here, directly opposite." There was a single bent nail in the wall.

She paused, her breathing ragged. "And it's still got that horrible smell. I'll never forget it." She gave a little sob, her eyes filling with tears.

"And what about the scratches?"

She moved again and examined the wall where she claimed the bed had been.

Eventually she answered, "They're here. They're still here. Exactly where I told you. Look."

She traced two tiny, barely visible scratches in the paint with her finger. She was smiling widely now, the tears forgotten, clearly elated. I moved closer, and the scratches resolved into three shakily executed letters: *EBC.*

ABDUCTED: THE ELLIE CANNING STORY

A documentary by HeldHostage Productions © 2019

ELLIE CANNING: TRANSCRIPT #11

One night the woman came down and said she'd had some good news. She didn't usually tell me anything about her life, so I was intrigued. Anyway, I asked her what the news was, and she pulled this thing out of her pocket and held it up. It was one of those sticks you pee on to see if you're pregnant.

"Look," she said. "Two stripes. That's a positive." And then she gave me this really strange smile and said, "So it looks like we won't be needing you after all, my darling."

And that's when I really woke up.

HONOR: AUGUST 2018

Honor thought long and hard before she took the phone call. She'd been expecting it, but it was still hard to know exactly what to say, how to phrase it. She knew there was going to be some regret, even sadness. A sense of bewilderment, too; it had all moved so far, so fast. It was going to start moving even faster soon—she could feel it. Fortunately, she had managed to arrange a television interview just hours before Suzannah's arrest was made public. The girl had made a good impression. She'd been calm, hadn't exaggerated; if anything, she'd underplayed her terror, had made very little of the bravery of her escape. Honor's phone hadn't stopped dinging since it aired. She hadn't even looked at what was happening online but assumed that #EllieCanning was currently trending. That the Twitterati were mobilizing in support of her—building a sympathetic, eager-to-hear-more audience. Or should it be fan base? The story was already big, but now that the motive behind the abduction was public knowledge, it was going to get even bigger. So making sure that Suzannah understood exactly where she stood was vital. A line needed to be drawn if Honor was to stay in control.

"Hi, Suzannah." She was unexpectedly nervous. "How are you?"

"How am I?" Suzannah gave a not-quite laugh. "I guess I feel like I'm stuck in a nightmare. Like life's just taken a turn for the surreal."

Honor could hear the barely controlled terror in Suzannah's voice. She sounded manic, like she was on something.

"I guess you know . . . of course you know. I've been charged, but I'm out on bail."

"I did hear. Yes."

"I just saw that Channel Ten interview with the girl, and apparently it's going viral. A colleague from school rang to tell me there's some Twitter account called @JusticeForEllie, and they're putting up old videos of me—photoshopping them and making it look as if I'm some sort of maniac. I can't even look. Anyway, I thought you might have some idea about what I should do—or if there's anything I can do—about what they're saying."

The silence stretched out as Honor tried to work out how to say what needed to be said. "I can't do that, Suzannah. There's a conflict."

"A conflict?"

"I'm representing Ellie. Until this is all over, I really shouldn't talk to you. I certainly can't give you any advice."

Suzannah gave a disbelieving laugh. "You mean that until this is all over, we aren't friends?"

"I suppose." She made sure her reluctance was clear.

"And after, when it's all over? What? I'm supposed to pretend it never happened?"

Honor said nothing.

"And how do you imagine this will ever be over?"

Honor could feel the heat of the other woman's anger, even over the phone.

"You know that one of us must be lying. That it's either her or me."

"Yes. Of course I do."

"And so you've made your decision? You've chosen her?"

"I'm a professional. I have to. It's got nothing to do with what I believe."

"Nothing to do with what you believe? That's absurd."

"I'm legally contracted to advise Ellie, to manage her interests to the best of my ability. It's my job. I can't just dump her now. She's only a kid, and she's got no other support. Her mother—well, her mother can't help. She's got no one else."

"And doesn't that make you wonder, Honor? The fact that she has no one else? Maybe there's something wrong with her. Maybe she's damaged. Sick. Why else would she be saying these terrible things?"

"From what I can see, the girl's as psychologically healthy as anyone could be after this sort of experience. And it makes no difference. I can't dump her now. It wouldn't be ethical. Handling this sort of situation is impossible, even when you're an adult. All the media attention—it can be completely disorienting. You know that better than anyone. And Ellie's only a child. It could destroy her."

"But what about me? I've been charged with abducting someone I've never even seen before. This girl's delusions could end up sending me to jail. *Jail.* For years."

"I don't think it's going to come to that." Honor tried to be reassuring, but the other woman disregarded her efforts, her voice rising.

"And you know I'm pregnant, don't you?"

"So I heard. Congra—"

"So what's going to happen to my baby if I have to go to jail?"

"Oh, Suzannah, I'm sure it's all going to work out. I've told the police, and Ellie for that matter, what I think. How unbelievable this all is . . ." Honor trailed off, took a deep breath. "And I want you to know that I would never . . . I would *never* have taken her on if I'd known you were involved."

"But I'm not." Suzannah's indignation made the phone vibrate. "I'm not involved. That's the thing. The girl has accused me, but it's insane. I've never even seen her before."

Honor waited a beat. Two, three, four. "Okay." Her response was painfully neutral.

"Well, thank you for being honest. I guess we won't be seeing you in the near future?" Suzannah was clearly making an effort to contain her emotion, but Honor could hear the slight tremor.

"No. I guess not. It wouldn't be . . . appropriate." Having to speak so bluntly made her voice harsh, and the silence that followed was drawn out, potent.

Then: "Honor?"

"Yes?"

"You must know it's not true, what the girl is saying. You do know *that*, don't you? She's lying. You've been here. You know me."

"Perhaps . . . perhaps there's just been some terrible . . . mistake?" Honor knew that Suzannah wanted her to proclaim her faith in her with some sort of certainty. But she couldn't.

"A mistake. That's what you think. Really?"

"I don't know. I can only go on what Ellie says. Whatever it is that the police have found. I have to go with that. That's all any of us can do."

"But what about what *I* have to say?"

"What do you mean?"

"Why doesn't that mean as much?"

Honor took another deep breath. "But there's so much evidence. Her memories. The DNA. It can't be ignored. And what reason would Ellie have to lie? I can't see it."

"But what reason would I have for doing what she says I've done? That makes no sense either. Why would I want to keep her here—to impregnate her, for God's sake? It's grotesque. It's not as if I was trying to get pregnant. I haven't even thought about having a baby since . . ." She paused. "This pregnancy came completely out of the blue. It was an accident."

"Look"—Honor was completely businesslike now—"there's no point in going over this with me. This is stuff you have to discuss with Hal—and the police. I'm just Ellie's agent. There's nothing I can do about it."

This time Suzannah's response was slow in coming, and her words were measured. "Okay. You're right. Of course there's nothing you can do. I'll talk to Hal." She sounded calm, but Honor could feel the sharp edge of the other woman's fear.

Suzannah might have trained as an actress, but she was out of practice. Or maybe the part was way out of her league.

ABDUCTED: THE ELLIE CANNING STORY
A documentary by HeldHostage Productions © 2019

ELLIE CANNING: TRANSCRIPT #12

I had to get away. And I had to do it fast. I knew there was no way I was going to escape if it involved some sort of physical confrontation. I'd been in bed for so long, and even if I wasn't so out of it anymore—I'd been trying not to eat or drink too much—I was still pretty weak. The only way I'd even have a chance of escaping was if I could stop the woman from locking the restraint.

I told her I needed to pee, so she undid the belt thing and helped me to the toilet. After she'd locked it back up, I distracted her by knocking the bowl of soup she'd brought me onto the carpet. She had to go into the bathroom to get a wet cloth, and while she was gone, I grabbed her keys, which she'd left on the bedside table, and unlocked the belt. By the time she finished cleaning up, I'd pretended to fall back asleep. She wasn't suspicious—she just kissed me good night and left.

After she'd gone I waited for what felt like forever. I didn't have a clue what time it was—it was always dark in the room when the light was off—but I assumed it was night. I heard doors closing and footsteps and muffled voices from upstairs. And then finally, when it was completely silent, I got out of bed and tiptoed across to the door. I don't know what I'd have done if she'd locked it, but she hadn't—there wasn't any point, was there? I was out of the room. There were two staircases, one on the left and one on the right, so I had to choose. I didn't have a clue where either of them led, but I chose one and crept up, hoping the door at the top would also be unlocked.

Actually making it to the top of the stairs was, like, really hard.

I'd barely used my legs for weeks, other than the walks to the bathroom, and I was so shaky and nervous that I actually crawled up. I was scared the door at the top might be locked, but it opened easily, too. I remember it creaking a little, but nothing happened. There was a light on, so I could see that the door opened into the hall, and then at the end of the hall was the front door. I crept down the hallway to the front door, and then I was out.

That's when I really started to be afraid. More scared than I'd ever been in the room. I almost wanted to go back inside, to get back in the bed, pull up the covers, and go back to sleep. There was no moon that night, so once I got past the house, it was really dark; it took ages for my eyes to adjust. It was really cold, too—I hadn't expected that. All I had were those silky pajamas she'd given me. I had socks, but no shoes. I followed the driveway down past the mailbox, and then I walked along the road trying to get as far away as I could. My legs still weren't working properly, so it was slow going.

After that it's all a bit of a blur. I think I must have walked for hours. I had no idea which way to head, so I went one way along the road and then the other. Then I got even more confused—I couldn't work out where I'd escaped from, which driveway was safe to go down . . . And I was feeling kinda crazy and paranoid. Worried that wherever I went, maybe the people would be in on it, that it was some sort of giant conspiracy. I mean, I had no idea what was really going on. It was like one of those crazy movies where they've been in some sort of alternative reality where everyone's actually aliens.

I was hoping I'd get to a town or something, where there was somewhere safe I could go to—a servo or a police station, something like that. But I was literally in the middle of nowhere. I just kept walking and walking, and eventually I was so tired and cold, I could barely stand up. And then I saw that hut and went in, and there was that disgusting old blanket . . . and I just wrapped it around me and collapsed.

SUZANNAH: AUGUST 2018

I woke up to the familiar, low murmur of the ocean—a sound from my childhood. I closed my eyes again, thinking I must still be asleep, waiting for this pleasant dream to fade, another to take its place, but the incoming tide of nausea assured me that I was truly awake and that the waves of sound were real.

I'd just worked out that the noise was, bizarrely, the sound of traffic when Chip came into the room.

"It's the fucking media." He spat the words, clearly agitated.

"What?"

"There are television crews down at the end of the drive, and I don't know who else. Newspaper journos. Podcasters. Sightseers, probably. I don't fucking know. There's at least a dozen vans out there. A couple actually started coming up the drive, so I threatened them. I've closed the gate and padlocked it so they can't get in."

"What did you threaten them with?"

I was expecting strong language, maybe even a lawsuit.

"My twenty-two." He grinned unexpectedly. "Don't worry—it wasn't loaded."

"Oh shit." I pulled the covers over my head and closed my eyes, visualized a sunshiny morning on a tropical island.

Lapping water. A hammock swaying between palm trees. This was clearly the wrong image for someone in my condition, and I only just made it to the bathroom in time.

The three of us ate breakfast together. Chip was talking to his brother on the phone, breaking off occasionally to relay information and give out terse directions.

"Hal says you're both to stay inside," he said. "They'll probably have some sort of supersonic telephoto lens . . . He says it's possible they'll jump the fence, so they could be in the yard. If they get to the door, you're not to answer it. And you're not to take any phone calls from numbers you don't know. Actually, you should turn your mobile off. Pull the plug on the home phone. If anyone desperately needs you, they can call Hal. And, Suzannah, he says you should probably stay away from the internet, too. Whatever you do, don't google yourself."

Chip disconnected. He stared into space for a moment, then stood up. "I'm going over to my place. I'll go through the back paddock so they can't see me. I'm going to bring the dogs back. That should make them think twice about coming any closer. You two stay inside until I get back."

Mary had barely spoken a word all morning. She sat at the breakfast bar, hunched over her bowl protectively, spooning soggy Froot Loops into her mouth. She was taking longer than seemed humanly possible, sloshing each spoonful noisily before swallowing. I avoided watching her as I nibbled my dry toast.

As soon as Chip left, she perked up. "I wanna go up to the mailbox again, Suzie. Why can't we go?" The ends of her hair drifted into the milky mess of her bowl.

"Chip says we need to stay inside. There are people up there that we don't want to talk to."

"People?" Her eyes lit up. "Why don't we want to see them?"

"Because . . . because they'll want to talk to us, and we don't want to talk to them."

"Why not?"

"Because they're not our friends."

Mary leaned toward me, her soaked dressing-gown sleeve smearing milk across the table, and whispered conspiratorially, "Oh, Suzannah. Haven't you noticed? You and me, we don't really have any friends. We're just not that type."

I busied myself with housework—cleaning the kitchen, throwing on washing—and then wrangled Mary into semiappropriate cold-weather clothing, a pair of green-and-purple harlequin pants, worn under a hoop-skirted mid-Victorian confection, overlaid with a dark-gray knitted tunic designed to look like medieval armor for added warmth (all taken from my collection of stage costumes). I got her to sit quietly with some coloring-in, the TV blaring as backup.

But after more than an hour of this enforced busy-making, I could resist the siren song of the internet no longer. I googled Ellie's name initially rather than my own. There were already a few interviews, all remarkably similar in content and tone: the interviewers bordering on reverential, Ellie herself composed, self-deprecating, unaffected, serious, and so, so sincere. There was nothing of the victim about her and nothing in the least confrontational. There was no anger or outrage: she was careful to never mention her alleged abductors and, despite the journalists' efforts, reluctant to comment on the clearly flawed system that had allowed her disappearance to go unnoticed. All the details of her ordeal were cleverly glossed over; Ellie merely expressed her deeply felt relief over her escape and her hope that she would be able to get on with the rest of her life. She was entirely media-friendly and utterly, utterly convincing.

I browsed the newspaper accounts, scrolled through all the #EllieCanning tweets, listened to a few talking heads pontificating on the bizarre nature of the kidnapping, their intense admiration for Ellie: her determination and fortitude, her remarkable lack of self-pity—what an excellent role model she was for her generation. A couple of teenage girls had recorded their take on the story—a confused analysis that seemed to be more concerned with Ellie's perceived attitude and her looks than the serious aspects of the abduction, and featuring a tutorial on how to achieve her signature look (pale foundation, concealer, gray eye shadow, kohl, salt spray for the messed-up hair), as well as a conversation about how Ellie's escape—her empowerment!—had already made her, like, *so* iconic.

My own web presence was a significant contrast. Just a few months ago, the hits would have been minimal: my very brief IMDb bio and a few articles of the "Whatever happened to" variety, detailing my exit from acting into teaching and motherhood and illustrated largely by pictures of me taken from the show, with perhaps a wedding photo thrown in for contrast. There were a couple of dedicated *Beachlife* fan sites, too, but these tended to focus on the characters' dramas rather than the actors' life stories. Now, in just the few days since my arrest, the links had multiplied exponentially. The fact that the case was sub judice had restricted commentary by most of the respectable media outlets—they could mention only my name, the fact that I was a teacher and former soap star, and that I had been charged. One broadsheet had made a valiant attempt to broaden the discussion, with an outraged young feminist arguing that my transgression was yet another instance of the ways in which internalized misogyny forced women to replicate patriarchal power structures.

Legal ramifications appeared to have little effect in other places. The number one link took me to a site called 180Degrees, which had scooped up all the available facts and run with them. Their piece managed to insinuate that not only was I a failed actor of negligible talent, but I was also embittered and barren, with a sinister character and a dubious past. According to "unnamed sources," I was an unpopular figure in the town—a bad teacher and social climber to boot—and my connection to the rich and influential Chip Gascoyne made me even more suspect. In the accompanying image, another one that must have been taken outside the station just after my arrest, I looked frankly hideous—my body hunched, hair flying around my face, my expression vindictive. Like Ellie, I had earned my own Twitter hashtag, and the accompanying tweets were horrifying to view. Of course most threads linked to the 180Degrees piece, and the comments ranged from the mildly alarmed—the types who wondered how someone so clearly disturbed had been allowed to teach young people—to those that questioned why I was given bail. A few called for royal commissions into foster care and private schools. A frightening number suggested that I should be sterilized, that my baby should be adopted out (or aborted), that I should be thrown into prison and the key destroyed. I was described as a bitch, a witch, a sicko pervert. The invective was impressively nonpartisan, coming from all directions: young and old, men and women, left and right. But the fact that I'd created some rare form of community cohesion by being universally loathed was of no comfort at all.

These were only the public sites, the ones I could see—the open forums, the less mainstream and sometimes completely dodgy news sites. Their dodginess didn't seem to matter—whatever they reported, regardless of whether it was true or false, would be accepted by some, and often by many, as the truth. And then there were all the other sites that couldn't be seen, the private forums, Facebook pages, Snapchat communications, where the gossip moved like wildfire, where stories could be shared by hundreds, thousands, without any threat of exposure or censure. I'd seen it happen to others, though never had I imagined being the subject of this deadly game of telephone. I might as well forget the formal legal process: this was where I was being tried, by these thousands and thousands of people who had nothing at stake and who were enjoying every moment of their own outrage. It was completely beyond my control.

When Chip arrived back with the dogs, it came as something of a surprise, to me, at least, that Mary was a dog lover. My grandparents had had German shepherds—spoiled family pets—when I was a child, but somehow I had never really considered that Hugo, the shepherd who'd already been an old dog when I was a small child, had once been Mary's childhood pet. Chip had two almost-retired working dogs—black-and-white border collies, Rip and Ned, siblings I had met on only a few occasions, who were slavishly loyal to Chip and almost embarrassingly indifferent to me. But Mary was another matter.

Initially, Chip tried to get her out in the backyard with them, teaching her to use some basic commands, but Mary tired of this quickly and so did the dogs. Instead she huddled with them on the front veranda, ignoring the arctic outdoor temperature, her beloved television programs forgotten. For the rest of the afternoon, I sat in a patch of sun and watched as Mary regaled the patient duo with stories about her youthful exploits, real and imagined, the dogs' attention assured by her petting and the cereal she shared with them, doled out piece by piece, straight from the packet.

I wasn't sure if the dogs were protecting us from the barbarians at the gate, but they were saving my sanity, even as they added to my Froot Loop bill—pun, metaphor, irony, whatever, intended.

ABDUCTED: THE ELLIE CANNING STORY

A documentary by HeldHostage Productions © 2019

ELLIE CANNING: TRANSCRIPT #13

After a couple of days, I had to leave the hospital—they needed my bed—but I really didn't want to go. My foster parents didn't want me back, and there was no point going back to school.

There was no way I was going to my mother's. I'd turned eighteen, so the department wasn't legally responsible for me anymore. There was literally nowhere for me to go. That's when Honor came on the scene.

Once the media knew Honor was involved, things calmed down. Before that it was nuts. Some journalist had even dressed up as a nurse to get into my hospital room.

Honor fielded all the calls, and then I made an official statement. I was able to make sure that what went on the record was true and not just speculation. The police told me what to say and what not to say. I had to be careful to leave out any information that might identify my captors before the police could do their job.

At first I resisted Honor's advice that I be paid for interviews and appearances—it didn't really seem right. But my life had changed because of what happened to me, and not necessarily for the better. I wasn't going to be able to go back to school or to Manning. Honor offered me a room at her place, but I was eventually going to have to find somewhere to live, and for that I needed money.

And even though Suzannah Wells had been charged, the committal hearing was still four months away. And we had no idea about the trial itself. It seemed as if it was going to be a long, boring wait.

SUZANNAH: SEPTEMBER 2018

I had work that had to be handed back to my classes, and there were a few things I wanted to collect from the staff common room and the drama room, so I rang to arrange a suitable time. Tania was civil but cold: I wasn't to be on the grounds between nine and three; 4:00 p.m. would be best, as most of the children would have left by then. I wasn't naive; I wasn't even hopeful. I had a pretty clear idea about what was going to happen when I turned up at the school, how my colleagues would behave, but I wanted to go anyway. I wanted to see it for myself, perhaps.

But first I had to get through the small crowd still gathered at the bottom of the driveway. I donned dark glasses and wore a padded jacket with a hood that I pulled as far down as I could and wrapped a scarf over the bottom half of my face, but even so there was no disguising my identity. Who else could I possibly be? I pulled up to open the gate, ignoring the clamor, the shouted questions, the flashing lights, sliding back into the car and locking the doors as quickly as possible. I looked straight ahead, drove through slowly and determinedly, then sped off down Wash Road. I didn't get out to close the gate, and I didn't look back.

When I walked in, the still-crowded common room was silent for an almost imperceptible moment. The resumed conversations were stilted, tense; necks were carefully angled, heads deliberately still as I made my way to my desk. Everyone was trying so hard—too hard—to act as if it were no big deal. When they came, the greetings were offhand and oh-so-casual, as if nothing had changed.

Only Julia made an effort to speak to me. She asked how I was holding up, and then, without waiting for a reply, launched into a long story, telling me about her weekend trip to Sydney, her trip back early this morning, the mess her housemate had left in their kitchen. Julia's stories tended to drag out inexorably, and where I would once have tried to move away as quickly as possible, today I found her conversational meanderings comforting. And listening to Julia saved me from making eye contact with anyone else, excused me from confronting their ill-disguised curiosity. Eventually, Sarah Bower, the principal's PA, bustled over to us.

"So sorry to interrupt, ladies, but you're wanted in Tom's office as soon as possible, Suzannah." Her words were ice-tipped, her expression frozen.

I gathered the few odds and ends I'd come for and made my way back across the room. This time all pretense at normal behavior was dispensed with—heads turned blatantly and the silence was charged. I could hear the soft murmur begin as soon as I exited.

I handed Tom the folders I'd brought in for my Year Elevens and the marking sheets for their last performance. "Do you want me to sort out some class plans for whoever is relieving?"

"No. It's fine." He didn't quite meet my eye. "We've got a replacement coming."

"An actual drama teacher?"

"Well, English and history primarily, but apparently he's had some experience in amateur theater. He should be able to sort something out."

"Will you keep my job for me?"

"We'll see what happens. You know I have to go through the department. It's not just my decision." He changed the subject. "Now, have you got what you needed from the common room?"

"There wasn't much, really. A few books, some notes."

"No sense leaving them; things tend to disappear. You know what it's like."

I nodded, smiled. I knew what it was like.

Tom gave a tepid smile, shook my hand, thanked me for my hard work, wished me all the best.

I turned back at the door.

"I didn't do it, you know, Tom." His expression was neutral. I didn't stop there, though I knew I should. "What this girl's saying I did. It's utterly ridiculous. Why on earth would I kidnap anyone? It's crazy."

"You're right," he said eventually. "It is crazy. But sometimes people do crazy things, things we can't ever understand." His voice was all gruff sympathy now, full of a pity I didn't want to hear.

ABDUCTED: THE ELLIE CANNING STORY
A documentary by HeldHostage Productions © 2019

ELLIE CANNING: TRANSCRIPT #14

I guess every teenage girl fantasizes about being a celebrity, but I could never have imagined the media craziness surrounding the case.

It was as if I'd fallen into the plot of some Hollywood movie: one moment I was a pretty average Australian schoolgirl, getting ready to do my final exams, making plans for my future, and the next thing I knew I was locked in a bedroom, drugged out of my brain, the prisoner of two madwomen.

And then, after I escaped, before I'd even processed what had happened to me—I was still dazed and confused and falling asleep at random times, and so unfit I could barely make it up one flight of stairs without panting like an old lady—there was a crowd of journalists following my every move, shouting questions at me, microphones shoved in my face every time I went outside.

Right from the start, the media were over the top about my story. I still don't really understand why, but for some reason it really hit a nerve. Everyone wanted to talk to me; everyone was so fascinated by what happened. And most people were nice, like they really genuinely cared what had happened to me. My biggest fans were probably teenage girls. I'm not sure why—whether it was my story or just that I seemed like one of them ... Anyway, for whatever reason, everyone was so amazingly supportive and caring. And I know it sounds cheesy, but I felt really lucky, really blessed.

HONOR: SEPTEMBER 2018

The girl herself was more than Honor had hoped for, better than she'd expected. From the first moment she hit the public eye, they'd loved her—how could they not? Ellie was pretty, she was poor, she'd had to work hard, she'd been neglected by her family and the system, and then she'd used all her not inconsiderable smarts to escape what might have been a sticky end by the skin of her teeth. She'd had so many obstacles to overcome, and yet she'd emerged triumphant. Some of the narrative elements could have been improved, of course—if there'd been a man involved, the story would have been more conventionally titillating, perhaps excited a different sort of audience. But Honor wasn't sure if that would have made it bigger. However appalling it was, a man abducting a young girl wasn't that remarkable; being kidnapped by a seemingly respectable woman was something else again. And because it was something unexpected, it was even more sinister. In this scenario nobody could be trusted—no one could be safe.

There was something perversely rousing, it had to be said, about pitting these two very different women against one another. And, as expected, the crowd was cheering for the golden-haired damsel in distress and not the dark and bitter crone. One had all the moral weight, the popular appeal; the other faced community hostility and loathing. Honor was filled with pity for Suzannah, of course she was; the imagined monster they were excoriating bore no resemblance to the warm and engaging woman she knew, but there was no denying that all the online vitriol directed at Suzannah had been good for Ellie—and for

Honor, too. She'd made it her business to check out every site that featured Suzannah and to read the comments. Much of it fueled the outrage: the students who didn't like her; the parents complaining about her bad marks, dodgy teaching methods, her retrospectively suspicious behavior; the former colleagues who thought she was bigheaded; the stories about her youthful indiscretions; the rumors of a manufactured relationship with her gay costar. Someone claiming to have been a midwife in the hospital when Suzannah's daughter was born had even hinted she suffered from postnatal psychiatric problems that may have led to the infant's death. Honor had no doubt that almost all of it was fabricated. This sort of publicity always encouraged the nasties to crawl out of the woodwork. What could be more thrilling to the self-righteous than to join a crusade against such a vile predator?

Honor was honestly impressed by her new client's behavior. Ellie had listened respectfully to everything she'd told her, had happily taken her advice on every aspect. Honor had explained what was permissible legally, how she needed to avoid any suggestion that her public appearances could be considered prejudicial. "If they try to get you to discuss the case directly—and they will, especially the surrogacy angle—deflect. Talk generalities."

When she explained that an appearance on a certain show, although immediately lucrative, would blow Ellie's chances of a hard-to-get, less financially attractive but ultimately more advantageous post-trial exclusive, the girl had agreed to wait. She'd kept her Twitter feed completely anodyne—not even retweets of anything controversial—and her Instagram was almost exclusively (and lucratively, as her followers increased) brand-based. Most importantly, she'd listened to what Honor said about what her approach should be, what tone to take. "The media love you right now, and they'll love you more if you keep it together. Try not to seem too vulnerable. Victimhood might be the new black, but people still like to think you're capable of being brave—that you can take some things on the chin. The more serene you are, the more outraged the public will be."

And thus far Ellie had been impressively circumspect in all her interviews: she'd come across as quietly courageous, self-deprecating, generous. And most importantly, authentic.

One thing they had argued about was Ellie's living arrangements. Honor had initially suggested she go back to Manning until the committal hearing, had thought it best to lie low, to make only carefully stage-managed appearances. Honor would pay rent on a flat, but maybe Ellie could get someone to move in with her. She could even look for part-time work. She must have friends, some sort of support network in town, surely?

"It's not ideal, and it's possible that the media will bug you for a few weeks even there," Honor had explained, "but if you're in Sydney, they'll be buzzing around like flies every time you take a shit."

But Ellie had point-blank refused. "I'm not going back to Manning," she'd said. "I'm never going back. I can't. You don't understand."

She'd refused to elaborate, insisted she wanted to move to Sydney, that she'd get a job, find her own place; she was eighteen, after all.

They'd eventually reached a compromise, and Ellie moved into the spare room in Honor and Dougal's place until the money started rolling in and she could rent her own flat.

They'd disagreed, too, about romantic entanglements. Honor's advice, strongly given, was that Ellie should stay clear of any relationships, serious or not, until the committal at the very least. But she couldn't guard her every minute, and there'd been endless possibilities. What young woman wouldn't be tempted by all the attention? Young men who were equally entranced by Ellie's beauty, her sudden celebrity status.

She'd been particularly concerned when Ellie began to show an interest in a journalist, Jamie Hemara—a handsome New Zealander connected to the notorious online scandal rag 180Degrees. The maverick site, which depended on anonymous sources and displayed a shameless genius for selective cutting and pasting, was one of the most scurrilous around, trading in celebrity gossip and political scandals. It was constantly under investigation, threatened with lawsuits—contempt of court, libel, perverting the cause of justice. Its country of origin and ownership were impossible to pin down, and prosecutions never seemed to get far. It had frequently been forced to pull stories when the law got involved, but by then they'd already been shared thousands of times, and the damage done. Jamie Hemara's byline only ever appeared above the website's occasional straight offerings, but there was no doubt he was responsible for much of the muck, too.

When she'd first found out about Jamie and Ellie's "hot new relationship" (via Instagram, naturally), Honor, working late, had rung Ellie immediately and warned her off. She'd pointed out gently that, at twenty-eight, Hemara was far too old for her and that he was a notorious womanizer and a hard partier with something of a serious coke habit. But Ellie had dug in her heels. "It's not going to get serious," she'd said. "I'm only eighteen. But I like him, Honor. And I need some sort of social life. What am I meant to do? Stay home and watch Netflix every single night? It's getting a bit boring."

Honor had sighed. This was a battle she would lose eventually, but she had to try anyway. "Right now men are a dangerous luxury, Ellie. And male journalists are even more dangerous. You have to be careful."

"Are you saying he'll use me?" Ellie's laughter was equal parts scorn and disbelief.

"I'm sure he thinks you're wonderful, but journalists can't help it. They're always looking for an angle. If you were his granny, he'd be working out how to get you into a badly run nursing home so he could write an exposé. It's nothing personal. I was one of them. I know exactly how it works."

Dougal had been a little harder to manage.

"I really don't understand why she needs to stay here, Honor," he'd said when she told him she'd offered Ellie a place to stay. "Can't she just get a room in a hotel or something?"

Honor was surprised by Dougal's attitude. Over the years, her husband had offered up very little in the way of opinion when it came to her clients. On the odd occasion that he'd been called on to accompany her to some function or other, he might have expressed his distaste for a particular client, or, rather less frequently, his interest or admiration, but mostly he'd kept his distance.

"And I don't understand why it bothers *you* so much," she'd countered. "It's only temporary. I've already explained this." She'd swallowed down her impatience, made herself speak calmly. "She really needs some sort of guaranteed cash flow first, and she doesn't have that yet."

"Well, why can't you give her some sort of an advance? Help find her a place. Isn't that what you usually do?"

It was a Saturday morning, Ellie still in bed, and Dougal was sitting at the breakfast table with his morning newspaper spread open in front of him, a cup of tea at hand, doing his best impression of an old-fashioned paterfamilias. He peered at Honor over his reading glasses, his lips drawn together primly. He looked, suddenly, shockingly, every one of his sixty-five years.

"But she's so vulnerable right now, and she's really just a kid. She's only just turned eighteen. She's clueless."

"Why can't she get into some sort of share house? With people her own age?"

"There's no one she can move in with—her friends are all still at school."

He raised an eyebrow, clearly unconvinced.

"This is the easiest route to take, believe me," said Honor. "It suits me to have her here right now because at least I can see what she's doing, even if I can't control it completely. I can make sure she's not going out *every* night and getting drunk and taking drugs and hanging with all the wrong people. She needs to be in top form—so many people want to talk to her. She's got so much happening, it would be a pity to stuff the whole thing up. Right now she needs a responsible adult looking out for her." She took a deep breath. "Dougal, I'm not sure what the problem is. It's not like she's causing any trouble."

"I just don't . . ." He paused, modified what he was going to say. "It's just awkward, having her here."

"Awkward? In what way is it awkward? I'd have thought you'd be enjoying having a young person about the place. I'm enjoying it."

He leaned toward her, lowered his voice. "I don't trust her. I can't even tell you why, but there's *something*."

"Is it because she's not from a nice middle-class background? Are you worried she's going to help herself to the family silver?" She laughed, held up a teaspoon. "Oh, for God's sake, Dougal. You're such a snob." She shook her head, tapped him lightly on the back of the hand with the spoon.

He had the grace to look slightly uncomfortable. "Of course it's not that. It's . . . You're right. She's everything you say she is—intelligent, thoughtful, polite. Yesterday she bought me two bagels from that place in the Cross because she'd heard me telling you how much I like them. And then we had a thoroughly engrossing conversation about the book I was reading—a history of Hitler's invasion of Czechoslovakia. It turns out she knows quite a lot about it. And then, not five minutes later, I overheard her talking to that journalist she's seeing, that Maori fellow. She sounded like, I don't know—like a . . ." He fumbled for the term. "Like one of those phone-sex women."

"She sounded like a phone-sex woman?" Honor couldn't help laughing again. "Dougal. You're a bloody old prude, as well as a snob. She's just young."

"Don't be silly. You know I couldn't care less about her bloody sex life. It's the fact that she can turn it on and off so easily. She can act like a virtuous schoolgirl—the perfect granddaughter to me, in fact—and then five minutes later she's channeling the whore of Babylon. And yes, I know, you'll say that's just girls, that I'm old, that I've forgotten. But I haven't. That girl is too much. Too smooth. She's too good to be true." He paused for a long moment, and when he spoke, his voice was deadly serious. "And she's dangerous."

"Dougal, my darling. Ellie's not dangerous, she's just a child."

"That's the thing, Honor." His eyes were full of pity. "She's not actually a child—and you're not her mother."

SUZANNAH: OCTOBER 2018

The ringing of Chip's mobile woke me. It was still dark. I closed my eyes again, pushed my face into the pillow, willing sleep to return.

I must have managed to drift off while he was on the phone, because when I finally opened my eyes, Chip was back in bed, leaning up against the headboard with his head flung back, his eyes closed, mouth an angry line.

I touched his arm gently. "Chip? Who was it? What's happened?"

He took a deep breath before he responded, still not opening his eyes or turning toward me.

"That was Hal. Apparently you're big news again today. On the internet."

"What is it now?" I struggled to sit up. "But there's been nothing new, has there? She hasn't said anything else?"

Chip turned to me, his voice weary. "That's the thing. It's not something new. And *she's* not saying it. This is old news, apparently. You really should've told Hal about it, Suze. He might've been able to prepare for it somehow. It's too late now, even if this stuff isn't going to be admissible."

"What stuff?"

"It's that bloody website, 180Degrees. They've dug up some dirt on you from the eighties. It's like they've got some sort of vendetta."

"What kind of dirt?"

"Filthy dirty dirt." He tried to smile, to make it into a joke. "You clearly had a more interesting youth than I did."

"I don't have any idea what you're talking about—" I began.

And then, suddenly, I did.

By the time I was in my late teens, I had everything any girl could possibly want. At sixteen I had scored, with very little effort—I'd just done a screen test on a whim—a plum role on what was destined to become one of Australia's best-loved soaps. On screen I was Gypsy, the show's sweetheart: a girl-next-door surfie chick, an integral part of a loving but chaotic family, a close-knit surfing community. In real life I was living the teenage dream. With Mary permanently AWOL and Nan and Pop too old to have much of an impact on my decisions, I was independent in a way that most of my peers weren't. More importantly, I had money. I was also famous. I may not have been Kylie—I'd never learned to sing, and my hair wouldn't take a perm—but I was the next best thing. Smart, but not scarily so, dark-skinned and doe-eyed and not too "up myself," I was everybody's daughter, sister, best friend, and girlfriend—a Mediterranean Gidget without the bangs.

I floated through life, not giving too much, taking what I wanted, imagining that I somehow deserved all I'd got—the success, the admiration, the occasional trip up the red carpet, the cameras flashing—and thinking, too, that I had power, over men, over the world, over my future. And I thought, silly young thing that I was, that the power was real, that it actually meant something, that it would last.

What I didn't have at that age was anyone to guide me. My grandparents had done their best to raise me, but they were bewildered by the way my life had turned out. They'd already had their hearts broken by my mother, and they'd had to work hard to hide their disappointment—and their fear—when it looked as if I was going to be swallowed up by that same world. I knew that, despite all the clear evidence of my success, they'd never stopped being afraid that eventually I was going to go off the rails, too.

And eventually, inevitably, off the rails I went, although my derailment certainly wasn't as tragic, or as long-lasting, as my mother's.

Thankfully my grandparents didn't have to witness any of it, not that I would have been inclined to modify my behavior for them. Pop had died and Nan's once-sharp mind had begun to fade and she'd moved into an old people's home, her connection to reality rapidly diminishing.

By the mid-1990s, *Beachlife* had been running for almost a decade and the storylines were getting stale, the ratings beginning to lose momentum. Like the *Titanic*, once damaged, these big soaps tended to sink rapidly. First we lost a few of the biggest stars, most moving on to other soaps, the big screen. In all my years on the show, I'd been complacent about my future prospects. My agent hadn't worried either. So when management decided to kill me off in a bid to up the ratings, I was shocked and unmoored. There was a requisite fifteen minutes of public sadness over my tragic "death," but once I'd made my exit from the show, I was no longer a hot property. Although I was pretty and talented, I was limited—too well known, not well enough trained, and not, it had to be said, all that ambitious. My agent was apologetic— there was nothing going—my identity, my signature looks, were so tied up with the show, and with being Gypsy . . . It was over, and unlike Kylie, I had no plan B.

And I clearly needed a plan B. I wasn't by any means a spend-thrift, but apart from buying the apartment in Bondi with a deposit large enough to leave me with only a minuscule mortgage, I was broke. A small fortune could easily trickle through your fingers when you bought whatever clothes or food or cars or holidays you desired, with no thought for a future that might be leaner.

Until then my private life had been relatively tame, as far as soapie starlets go. There had been no sordid scandals, no love triangles or lesbian affairs to cover up. I wasn't big on partying or clubbing; the only red-carpet affairs I attended were the ones management told me to go to.

I'd had two serious boyfriends. The first was the lovely, and as it turned out extremely gay, Sebastián Mendes (although he stayed in the closet until the beginning of the new century). He played Mick, my surf lifesaver love interest on the show. Seb and I were an item for a few years and lived together for almost twelve months, with the blessing of the studio. We had a great time, and though I imagined I was in love for a short while, it was an easy relationship, without any intensity—just two mates having fun.

My second serious relationship—when my own star was at its peak—was with one of the film editors, Dylan Menzies. Dylan was older, and though he was extremely good-looking in a slightly sinister way, nobody would ever describe him as lovely. He was sharp, slick, ambitious, opportunistic. He ran with what my nan would have called a fast crowd—clubbers and druggies, low-level crims—in a world that I knew existed but had somehow avoided. We broke up after a tempestuous yearlong relationship—his penchant for drugs and other women too much of a challenge to my own innate conservatism.

It'd been a year or so since our breakup when I bumped into him at a club. It was a few weeks after I finished on the show, there was no work on the horizon, and my bank balance—and sense of self-worth—was rapidly dwindling. He'd persuaded me to go to a party at Edward Levant's waterfront mansion. I *knew of* Levant, and though everyone who was anyone knew Levant, I'd never actually met him. A millionaire back when the term meant something, he was a constant presence on the fringes of the film scene. No one (in the pre-*Underbelly* world) seemed to know much about him, where he'd come from, what he did, or why he had money. There were all sorts of rumors—that he was the head of an international drug syndicate, that he sold arms, that he dealt in human trafficking—but no one seemed to care. We were young, we were having fun, and people like Levant provided money, glamour, a place to be seen, and people to be seen with, and that was all that mattered.

According to Dylan, Levant wanted to get into the film industry. He was looking to invest, perhaps head a production company, and

Dylan thought there might be an opportunity there for me. And as there didn't seem to be anything else looming on my horizon, how could I resist?

I met up with Dylan at a nightclub in Darlinghurst and had a few drinks. Very uncharacteristically, I was coked up, too. "For fuck's sake, Suzannah," Dylan had sighed, only half joking, when I'd initially declined, "you can't turn up to Eddie Levant's place straight. You'll get us thrown out."

So I had shared a line, or maybe two, and when the taxi set us down outside the imposing stone gates of Levant's Point Piper mansion, my inhibitions were pretty loose. And by the time I'd had a few glasses of Bollinger and shared a line or two more with a couple whose names I never bothered to ask, they were nonexistent.

The following day, I woke up on the floor of a holding cell at Kings Cross police station, having been arrested after a police raid at Levant's. I had no memory of what I'd actually been doing when the shit hit the fan the night before. It was only when my agent bailed me out that afternoon that I found out what had gone on. Apparently when the police descended, I'd been in the basement, where our host kept a fine assortment of bondage gear, appropriately dressed (or undressed, depending on your perspective) and ready to play house.

It hadn't been a huge thing in the press at the time—there'd been some much bigger names at Levant's that night. A couple of super-models and visiting American actors had been among those arrested, and naturally the tabloids had focused on them. But I had been listed among those charged, and though it hadn't exactly harmed my already floundering career, it hadn't helped either. The charges against me were dropped the following day, and by the next week, the affair was nothing more than yesterday's fish-and-chip wrapping. My career had more or less ground to a halt soon after, though that had nothing to do with the arrest.

On the advice of my agent, who was refreshingly, if brutally honest, I'd decided to pursue an ordinary life. I enrolled in an arts degree, majored in English and drama, then did my high school teaching diploma. And life, as my agent had assured me it would, had gone on.

I'd met Stephen in my first year of teaching, married him the following year, and a little less than twelve months later, Stella had arrived. I can remember laughing with Steve about my single criminal escapade, and that was probably the last time I'd ever mentioned it. In fact it was probably the last time I'd thought about it; far bigger and harder things had happened to me since.

I put off looking for the story until Chip had gone. He grunted his goodbye, not quite meeting my eye. Mary was in one of her compliant moods, happily entranced by the morning cartoons. The dogs were lying in a sliver of pale sunlight on the veranda, enjoying their brief respite from Mary's attentions. I made myself a coffee, then sat at the table with my laptop and googled my name. I had to scroll down a little to find the 180Degrees link, which gave me some hope. Clearly the story hadn't gone viral. Yet.

KIDNAPPER'S S&M PAST

Ellie Canning's female alleged abductor, Suzannah "Gypsy" Wells, arrested in Sydney raid in nineties. Connections with drug lord Eddie Levant revealed.

I scanned the story. While it was surprisingly light on outrageous innuendo, it somewhat less surprisingly failed to mention the fact that the charges had been dropped. There was some background on Eddie Levant—his underworld connections, his 2005 conviction for money laundering—and then the history of my alleged part in Ellie's abduction was related again. Though no links between the two events were made explicit, they didn't need to be. The damage had been done.

The story was accompanied by another photo—one that I'd never seen before—taken at Edward Levant's party. It hadn't appeared at the time; I really had been small fry, not worth the newsprint. I didn't recall posing for the shot, but then I didn't remember much about the night in question at all. The picture was so hazy, so out of focus, that I suspected I wasn't even the intended subject. Still, it was recognizably me—a much younger and thinner version, maybe, but indisputably me. I looked more silly than threatening, dressed in what looked like costume-party bondage gear—a leather belt and shiny chaps, a whip in one hand, plastic handcuffs in the other. I was topless—another detail I'd somehow forgotten—and in a gesture typical of the confusing times we were living through, some puritan at this absurd scandal rag had felt compelled to cover my pert little breasts with a black modesty strip.

The following day, there was more. Again, it was on 180Degrees, and again it was the sort of story that no reputable newspaper would dare touch.

EXCLUSIVE: SUZANNAH WELLS'S INAPPROPRIATE RELATIONSHIP WITH STUDENT REVEALED

A former student at an elite NSW private school has told 180Degrees that Suzannah Wells, the Enfield Wash drama teacher charged with the abduction of 18-year-old Ellie Canning, was forced to resign from her teaching position in 2015 after developing an inappropriate relationship with one of her senior students.

The source, who wishes to remain anonymous, says that Wells was forced to resign from Manning College after complaints were made by the girl's parents. "There were rumors flying about that they'd had a lesbian relationship, but it was all kept really hush-hush.

No one could really work it out." While both the girl and her parents have refused to comment, it is possible that Wells may have been grooming the girl as a potential surrogate.

After her departure from Manning College, Wells worked as a substitute teacher in Sydney. In 2018 she took up a full-time position at Enfield Wash High School.

Even with the distance of years, I still couldn't see what I'd done wrong when it came to Taylor Abbott. Or locate the precise moment I'd overstepped. Or why I'd been chosen to be the scapegoat for her failure. Taylor Abbott had come to Manning College from a boarding school in Sydney. I hadn't been told the full story, but there were rumors that she'd been asked to leave the school for one of the usual reasons: drugs, boys, or booze, or a combination of all three.

It was true that I'd encouraged her in class, given her good marks for her performances. She *was* good, a natural. But she was in no way favored, a teacher's pet. She was far too spiky, too cool for that.

New senior students were assigned a teacher for the first term, which meant weekly meetings, and I'd been made her mentor. These meetings were conducted in a classroom—in my case, the drama room—at lunchtime, the door left open, as it must be when you're alone with a student. The meetings were never what you would call private. There'd be other students in and out, other teachers, sometimes a bunch of kids queued outside, waiting to use the room for rehearsals. These meetings were always brief, always quite formal, the mentor's job circumscribed—a matter of box-ticking, really. Was she settling in? Was she having any difficulties with any of her subjects? With other students? Staff? With course content? I was just there to answer any of her concerns—but as far as I was aware, and as far as she let on, Taylor was settling in well enough.

I'd met the girl outside school just once, by chance, at a café. Taylor had been there alone, waiting for a friend, she said, and I was on my way out, but I sat down at her invitation and chatted for a few minutes. We discussed school, the timing of assignments, her logbooks. I remember saying something encouraging about her proposal for her individual performance piece for her final exam—she'd decided to do a monologue from a modern adaptation of *Medea*. It was a little bold, perhaps, more confronting than the usual student fare, but it was nothing she couldn't handle.

About halfway through the year, things changed. Taylor began to miss classes, and she turned up once or twice very obviously hungover, sometimes drunk or stoned. She failed to hand in several assignments, missed an assessable performance. I tried to talk to her, but she brushed me aside. When I finally informed the head of the department, she told me that Taylor was in danger of failing not only drama but most of her other subjects, too. Mandatory work wasn't being completed; she was disruptive in class. Her attendance was only sporadic. She wouldn't get the marks she needed for university; indeed, it was unlikely she'd receive any leaving qualifications at all.

Eventually the situation reached a crisis point, and her parents had to be informed. She was failing every subject by this time, but her downward trajectory in drama, where for a short time she had been coming top of the year, had been the most profound.

When the complaint came, shockingly out of the blue, her parents were gunning for me. I was accused of breach of care and additionally of inappropriate behavior, of attempting to establish an inappropriate relationship, whatever that meant. The accusation was ludicrous, dismissed in private by the head of school and all the staff, by everyone who knew me. But the girl's parents had money and clout. They would take it no further, they said, if I left the school. They had done their research; they knew who I was and knew my background. I'd been up-front about the arrest when I applied for the job—it had been a youthful indiscretion, the panel had agreed, and not one that was likely to be repeated. And it would in no way color my behavior with the students. The head and numerous teachers came to my defense when the allegations were made, but ultimately it was a board decision. The board was naturally more concerned with the reputation of the school than with the truth or the well-being of staff, and I was asked to resign. It wasn't a sacking—that was made very clear. I was offered a reasonable, in fact generous, package—six months' salary, additional superannuation—ensuring I'd go quietly. They gave me a stellar reference; I signed a nondisclosure agreement and took a few months off to nurse my wounded pride. I moved back to Sydney and worked as a temp until Mary turned up like a bad penny and the job in Enfield Wash came along.

The piece on 180Degrees insinuated that the girl at Manning College had a fortuitous escape, that I'd obviously had my eye on her as a possible surrogate—that it was a near miss for her. I genuinely enjoyed teaching teenage girls, but when I looked at them—their clear eyes, their not-quite-formed faces—what I saw wasn't a potential breeder of a longed-for child, but my own child, my own daughter, who would have been a teenager then, had she lived.

Sometimes it was impossible not to allow the fantasy, to imagine my own girl at fourteen, fifteen, sixteen—miraculously, gloriously, incandescently alive.

This time I'd seen the piece before Hal and rang to alert him. And this time he wasn't surprised—I'd told him the story yesterday, when he'd asked whether there was anything else in my past that might provide a headline.

"Twenty, even ten years ago, it wouldn't have been an issue," he sighed. "*Sub judice* actually meant something. But it's a new world. These online outlets don't let a minor thing like the law get in their way." Like the Levant article, there was little we could do in the way of damage control. "We could try and sue them, but even though that arsehole Hemara lives in Australia, the site registration is impossible to determine. There's nothing we can do. If the case goes to court, we can ask that the jury refrain from taking any of these stories into account . . ."

"But can't we just tell them the truth—maybe get the head in to tell them what really happened?"

"I suppose we could get her in as a character witness if it comes to that, but we can't address this specific allegation. We just have to hope that no one in the jury has heard about it."

"But it's not true. There was a girl, and there was an accusation, but I only resigned to make it all go away. If it'd been true, I'd have been charged. And I certainly wouldn't still be teaching. Doesn't the truth matter?"

Hal took a while to answer. "I'm afraid truth isn't the only thing that matters in law, Suzannah. And out in the real world, it doesn't matter at all."

ABDUCTED: THE ELLIE CANNING STORY

A documentary by HeldHostage Productions © 2019

VOICE-OVER

Despite the risk of legal action, a number of accounts that shed a less than flattering light on Suzannah Wells's character and past were made public while the case was sub judice.

These included Wells's daughter's tragic death from SIDS, her sham affair with gay actor Sebastián Mendes, and her arrest on drug charges in 1996. In September 2018, the news website 180Degrees published an interview with an anonymous source who claimed that Wells was dismissed from an NSW private school due to her "inappropriate relationship" with a teenage girl in 2015.

MADISON COSTELLO*: INTERVIEW TRANSCRIPT

Um, yeah. So this was all a while ago now; I was only a kid, just turned seventeen. I'd had to move from a boarding school in the city to this shitty little private school in Manning. Like, I don't know if you've ever been to Manning? You may as well be dead.

Most of the kids at the school were morons, and the teachers were crap. The only halfway decent one was Miss Wells, the drama teacher. Well, anyway, that's what I thought. It started off okay. I mean, she was my mentor, and we'd have these meetings where I'd just tell her what was going on—you know, with friends, schoolwork. And I was doing pretty well in drama, too. Like actually coming top for a while. I got really into it, and I was rehearsing every afternoon. I'd go down to her office, and I'd go through my IP—that's the individual piece for the exams—and she'd direct.

But then it got sorta weird. She started asking if I wanted to meet outside school. At first it was only coffee, but then she suggested I come over to her place to rehearse, and I thought, yeah, why not? She said not to tell anyone, so I should have known, shouldn't I? Anyway, when I got there, it was clear that she had something else in mind. She was dressed really weird, way too sexy for someone that old. She gave me a drink—something alcoholic—and I think there was something in it?

Anyway, she started to make, like, moves or whatever, and I . . . well, it was hard to, you know, it was hard to resist. It makes me sick just thinking about it.

And that's when things started to go bad. In my life, I mean. I didn't want to go to school after that—I couldn't face it, y'know? And I started getting into drugs and drinking. All that shit. And fighting with my parents. I guess I was pretty traumatized. I know she's a woman, but . . . it was still child abuse, wasn't it? And now, after what she did to Ellie Canning . . .

*Not her real name

SUZANNAH: OCTOBER 2018

Chip flinched as I walked past the kitchen table, where he sat reading something on my laptop. I looked over his shoulder, saw the flash of the browser screen minimizing. He turned and said something banal and cheery, which only made his attempt to hide whatever he'd been looking at even more obvious.

Later, when he'd gone to bed, I looked through the browser history, clicked through until I found what he'd been reading. It was an old article written a few years back, from some syndicated pop psychology website. It had been reposted and updated since the abduction and had more than a million reads by now.

THE PSYCHOLOGY OF THE FEMALE KIDNAPPER

We were a rare breed, apparently. Usually suffering from some combination of personality disorders, including narcissism, generally in combination with Machiavellianism and psychopathy, which meant we were honorable possessors of the dark triad. That was, if we weren't also suffering from actual diagnosable mental illnesses, which was also in the cards. Diagnosable mental illness aside, we might just appear to be regular members of the community, or even work in the caring professions (nurses, teachers) with no apparent social or psychological difficulties. We might have had trauma in our younger days—abuse, neglect, tragedy—but then again, we might not. The article provided very little in the way of reassurance—these women were almost impossible to detect, being naturally secretive and masters of disguise who were able to hide their real selves very effectively.

Most often females involved in kidnappings were working with others, usually men, as half of a folie à deux or because they were in some sort of hostage situation themselves. On the odd occasion that such women worked alone, the victims were almost always children, taken for reasons that had more to do with love than money or sex.

There were numerous instances of infertile women murdering mothers and taking their babies, either to satisfy their own thwarted maternal instincts or at the behest of their husbands or lovers. However, abductions involving forced surrogacy were incredibly rare; indeed, until the notorious Canning abduction, they had received very little in the way of scholarly attention.

I slammed the computer shut, not even remotely excited to learn that one day I might be credited with opening up a whole new area of study.

Chip was lying on his back in the dark room, his eyes closed, arms folded under his head. Sleep gave an unexpected softness to his usually harsh features—the defined jaw, jutting nose, slightly hollow cheeks. I watched the slow rise and fall of his chest, felt my own constrict painfully. How quickly I'd become accustomed to having him in my bed, and how badly I wanted him to stay. How desperately I wanted this future—Chip, me, our baby—to work.

His eyes flickered open. "What's up?" He sounded wide awake.

"What are you thinking about?"

"Nothing much."

"Are you wondering whether I'm a psychopath?"

"No." He didn't turn his head to meet my eyes but gazed at some point on the ceiling.

"Do you think I'm lying?"

"No."

"Do you actually think it's possible that I did it? That I kept that girl here."

"No."

"But you can't really know, can you?"

He took a while to respond. "I know you."

"No, you don't. Not really. We've slept together, and I'm carrying your child. But that doesn't mean you know me." He went to speak, but I couldn't stop. "You *have* to be wondering. There's so much evidence, and none of it can be disproven. You must be wondering whether it's all a fantasy—this me you think you know. You do understand that I've actually been trained to . . . to *be* other people. To pretend. That's my job. So how do you know I'm not acting? How can you trust anything I say? How can anyone?" I could hear my voice getting louder. Faster.

"Suzannah." He was there beside me, holding my hand. "It's okay." He led me over to the bed, pushed me down gently, then sat, his arm slung around my shoulders like a kindly big brother.

He gave me a little shake. "Now, if you'll just shut up and listen to me for a moment. Three things. Firstly, I was only on that site because some arsehole—and I'm not saying who—sent me the link and I stupidly clicked on it. Not because I was checking out whether you fit the bill psychologically. Okay?"

I swallowed. "Okay."

"Secondly, I trust that you didn't do it."

"Really?" I could hear my relief.

"One hundred and fifty percent."

"Okay." His arm had tightened into a decidedly nonbrotherly embrace, and he was moving in for the kill.

"Hold on." I pulled away. "What's the third thing? You said there were three reasons."

"Oh, right." He sounded slightly reluctant. "Well, you were saying that you could be acting, that you could be putting this whole thing on."

"Yes?"

"Yeah, well, I wasn't going to mention it, but I've been watching old reruns of *Beachlife* on YouTube." His tone was bland, his expression unreadable.

"And?"

"You were pretty hot back then."

"Thanks. I think."

Another pause. "Have you watched any of it lately?"

"No. I've actually never watched it since."

"I wouldn't if I were you. It'll only depress you. I know it was a soap, but the plot was beyond bad. That episode where you won the surfing comp? I mean, you looked pretty good, but you couldn't surf for shit—"

"Chip!" I pushed him in the shoulder. "What's *Beachlife* got to do with anything?"

"I know I'm not any sort of expert, and I don't want you to take this to heart, Suze, but frankly, if Gypsy is any indication, I don't think your acting would be anywhere good enough to pull off something as serious as this."

"What?"

"You're not exactly Meryl Streep, are you?"

I was gobsmacked. "You know, I actually won a couple of—"

"Now, don't get your knickers in a twist, mate." His expression was deadpan, his rustic drawl pronounced. "I reckon it's a good thing you're a shit actress."

"How is that a good thing?"

"It's proof that you're telling the truth. I doubt you could lie your way out of a plastic bag."

I wasn't sure whether he was joking and didn't know whether I should be laughing or crying, but Chip was pushing me back on the bed, moving his body over mine, and now was not the time to do either.

SUZANNAH: OCTOBER 2018

"I'm afraid we've got problems."

Hal had arrived unannounced. His company, even with the prospect of bad news, was at least a distraction. It was early in the evening, and I was trying to persuade a contrary Mary that having to eat dinner before dessert did not constitute a form of torture outlawed by the UN. Chip had driven to Orange to attend some sort of agricultural-equipment fair over the weekend, and I was tired and short on patience. I was also feeling lonely.

"What now?"

"Let's go worst problems first, shall we?" He didn't wait for me to respond. "Sally O'Halloran."

"Has she refused to be a witness?" I could imagine she'd be loath to stand up in court and talk. Mary's carer was a quiet, sometimes surly woman who had never been entirely friendly toward either me or Mary. "Can't we subpoena her?"

"I'm afraid it's more complicated than that." Hal took a deep breath, gazing at a point somewhere to the left of me. "She is a witness, as it turns out. Only not for us."

"What do you mean?"

"It seems she made a statement to the police herself. Quite independently. For the prosecution."

ABDUCTED: THE ELLIE CANNING STORY

A documentary by HeldHostage Productions © 2019

SALLY O'HALLORAN: INTERVIEW TRANSCRIPT

I grew up in Enfield Wash, lived here all my life. I work part-time at the nursing home in town, and I do a bit of private work, too, looking after old folk in their homes. I was hired to look after Mary Squires three days a week. I'd looked after the old lady for about six months, and even though I didn't know it, I was there when Ellie Canning was imprisoned down in the basement. I got a huge shock when I heard what happened.

It's weird how things become clear. I didn't think anything of it at the time, but a few times when I was out there, just after the July holidays, I actually heard these noises—it must've been the girl crying or shouting—coming from the basement. I'd been told from the start that I shouldn't go down there—and the door was always kept locked. When I brung it up with Suzannah, she just said that it must have been a bird or something, maybe a possum, and not to worry about it. So I didn't. But when I mentioned it to the old lady, she said it was "the girl." I never thought she was telling the truth—she said so many crazy things—but she was, wasn't she?

As soon as I worked out the dates, I contacted the police.

It's terrible to think, isn't it, that that poor girl was down there all that time. And I could of done something about it. I have these nightmares sometimes.

I guess I was shocked about it being Suzannah Wells? I mean, she seemed okay. She wasn't all that friendly—she never wanted me to stay back and have a chat or anything like that. If anyone had asked, I'd have said she was a bit up herself, maybe. But I had no reason to be suspicious. But why would someone like her move to Enfield Wash? It's a bit strange when you think about it.

And you know, her poor mum's probably had a lucky escape, now that I think of it. Suzannah was always asking me about the Franchise, when it was likely a room would come up. Who knows what she might of done once she really got desperate to get rid of the old lady. I mean, she had a new bloke and a baby on the way. Who'd want their demented mum around? I feel sorry for that poor old lady. When she's not in a mood, she's as sweet and docile as they come. And what's going to happen to her now?

SUZANNAH: OCTOBER 2018

"What was the other bad news, Hal? You said there was more."

I was still recovering from the Sally O'Halloran bombshell. I'd made a cup of tea for me, poured a whiskey for Hal, and called Mary in from the veranda and supervised her painfully slow eating of lunch. She was back out with the dogs now, no doubt filling them in on her exploits in the nineties.

"It's your mother's police interview. It's been judged admissible."

Mary's police interview on the day I was arrested had been in legal limbo, with Hal claiming that her testimony was undermined by her psychological condition and the prosecution determined to prove that she was completely compos mentis.

"How can it be judged admissible?"

"Apparently they've got expert opinion on their side. According to their experts, based on a report by her doctors here and in Sydney, Mary's condition fluctuates. Basically, if she can engage in coherent conversation and appears to be lucid, she probably is."

"Oh. But I don't understand why it's so important to them anyway. What on earth did she say?"

Hal pushed a file across the table. "Here. Read the transcript, and you'll see what I'm worried about. It'd be hilarious—only it's not."

This is a transcript of a police interview between Mary Squires and Detective Inspector Hugh Stratford of the Enfield Wash Local Command in regards to the abduction of Eleesha (Ellie) Britney

Canning and tendered to the Lower Hunter District Court for the purpose of committal. The interview took place in the presence of Hal Gascoyne, solicitor, acting on behalf of the witness.

HS

Miss Squires, thank you for coming.

HG

I'd just like to have my objections to this interview noted. As you know, my client suffers from a form of dementia. Her memory is completely unreliable, and her understanding is severely compromised. I doubt that her statement will be of any evidentiary utility.

HS

Thank you, Mr. Gascoyne. Your objections have been noted.

HG

And if she becomes in any way distressed, the interview will be terminated.

HS

Noted. Can we begin?

MS

Go for it, Mr. Pig.

HS

Miss Squires, can you tell me whether this young lady has ever been in your home? For the record, I am showing the witness a copy of a recent photograph of Ellie Canning.

MS

I like her hair.

HS

Has this young lady ever been in your home?

MS

Maybe.

HS

Can you be more precise?

MS

Maybe she has been in my home. I mean, it's possible, isn't it? It's not like I know everyone who's ever been there. That house is old. And what home are you talking about, anyway? Maybe you need to be a bit more precise.

HG

He means the house you live in now, Mary. The farmhouse.
Where you live with Suzannah.

MS

I don't know why she bought that old dump. Actually, I do. It was
so she could get into his pants. What's his name? Mr. Fish and
Chips. Is he your brother?

HG

Indeed he is.

MS

You don't look alike, do you? Girls never make passes at boys
who wear glasses. But I wouldn't mind your brother's slippers
under my bed, as my mum used to say. He's screwing my daughter, so I guess he's off-limits.

HG

Mary, Inspector Stratford wants to know if the girl in the photo
has ever been in your house. The one you live in now. With
Suzannah.

MS

That old pile? It's so fucking cold. Don't you think it's cold?
You've been in there, haven't you? It's the coldest place I've ever
lived, and I've been in some cold places. New York. London. Paris.

But Jesus. This place. You've been there, haven't you, Mr. Pig? It'd freeze the tits off a brass monkey, 'scuse my French.

HS

The girl, Miss Squires. The girl in the photo. Has she ever been in the house?

MS

What the fuck is a brass monkey, anyway? And since when do monkeys have tits?

HS

Miss Squires, I'd like you to concentrate. If you could just look at the photo one more time and tell me if you recognize the girl. For the record, I am showing the witness a photograph of Eleesha Canning.

MS

This photo?

HS

Yes.

MS

She's a pretty little thing, isn't she? Butter wouldn't melt in her mouth.

HS

But do you know her, Mary? Has she been in your home?

MS

Of course I know her. She's the little bitch who's got my Chanel pajamas.

ABDUCTED: THE ELLIE CANNING STORY

A documentary by HeldHostage Productions © 2019

VOICE-OVER

Having reportedly been paid in advance for print and television exclusives, pending the forthcoming trial, Canning quickly
became an Australian media favorite. Although she was unwilling
to discuss her abduction directly while the case was sub judice,
Canning was interviewed by numerous mainstream media outlets across Australia.

Some—like the new youth current affairs show *Woke!*—took a
serious approach, exploring some of the wider social implications
of Canning's ordeal.

[Cut to footage from *Woke!* interview]

INTERVIEWER

One of the things that people have been very disturbed by is the
fact that an eighteen-year-old girl could disappear for almost a
month without anyone reporting her missing. Does this shock
you?

ELLIE

Well, I'm not shocked, exactly. I mean, kids like me get used to being pretty much invisible. It does make me mad, though.

INTERVIEWER

And it's a wake-up call, isn't it, for the system?

ELLIE

Totally. There have to be better safeguards. There are so many vulnerable young people out there who don't have families to keep an eye on them.

It makes you wonder about the others, doesn't it? The ones who have gone off the grid without anyone noticing. It's a pretty scary thought.

~

VOICE-OVER

Others, like Sarah Smiley on *Good Morning Today!*, were more interested in talking about Canning's current activities.

[Cut to footage from *Good Morning Today!* interview]

ELLIE

Hi, Sarah. Thanks so much for having me on the show. It's very exciting.

SARAH SMILEY

Well, it's exciting for us, too. Your story has certainly struck a chord around the country. You've become quite the phenomenon. I read that you've just been voted 2018's number one girl in *Top Girl* magazine—beating some very strong Hollywood competition, I might add, with thousands of Australian teenagers voting you the girl they'd most like to be. How does that feel?

ELLIE

Oh, it's wild. My life feels totally crazy right now.

SARAH SMILEY

You've certainly come a long way.

ELLIE

I really have . . .

SARAH SMILEY

And we hear there's a romance blossoming between you and that gorgeous Jamie Hemara.

ELLIE

Er—that's gossip. We're totally just friends.

SARAH SMILEY

Mm-hmm. Sure.

Anyway, we're all dying to find out what you're going to do next.
We've heard you've had some very interesting offers. Not what
you imagined, I suspect.

ELLIE

Yeah. There was a time when I basically didn't know if I'd even
have a future. But now there's so much happening. Some days it
feels like I've woken up in some sort of a dream world. So many
people want me. Honor—she's my agent—she says she's never
seen anything like it.

SARAH SMILEY

And can you tell us about some of these offers? Are they all that
different from your original plans?

ELLIE

Well, what I originally wanted to do was to go to university. Then,
of course, all this happened, so I thought that was out. But I got
a letter from the university just last week saying that due to
my, um, special circumstances, and after considering my school
reports, they've decided to accept me anyway.

And St. Anne's, the college, has offered me a residential scholarship. Although I'm not sure that I'll even be going now—I've got

so many exciting things going on. Heaps of opportunities. Maybe I'll just take a gap year—or two.

SARAH SMILEY

And can you tell us a little about these exciting opportunities?

ELLIE

Oh yes! I've actually been offered a job as spokesperson for Girl Up, which is a new organization that's devoted to helping empower young women who've been in traumatic situations, helping them to regain their confidence and find their voices again. They've got this kick-arse program to optimize all the bad things that have happened to them to build up resilience. Anyway, it's a really amazing role, and it's just so humbling to be given the opportunity to help others, after my own experience.

SARAH SMILEY

Wow. That sounds fantastic—so perfect for you!

And we've heard that there's something else, something very special that you're going to announce, exclusively, here on *Good Morning Today!*

ELLIE

It is pretty amazing. It looks like I'm going to be the face of a new line of L'Andon cosmetics in the new year.

SARAH SMILEY

So, a modeling contract?

ELLIE

Yes! It looks like it. Isn't it mad?

SARAH SMILEY

Well, I don't think, looking at you—and can we have a close-up of this beautiful face? I don't think anyone would think that it's really a mad idea. I think most of us will completely understand L'Andon's decision—and we'll be cheering for you all the way.

ELLIE

Oh, thank you. You're so kind.

SARAH SMILEY

Can you tell our audience what this new line of cosmetics is going to be called, Ellie?

ELLIE

I actually think they could guess. It's going to be called Escape.

HONOR: OCTOBER 2018

Since taking on Ellie, Honor had deliberately kept her trips to Enfield Wash to a minimum. Too many people—both known and unknown—were likely to approach her to try and find out what she knew about the case, or about Ellie's current doings, or to tell her that they'd always had their suspicions about Suzannah.

But this weekend it had been unavoidable. The nursing home director had called her late last night to tell her that her father had had a minor heart attack and had again been sent to hospital for observation. While his condition wasn't critical, considering his state of health, anything could happen. He would probably require surgery—either in Newcastle or Sydney, depending on the availability of beds, surgeons, and all the rest. Honor should probably make the trip up immediately. She had delayed seeing her father for as long as she could, had made an appointment to talk to the hospital's resident geriatrician to discuss what needed to happen next and to make any necessary arrangements before visiting. The doctor had, as it happened, recommended that nothing be done, that her father return to his room at the Franchise. Surgery might be advisable further down the track, but at this point, his condition wasn't in any way desperate.

"It may be better just to leave it for now," she'd said. "He's really not in any immediate danger. And in cases like his, it's often best to let sleeping dogs lie."

They both knew what the doctor really meant was that in cases like her father's, where quality of life was already so reduced, being carried off quickly by a major heart attack probably wouldn't be such a bad thing.

After the meeting, Honor postponed the visit further, ordered a cup of barely drinkable coffee and a stale muffin at the hospital kiosk, sat down with a magazine, and did some quick calculations. It was nearly four o'clock now—if she managed to drag this out, official visiting hours would be almost over and she wouldn't have to hang around, even for appearances' sake.

She'd chosen a table in the gloomy recesses of the kiosk, figuring that if she kept her head down and appeared to be immersed in her depressing food and her even more depressing reading material (a women's magazine, with a small and blurry but satisfying image of a Lululemon-clad Ellie "out and about in Paddington" in its "Celebrity Snaps" pages), she would be left alone. But she hadn't figured the waitress into her plans.

The woman knew who Honor was immediately and delivered her query with the coffee and cake.

"So, how is she? The girl? How is she holding up?"

Honor's first impulse was to tell the woman to fuck off, but she put her magazine down, smiled politely. The waitress was tiny, thin, bent, her features small and tight. She looked like she'd had a hard life, could be any age from thirty to sixty, but her hostility felt ancient. It wasn't necessarily directed at her, though, so Honor kept her response friendly enough, if uninformative.

"She's okay. She has good days and bad days."

The woman gave a stiff nod. Something about her looked familiar, and Honor couldn't resist the question, even though she knew that it would inevitably extend the conversation. "Do I know you?"

"I was Cheryl Cruikshank. Howatt now. Not sure you'll remember me. We were in the same year, but we weren't exactly friends." The woman's reflexively defensive attitude was familiar, too.

"Oh yes, I do remember you." Cheryl had been a tough girl from a rough family. She'd been benign enough in primary school but developed into a fearsome and sometimes violent bully once hormones—and an understanding of her immutable position in the town's social order—had kicked in. She'd never really bothered Honor, who'd ranked too low in the social hierarchy to be deserving of full-scale enmity, and who'd been a tough enough cookie herself, but as she said, they'd never been friends either.

"So you married . . ." She trawled through the possibilities, names she hadn't thought of for years. "Jason Howatt?"

"No. Jase never married. Too much time in prison. He hasn't had a chance. I married Darren, his brother."

Darren Howatt had been a figure of considerable infamy back in their youth. A good five years older than Honor, he'd worked in his father's auto body shop, drove a souped-up panel van, and was always in trouble with the local cops for the usual small-time crimes: pub fights, drunk driving, antisocial behavior. Rumors of darker deeds swirled around him, too: drug dealing, arson, sexual assault.

"I think I remember him. And you've got children?"

"Four. We've got two grandkids already. And another on the way." Her smile was fleeting but genuine.

"Grandkids. Wow. You must be busy." Honor did her best to look interested rather than appalled.

"Yeah. Our youngest is still at school. Year Nine."

"Here?" Honor had no idea why she asked this—it was highly unlikely that any of the Howatt children attended boarding school—but Cheryl hadn't noticed, had circled back to her original conversational target.

"She was in that woman's class. That bitch who took Ellie." Honor was surprised by the venom in the woman's voice.

"Oh yes. I suppose it must have been a bit of a shock to the school community." Honor's response was measured, but the woman was enjoying her anger too much to be deflected.

"They shouldn't allow them around kids, sickos like that. And I don't understand why her and her loony mother haven't been locked up."

"I guess she's not really a danger, though, just living quietly at home. I mean, there are bail conditions, and I'm sure the police are keeping a close eye on her."

"Yeah. Well, that's a load of bullshit, isn't it? Not what you know, it's who you know around here." The woman's eyes narrowed. "If it'd been one of us, they'd be in jail and the key thrown away."

"Oh, I don't know that that's really . . ."

"Oh, come on. She's screwing Chip Gascoyne. Those rich wankers have always had this town wrapped around their little fingers."

"Maybe that was true back when we were kids, but things have changed a little, don't you think?"

The woman glared at her. "No, actually, I don't think. That woman's a fucking pervert, and she should be locked up and not let within a hundred miles of any kids. It's not just a principle—some of us still actually live here."

Honor ignored the barb, gave a sympathetic sigh. "I can understand why it must seem unfair. And frustrating. But there's not really anything that can be done." She paused. "Sometimes it would be better if communities could just deal with this stuff themselves. But we can't, can we? The law's the law."

"Yeah. Well, there's the law, and then there's justice." Cheryl's full smile, as unexpected as it was ghastly, revealed a row of blackened, stumpy teeth. "And some of us don't see why one has to wait for the other."

SUZANNAH: OCTOBER 2018

I woke in the middle of the night. Mary was standing silently beside the bed, gazing down at me intently, as if willing me to wake up. She looked like a wraith—her long hair wild around her head, eyes wide, a pale blanket draped around her body for warmth.

"What's wrong, Mary?" I kept my voice low, calm, steady. I had found her sleepwalking once or twice before and didn't want to startle her. If she woke up properly, she would be difficult to get back to sleep.

"There's someone out there."

"Out where? Outside?"

"Out there. In the garden." She pointed to the window. "Listen." This wasn't following the usual pattern—Mary's sleepwalking conversations were generally with unseen others and never made sense. She was awake.

I pushed the blankets off and sat up. She grabbed my wrist in her bony fingers and squeezed hard.

"You need to do something," she hissed.

"What?"

"Before they get us."

"Who's going to get us, Mary?"

"The villagers. They're out there. With their pikestaffs. Come and see."

She grabbed my shoulder with her other hand and pulled me, surprisingly strong.

"Stop, Mary. I'll get up." She let me go but hovered, breathing heavily, as I got to my feet.

She positioned herself behind me and pushed me toward the window.

"Go and look out, but don't move the curtain too much or they'll see us."

"Oh, for God's sake." But I humored her, crept over to the window, peered out. "If there was anyone here, the dogs would be—" But then I remembered: Chip had taken both the dogs with him.

"Can you see them?" Mary stood behind me, too close, literally breathing down my neck.

I couldn't see anything unusual, just the shadows of the dense canopy of trees that grew around the perimeter of the yard moving gently in the breeze.

"It's just the trees, Mary. It's just their shadows in the breeze."

"No—look over there." She pointed in the direction of the garage. Three forms, shadows elongated but distinctly human, were lined up against the back of the shed. It was impossible to make out which way they were facing, but they appeared to be doing some sort of bizarre dance, swaying this way and that, moving up and down, their arms sweeping back and across in long, fluid gestures. Each of them held something aloft. It only took me a moment to work out what they were doing.

They weren't holding pikestaffs, but their modern equivalent—cans of spray paint.

"Oh shit."

"So, can we shoot them?" Mary's fear had morphed into excitement. "What?"

"They're on our property. Isn't it the law out in the bush? I'm pretty sure we can shoot them."

"Mary." I turned her away from the window and led her over to my bed, pushing her down gently. "We can't shoot anyone. Not only is it illegal, I don't actually have a gun."

"Doesn't your cowboy boyfriend have one?"

"Oh, Mary. It's not . . . Anyway, Chip's not here."

"Did you scare him away? No wonder." She poked at my belly. "You're getting a bit tubby."

"I'm going to call the police. And then I'm going to make you a hot cocoa and take you back to bed. Okay?"

"Why would you want to call the pigs? They already want to put you in prison for what you did to that girl."

"You know I didn't—"

"There's only one way to handle this."

Mary was back at the bedroom window in an instant. She peered out into the night, shaping her fingers into a pistol, taking aim, firing.

It was impossible to know who might have been out there. Online attacks had been coming from all quarters. Most were from people who'd never met me, but some were closer to home and all the more frightening for that. It seemed that even during my brief—and I would have said relatively uncontroversial—time at Enfield Wash, I'd managed to make some enemies. Who would have guessed that a tiny disagreement about classroom bookings could be turned into a public assassination of my character, again compliments of 180Degrees:

> An anonymous source tells us that Wells was a constant troublemaker during her time at Enfield Wash High: "It's an under-resourced school, so most teachers work hard to share what we have as fairly as possible—but Suzannah Wells was utterly ruthless about never sharing her drama room with other teachers, even when it wasn't in use. At the time I just thought she wasn't a team player, or that she was big-noting herself . . . now I'm wondering whether there was some sort of sinister reason . . ."

And how could I have known that the supermarket employee who accidentally knocked a can of tinned tomatoes off the checkout and onto my foot had been utterly terrified by my response (it hurt; I swore) and would one day be eager to share her terror with the world:

> "I mean, it's not as if I did it deliberately, but the look she gave me. Honestly, I thought she was going to kill me..."

And then there were the revenge-seeking parents, frightening enough when I was just the annoying teacher stifling Junior's creative genius, but on steroids now that I was the villain du jour.

> The mother of a student at Enfield Wash High has spoken about having always had a sense of unease about Wells's relationships with some of her charges. "I did always wonder if her relationships with some of the girls were healthy. Her favorites always seemed to be vulnerable girls, not girls who had strong family connections, and not the students who displayed any particular talent. I ended up warning my own daughter to keep her distance from Ms. Wells—which is such a pity, as she's such a talented actor—although I couldn't really put my finger on what was worrying me. Anyway, it turns out my instincts were right."

This last "informant" was easy to work out: Linda Simmons, mother of Lexie, and a classic stage mum. She had cornered me in the school car park one afternoon earlier in the year. It was a gloomy autumn afternoon, and I had been in a hurry, running late after a staff meeting, worried that it would be dark before I arrived home. Linda didn't bother with any preliminary greetings but launched right in.

"I hear the Mallory girl has been given the main part in *The Crucible*."

"Well, yes. But Rebecca Nurse is a solid role, too. I think Lexie will find it—"

"Lexie's been waiting for this for years. It was always expected that *she* would be given the main part in her senior year. Miss Amber promised her."

I refrained from telling her what I really thought, which was that her daughter's determination to always be the center of attention didn't equate to her having talent, and instead said very mildly that I'd made the decision based on who was right for this particular role.

"But I don't understand why you would give it to Jess Mallory. Why would she be any good? Lexie's been going to drama classes for years. I doubt Jess has even been inside a theater. I'm worried—well, quite a few of us are worried—that she'll . . . spoil things. Are you sure she really is reliable? I don't want to seem mean, but I've always thought Jess was a little bit slow. Are you sure she'll be able to learn all those lines?"

It was true that Jess Mallory's talent was something of a surprise. She certainly wasn't one of the usual suspects: she wasn't part of the popular gang, she was something of an introvert, and she certainly hadn't had years of out-of-school coaching in drama and singing. But she could act. What I'd wanted to tell this mother was that art didn't necessarily come from smart, or pretty or respectable or outgoing. And not even from good or kind or hardworking. Her daughter, for instance, was all those things. But all the elements that had made Lexie a happy, well-rounded girl with abundant self-esteem didn't necessarily make her a great actor. I wanted to explain that art could come from places no one really wanted their daughters to go. I would have liked to tell her that Jess Mallory was tapping into experiences that her daughter didn't have access to, that there was something dark in her, something hard, something powerful. I didn't know what her life out of school was like—and to be honest, I didn't want to know. Most likely there was something that stopped her from feeling whole, feeling real, feeling *herself* in the way that Lexie so clearly did. And it was this lack that meant Jess was able to become others so easily, so authentically. Mostly I resisted the notion of the artists' wound, the idea that there's always something melancholic in their nature, stemming from some existential trauma, some sadness that can't be assuaged. But I had to acknowledge that there was an element of truth in it, too. Where there was darkness, there was damage—and with damage, sometimes depth.

But I'd said none of this. Instead I'd smiled, kept my voice breezy. "She'll do brilliantly. They all will."

"You don't think perhaps you've been out of it for a long time?"

At our only other meeting, the woman had seemed intelligent, interested, but now she was a lioness mother, her teeth bared, baying for blood. She looked me up and down blatantly, her lip curling. I suspected that I didn't even meet her expectations of what a schoolteacher should look like, let alone an actor.

"Perhaps things have changed a little since you were, er, active in the scene."

At this, I'd lost my cool. "Oh, I don't think so. It's like any art form—there are essential elements that haven't changed since, oh, ancient Greece, probably. I'd be happy to fill you in on the details if you'd like, but it's quite complex. It might take a while."

Her face had darkened with anger. "I'll be talking to someone about this," she muttered before stalking away.

I stood there for a moment, feeling vaguely unsettled, wondering who it was she planned to talk to and what they would have to say.

I'd told the story to Bret Baker, a science teacher who'd worked at the school for almost ten years. He'd warned me that Mrs. Simmons could be dangerous to get offside.

"She's ambitious for her four girls. And vicious when she's thwarted in any way. A music teacher resigned after a complaint she made a few years back."

But according to Bret, Mrs. Simmons was the least of my worries as far as proactive parents went.

"It's the violent ones you have to look out for."

"Are you serious?"

"There are a few big families here with pretty solid criminal backgrounds—Cruikshanks, Howatts, Sharpes. They're all related, and even the ones who seem completely respectable can be pretty shady. They're fine if you stay on the right side of them, but if one of them gets pissed at you, the lot of them are likely to come after you."

"Do you mean physically?"

"It's possible. There was a young English teacher here a few years back whose car was stolen, set alight, and pushed into the Lock after she complained about one of the Cruikshank boys verbally assaulting her. There were abusive letters, death threats. No one could ever prove it, but everyone knew who it was. She didn't stay long after that."

I taught at least eight kids with the offending surnames. "Shit."

"And you don't have to upset them personally either," Bret added. "They've been known to go after people who have beef with their friends, or people who they don't 'approve' of, for whatever reason. There was this scientist who visited one year to give a talk about sustainable farming, and apparently he said something that must've challenged their worldview—Christ knows what—and two family heavies cornered him after the event and beat the crap out of him."

"But how do they manage to get away with it?"

"The usual. They've been here forever. People are scared of them. And they have connections."

Bret had laughed at my obvious dismay. "I wouldn't worry too much. I doubt any of that lot are likely to get too upset about anything that goes on in your drama class. And anyway, you're some old TV star, aren't you? They're not going to bother you."

It was almost two hours before the police arrived, and by that time the intruders had long gone. I'd persuaded Mary to go back to bed, and she was finally asleep. I offered to accompany them out to the shed, but the two officers—both male, one young, the other middle-aged—asked me to stay put. I watched from the veranda as they sauntered across the paddock and shone their flashlights over the shed, walked right around it a few times, then wandered back, flashing their torches this way and that.

I quizzed them about the damage.

"They've certainly done a job on your shed."

"Could you read what they'd written?"

"Oh, you know. It's just the usual rubbish. I wouldn't bother even looking at it if I were you. We can send someone out to clean it up in the morning."

"Really? That would be fantastic."

"They'll scrub it off with some sort of solvent—shouldn't cost too much. The car might be more difficult."

"The car?"

"It looks—"

"And smells!" the younger officer chipped in helpfully.

"As if someone's dumped a bucketload of, er, human excrement all over it."

"What?"

"Yeah. Maybe you can get out there with a hose first thing. But the frost might be a problem, yeah? Might be best to get to it before it, um, sets. Hopefully none of it leaked inside."

"There's not someone who can come and clean that up?"

The older officer scratched his chin, looked over at his partner. "You know anyone?"

"Yeah, no. Maybe just contact a cleaner? They have like those trauma cleaners in bigger places, but I dunno about here. You could try and get someone up from Sydney, I guess?"

"And what about finding out who did it?"

They seemed oddly uncomfortable. "I'm not sure it's going to be possible to identify them. You didn't try and get a look? See what sort of vehicles they were in? What they were wearing?"

"No. It was dark. I could see figures. They seemed quite tall. Male, I think. Adults or older teenagers, I guess."

"Maybe if you'd turned on your outside lights, they'd have taken off right away."

"But . . . I didn't want them to see me, to know I'd seen them."

"Why not?" The young officer looked genuinely perplexed.

"We're two women out here, alone—and they probably already know that, with the reports in the newspapers and everything. It seemed a bit of a risk, anyway."

"Yeah, no. These types really don't tend to be violent. It's just simple property damage. They usually just say what they want to say and then they go."

"But we couldn't possibly have known that."

"I guess not." He shrugged. "So, do you want to file a report?"

I was taken aback. "I'd have thought that was mandatory. Don't you have to?"

"Not necessarily." The older man shook his head.

"What would you advise?"

"Well, it's not like we'll ever find out who they are. And even if we do, there'll be no evidence. It would've been too cold for them to have been working without gloves, even if they happened to be that stupid, which I doubt, so there's no point trying to get fingerprints."

"Right."

"It'd really just mean a shitload of paperwork for everyone. You included."

"You don't have a list of . . . potential suspects you can investigate?"

"Not really. I mean, we do have some what you'd call regular offenders, but most of them are only kids. Bored on a Saturday night, looking for kicks. And there are a couple of idiots who see themselves as serious 'artistes.' But I'd say in this case, it's probably a little bit different."

"What do you mean, different?"

"Well, first, it doesn't look like kids. Kids don't usually stray too far from town; most of them don't even have cars. And if they do go out of town, it's for a good reason. You know, something highly visible, like silos, billboards. That sort of thing. They don't tend to deface isolated farmhouses."

"Oh."

"This is obviously a bit more . . . personal. You've been targeted for a reason."

"But doesn't that narrow things down?"

"Not exactly."

"What do you mean?"

"Well, it could be anyone, couldn't it?" Both men looked grave. "You've made a lot of enemies out here, Ms. Wells. Half the town thinks you should be locked up for good. There'd be a lot of people wishing they had the guts to do it themselves. A lot of people who'd say this is no more than what you deserve."

SUZANNAH: DECEMBER 2018

I had spent the last few months in a strange state of suspended anima-
tion, with my life put on hold indefinitely. Time blurred; the days were
hard to distinguish from one another. Chip left at the crack of dawn
every morning to do what had to be done to maintain his livelihood. I
envied him his escape into a world that seemed simple in comparison to
mine—farming might be physically harsh, brutal even, but it could be
understood and negotiated. I envied, too, the fact that he could direct
his focus elsewhere, even if it was only for a few hours a day.

I had decided early on that if I was to avoid going mad, I would
have to pretend that I was simply enjoying a well-earned break, taking
early maternity leave. Every morning I set myself some routine domestic
task—catching up on bills, gardening, unpacking boxes, rearranging
furniture. But by the afternoon, my (clearly inadequate) imaginative
reserves were exhausted, and I would slump on the sofa beside Mary,
half watching whatever program she was currently obsessed with and
sharing her dry Froot Loops. Somehow I still managed to keep the
anxiety at bay, pushed it to the furthest recesses of my pregnancy-fogged
mind and focused on the one bright point, the only certainty of my
current situation: the child who was growing within me. I was well
into the second trimester, the baby was kicking, and the nausea had all
but disappeared. I tired more easily but had yet to develop any of the
expected aches and pains. We hadn't asked to find out the sex, but all
the tests indicated a healthy fetus.

In early December, with only six weeks to go before the hearing, Hal came over to go through the prosecution evidence with us. Most committals were simple paper committals, with evidence supplied to the magistrate in the form of written statements, but Hal had asked for a physical hearing to garner more time, and in the hope that he might discover evidence to dispute the prosecution's evidence—or even better, find a witness whose story would make Canning's fall apart. If at committal the magistrate wasn't convinced that the prosecution's case could satisfy a jury beyond reasonable doubt, the charges would be dropped, the case dismissed.

Media interest in the case had moved on—mercifully, Ellie Canning seemed to have become the focus of the story, rather than me, or even the crime itself—but a small contingent of reporters (a motley bunch representing mostly oddball online sites) still gathered at the end of our drive, so it was easier to meet Hal here than in his office in town. Chip had made the trip into town to pick up our week's groceries and arrived home just before Hal. He, too, had increasingly kept clear of Enfield Wash over the past months, not so much because of the media, who didn't seem to worry him, but because of local attitudes toward us, particularly after the night of the graffiti. He hadn't said much—not wanting to worry me more, I guess—but he had made vague noises about certain people having too much time on their hands.

The three of us sat down at the dining room table, where we had a good view of Mary, who was out on the veranda with the dogs. I tried not to laugh as Hal did a double take. This morning, Mary was dressed in what she'd taken to calling her hairy-wear—an old pair of orange fluoro work overalls supplied by a thoughtful Chip when I complained about the endless washing that Mary's canine obsession was creating. She was sharing Rip's doggy bed, lying curled up against him, one arm caught underneath, the other stroking his nose. She muttered constantly and sometimes quite heatedly, but the dog seemed happy enough, eyes closed, tail thumping sporadically. Ned was nowhere to be seen; he either had his nose badly out of joint or had gone into hiding.

There were far too many documents for us to get through in a day—interviews, witness statements, scientific reports, photographs—but Hal had provided a précis of the critical elements. It was mostly what I'd expected. All of it nonsense, all of it fabricated.

And all of it completely irrefutable.

I read the girl's statement again, went through it slowly, made notes, trying to find anything—some little error that might be expanded into a gaping hole—that would cast doubt on her testimony.

We went through the list of physical evidence that provided proof of Ellie's incarceration. The paintings, the underwear, the cup with her DNA and drug residue, the hairbrush. Read through the witness statements that the prosecution had provided. Everything added up—but not to the truth.

Most of what was here wasn't a surprise, but the accusations, documented so officially and authoritatively, made the craziness real.

There were so many lies, coming from so many directions, it was impossible to know how I could even begin to refute them. The accusations were so lunatic, so preposterous. They made the small implausibilities (drugging a potential surrogate, for example) seem irrelevant.

Suddenly the reality of what it all meant, and what it might come to mean, crashed down on me like an all-encompassing black cloud. Years in prison, the removal of my child, the end of this burgeoning relationship with Chip. And Mary, what was to become of Mary? I wanted to curl up and howl.

"I don't get it. It feels like someone's just walked in and turned my life into something insane. Something hellish." Chip, who looked as desolate as I felt, squeezed my hand mutely.

"There must be something we can do, some way to show it's all lies."

Hal looked thoughtful. "The problem is that it's just so much easier to prove that something happened than to prove its opposite, its negative—to prove that something *didn't* happen. What we need is something that casts doubt on *her*, on Canning herself. Any doubt at all."

"But the girl is squeaky clean—no one's got a bad word to say about her. She's practically a saint."

"But if she wasn't here, where was she? Someone must have seen something, know something."

"But who? And how would we find them? You're talking about needles in haystacks."

Chip stated the obvious. "What about her phone records? I know she said it was out of power and that she hasn't seen it since she got in the car . . ." He looked at his brother hopefully.

"Yeah. That's all been checked. Her records are completely consistent with her statement. The last call she made was from somewhere near Broadway, just after her interview at St. Anne's."

"Do you have a copy?"

Hal dug it out of the teetering pile of documents and handed it to his brother. Chip looked at it briefly, then passed it over to me. No calls had been made from her phone after the date of the alleged abduction. And no calls had been made to her phone, either, just half a dozen texts—one from her mother, a couple of group texts between classmates, her foster mother hoping she was having fun in Sydney—but not many. I felt a moment's pity for Ellie. She'd gone missing from her life for almost a month, and there was no one to notice, no one who cared. There must be some sad story, some hidden pain behind all this.

"Pity we can't check her actual phone and look at her photos. I'd like to see if she's really the virtuous little thing she says she is." Chip looked at his brother hopefully. "Surely you know some dodgy techie who can find out that stuff for us? I thought no information was private these days?"

"I'm just a country barrister, not James Bond. Anyway, even if a techie found something on her phone, it'd be inadmissible—and completely illegal. But, barring a witness, that's exactly the kind of thing we need. A photo. A phone call. CCTV footage. Something dated, verifiable." Hal sighed. "But you're right—we're talking needles in very deep haystacks. At this point only Canning herself knows wh—"

He paused. "Actually, maybe that's it. Maybe we need to look at it another way. Maybe there's no point searching for the gaps in her story—maybe we need to consider what she *knows*."

"What do you mean?"

"Well, what does she know about you? Your past? The house? Mary?"

From her evidence, it was clear that Ellie knew an awful lot. More than was possible without having been here, without having met me.

"What if you make a list of all the things she knows, the things she shouldn't know or *couldn't* possibly know? That might tell us something about *how* she knows. Maybe there'll be a clue. Something that will help us make sense of it all."

"But what's the point," I asked, "when there's still all that DNA evidence? How can we refute that? It's all impossible." I could feel my voice thinning out, a *wahhhhh* developing. "It doesn't make sense. We can discuss what she knows—and the impossibility of her knowing it—until the cows come home, but it doesn't tell us *how* she knows. She's made her accusations, and we can't disprove anything. We can make guesses, but we can't prove anything."

Even I could hear the tinny shrill of desperation, the despair. I laid my head down on the table, overwhelmed by a wave of exhaustion.

"Or maybe everything she's saying is true and I've just gone completely mad."

After that night's Trouble, which took us longer than usual to successfully lose, Mary was adamant that she wasn't ready for bed, insistent that she needed something yummy, something chocolate. We were all out of chocolate, so I made her a cup of warm cocoa, which was too pale for her liking; added more cocoa to make it darker, which made it too bitter; and added sugar, by which time it was too cold and needed to go in the microwave again. Finally, everything was just right, and Goldilocks sat slurping noisily in front of the box.

Chip was skeptical about his brother's idea, but I was keen to follow his suggestion.

"Do we have to do this? I'm not sure that writing a list is going to help anything. And I'm bloody tired."

I sympathized, but at this point I was ready to try anything. "Come on. It might just, you know, shake something loose."

He sighed, looked longingly at the television.

I handed him a pen and a pad. "She's watching cartoons, Chip."

"I know," he said glumly. "It's a Looney Tunes special. I was kinda looking forward to it."

Once we began, the list of things the girl shouldn't know wasn't really as long as I'd imagined; in fact, it was quite limited. There were, naturally, all the things anyone could know about me, or that could have been discovered easily by the careful questioning of locals:

That I existed.

That I lived where I lived.

That Mary existed.

That Mary had dementia.

That we lived alone here together.

Then there were the other things that might take a bit of research: reading old newspapers, talking to people . . . but who?

The layout of the house.

That I'd been married and had a child. That my child had died.

Then there were the things that couldn't be explained, the things that Canning could only have known by being here:

That I owned the Alice Neel and Margaret Preston prints. That there was an old metal headboard down in the basement. That I'd kept my daughter's sippy cup.

These things couldn't be invented—they were all too specific. The girl, or an accomplice, had to have been here. She, or this accomplice, had to have seen these things—and scratched initials in the basement wall; planted the DNA samples, the hair, and the underwear; and stolen the silk pajamas while they were at it. None of this was completely implausible, of course. She could have broken in sometime when I was at work and somehow avoided Mary, or Mary could have seen her and forgotten all about it. But proving it was going to be difficult.

Proving it was going to be impossible.

There was one final thing that needed to go on the list: the one thing I knew Ellie Canning couldn't possibly have known—that only two people in the world had known at the time of her escape.

"There is one thing more." I was hesitant, not knowing where this might lead.

"What?"

"There's no way she could have known about the baby. I've looked at the dates. I remember working out exactly how pregnant I was. It was the day the Year Elevens chose their performance groups: July 18. And then I told you a couple of days later. Only you and I knew."

"What about your mother?"

"She didn't know until that night when the police were here, remember. At that point, when the girl was meant to be here, the night she made her escape"—I corrected myself—"the night she *says* she made her escape, it was still only you and me. And in order to know, the girl would have had to have been there, in *your* house. She would have to have heard me telling you *there*. We didn't ever discuss it here, did we? And you weren't around that following week. One of us must have told someone. Someone who told that girl. And I know it wasn't me." It wasn't a statement, but a question.

Chip was staring at me, stricken, his eyes wide, face pale. "Oh, sweet Jesus."

HONOR: JULY 2018

She knew what was going to happen the moment Chip walked in the door. There was something about the way he held himself, his shoulders square, the tension in his jaw, the cool wariness in his eyes. Honor had seen this look before, long ago, back when they were both kids. And from other boys, other men, too, so many times. It was always the same—that cold defensiveness that swamped everything, even pity, even guilt.

He had been Honor's first, but she'd never tell him that. Never give him that . . . satisfaction, if that was the right word.

She'd gone with him that first time without pausing to even think about it, to worry about the logistics, what lie she would tell her parents. What else was she going to do when he'd asked, in that deceptively offhand way of his, giving that slow sideways smile, whether Honor wanted to go out to Freezywater with him and a few of his mates? It wasn't going to be anything fancy, he'd said—a few of the boys had sleeping bags, but he was just going to sleep in the back of the old EH wagon he'd been doing up. He'd pick her up around six, would bring the steak, the sauce, the booze. She'd almost asked whether she should bring her own sleeping bag, but changed her mind at the last minute. Why tempt fate?

They'd half hooked up a few weeks earlier at a Bachelor and Spinster's ball out at the Boyd place. Honor never truly enjoyed those parties—they were really for the boarding school kids and their mates— and a drunken kiss with the suddenly desirable Chip Gascoyne, who'd been her classmate through primary school, had been the highlight of an otherwise dismal night.

The crowd out at Freezywater was a different bunch of kids. Most were townies, and the farm kids weren't the children of rich graziers, but hardscrabble "cockie" farmers who sent their kids to the local schools rather than to board in Sydney or Melbourne. She didn't have to worry about anyone smirking about her too-broad accent, her bad perm, her jeans that weren't quite the right cut or color, the fact that she wasn't heading off to Women's or Wesley or St. Anne's, but staying put and taking up a job as a cadet at the *Clarion*.

Honor had known these kids all her life—they were schoolmates, neighbors, children of her parents' friends; it was like being with family. And Chip was comfortable there, too. Unlike most of the other rich kids, he'd stayed mates with the local boys. He'd always had that knack, Chip, of getting on with everyone.

But no one else mattered, anyway. All she could really see was Chip. Those blue eyes, crinkling at the corners, reminding her of some old movie star—Paul Newman, maybe?—and that thing he did when he walked, a sort of saddle-shaped swagger that made her think he should be wearing spurs, packing a pistol, cracking a stock whip. His voice, that drawl that spoke of money, privilege, arrogance, and that deep, dark laugh that promised something else entirely. Oh God, everything about him made her feel almost sick with anticipation.

All the things she usually enjoyed doing at parties seemed suddenly completely pointless: drinking, bonging, sitting in a stoned circle watching the flames leap and flicker, or gazing into the vast and glittering sky, listening to the boys tell their bullshit stories, because in the main it was always the boys who directed nights like those, who told jokes, strummed guitars, provided what passed as entertainment.

That night all Honor was conscious of was the way time seemed to stretch and shrink simultaneously, of wanting the night to move quickly and wanting it to never end. And she had been waiting all night for that one moment: the moment when Chip stood up, stretched slowly, and muttered something about needing to hit the hay. The moment when he looked down at her, curled at his feet, looking upward, expectant. The moment when he offered her his hand and gave her that smile, that lift of the eyebrows. "You coming, Fielding?"

It had been a typical teenage romance, over almost as soon as it had begun. She and Chip had met up at the occasional Wash event in the years since, and if she'd been asked, Honor would have said that the adolescent spark had been well and truly extinguished. But they'd met up again in Sydney a few years after his wife's death. Honor was walking past a Woolloomooloo art gallery one evening after a work dinner, had noticed the small crowd, and when she looked in, had been amazed to see Chip there. She knew a couple of the art-world types milling about, so she had sauntered in. She went straight to the champagne, found a dim corner, where she pretended to gaze admiringly at an origami display, all the while watching Chip. He was talking to an intense-looking girl, clearly an artsy type, with her sleek black hair, red-rimmed glasses, knee-length skirt, fine wool cardigan, her clumpy but expensive brogues. Honor wondered momentarily whether the young woman was a romantic interest, but then she recognized Chip's expression—his impatience to move on evident in the tapping of fingers against his glass, the slightly panicked look in his eyes. She sipped at the too-sweet bubbles, watched him for a few minutes more, amazed that her heart still beat so fast at the sight of him even now. He was not the young god of her memory, but he was still the sexiest man she'd ever known. His wild hair tamed, gray at the temples, his toothy smile, his long, strong fingers curled awkwardly around the delicate crystal stem of his glass. She despised herself for it, but she was breathless just looking at him. She took a second glass of the sparkling—it really was cheap and very nasty—and walked over to where he was standing, bumping lightly into his shoulder.

He turned to apologize. "Honor." He'd been surprised, but his smile was genuine. "What the hell are you doing here?"

She told him a partial truth—work dinner, just walked by, thought she'd take a look. "I wasn't invited, but I know half a dozen people here—they'll vouch for me. I won't nick the masterpieces. But what about you? What are you doing so far from home?"

"It's, ah . . . Gemma's cousin Beth is one of the artists. I thought I'd better come—she and Gemma were pretty close. Beth used to visit quite a bit at the end. That's her over there." He gestured toward the girl with dark hair, who was talking to a woman Honor knew was a serious, and seriously moneyed, collector.

"I saw you two talking. I thought she might be your new squeeze."

"Oh God. Beth?" He looked horrified. "No way."

"She seemed quite keen, I thought."

"You're not serious, are you? Last I heard she was a lesbian. I mean, I know these things can change, but—"

She laughed. "This isn't really your scene, is it?"

"Oh, I dunno, Hon." He gave a rueful grin, crossing his fingers. "Art and me, we're like that."

And then it happened. He looked at her—and it was a look that set Honor's heart racing again, reminded her of the girl she once was, the boy he'd been—and asked the question she'd been wanting to ask from the moment she'd seen him: "Do you want to get out of here?"

It was a cliché—in fact, the whole thing was one glorious cliché— but she enjoyed the moment, anyway.

They headed back to his Kings Cross hotel room with a stolen bottle of the bad champagne and fucked before they'd even drunk the first glass. It was good, better than she'd imagined. And it had left both of them wanting more.

Later, when she told Dougal her decision, he'd agreed without question, pleased. "It'll be good for you to see your father more often," he said. "You know he might not have all that long. And it'll give you some downtime. And being in the country," he added, "is good for the soul." Dougal was always worrying about the state of her soul.

Two months later, the Randalls' property went on the market. The family had stopped farming years ago, sold off the land around them, and now they were selling the remaining five acres and the homestead. The house was old, desperately in need of a new kitchen, an extra bathroom, a paint job—but renovations would give her something to do. An added excuse for frequent visits. And even more appealing: the house was on Wash Road, less than a kilometer from Chip's.

Tonight Honor knew what was coming, but she tried to postpone the moment, pretending that nothing had changed. She wasn't going to precipitate things; that would make it all too easy. For him. Instead, she poured him a drink and pushed it into his hand, told him about the day's successes: the memoir deal wrangled for an aging rock star, a six-figure exclusive for a new-mum soap star, news of a client's million-dollar contract with Netflix. "Here's cheers," she said, "to sweet, sweet success."

Honor knew that only a few months earlier, these stories would have excited Chip. He loved hearing these tales, was simultaneously thrilled and disgusted by the excess. He enjoyed calculating the farm machinery that could be purchased with such sums, how many men could be employed for the cost of one ultimately forgettable performance. He loved to act the philistine man of the land in these conversations. But tonight nothing she said moved him. He sipped his drink, smiled on cue. When he cleared his throat, ready to say what he'd come to say, Honor ignored him. She wasn't ready. She started another story, but he interrupted.

"Honor." He grabbed her hand. "We have to talk."

Naturally, he did all the talking. What was there for her to say? She didn't bother begging or pleading, making claims. Didn't bother turning on the waterworks, or even showing any anger. These were their agreed-upon rules of engagement: no strings, no exclusivity, no promises.

But she did have one question.

"Why is it so serious with Suzannah? I don't get it. You've only known her a few months."

"Why?" He blinked, brought his attention back to her. He'd been staring off into the distance. His body was upright, taut with nervous energy. Even so, Honor could see how soft he was getting; he had the beginnings of a paunch, his shoulders sagged. His shirt was untucked, and she could see how pale his skin was, its crepiness. The old man under the middle-aged man's body.

"She's pregnant. Suzannah. We're having a baby." Honor didn't flinch, but his words were like a physical blow. "And I . . . I want to be a part of it all."

She couldn't help the bitter little laugh. "You're almost fifty, Chip. Aren't you a bit past all that?"

"I dunno, Hon. If you'd asked me this time last year, I'd have said there was nothing I wanted less. But now . . . I'm sorry, Hon. I really didn't expect this to happen."

Honor could hear the pleading in his voice. He could have his true love, play happy family, but she wasn't going to give him her blessing.

SUZANNAH: DECEMBER 2018

"You and Honor?" Things were beginning to shift, to take on a radically different shape. "She told me you'd had a thing when you were young . . . kids, she said, but I had no idea . . ."

"It was nothing. Really. Honor and me, it was—"

He stopped. The room had gone suddenly quiet. Mary had turned the television off and was gazing at us intently.

"That woman you were just talking about. The good-looking one."

"Honor?"

Mary nodded. "What happened to her?"

"What do you mean?"

"She hasn't been over for a while."

"No. I suppose she hasn't."

"Isn't she your friend anymore?" Mary looked worried. "Maybe she thinks I told you? Because I didn't, did I?"

"Told me what?"

"About her coming here that day."

"What day? Did she come when you were here on your own?"

"No. Nurse Ratched was here. She'd made me go to bed and tried to lock the door. I came out to see what they were doing . . ."

"And what were they doing?"

"She was coming up from the basement stairs with a plastic bag. The one who brought Hannibal Lecter to dinner. She said she was getting something from the laundry."

"Why didn't you tell us?"

"It was something to do with your birthday. A surprise. She told me not to tell you. So I didn't. I like surprises."

"Oh, Mary. My birthday's not until February."

"And she said if I didn't say anything, she'd get me that peppermint ice cream, the one I really like, with all the crunchy bits. But she hasn't, has she? I'm still waiting."

Mary turned back to the television, picked up the remote control, and then swiveled around, her eyes wide.

"I know what she was doing down there. I'll bet that bitch stole my pajamas."

Chip phoned his brother early the next morning, before Mary was awake, eager to tell him what we'd discovered. We'd gone over and over our suspicions—now solidified into certainty—through the night, but were no closer to understanding how Honor was involved or, more importantly, why.

Hal wasn't impressed. "I know it was my idea, but this is a dead end. The fact that you told your mistress that your new girlfriend was pregnant isn't proof of anything except adultery." He spoke bluntly despite the fact that he was on speakerphone. "Honor didn't have any previous connection to Ellie Canning, did she?"

"Well, not that we know of, but what if—"

"*What if* won't cut it, Chip. This isn't a crime novel."

"What about Honor's visit, the plastic bag she took away?"

His brother gave an irritated sigh. "Oh, come on. Any evidence provided by Mary is highly suspect. She can't even remember what century she's in half the time. It's what we'll be arguing if this goes to trial, anyway. We need to get rid of that police statement altogether, not argue that she remembers things differently now."

"Can't you just check? See if Sally O'Halloran's connected to Honor in some way? Hire someone to run a background check. See if her bank balance has gone up or something?"

"I'll talk to our investigator—maybe he can ask around discreetly. It won't hurt. But look, even if we find she has some sort of connection with Sally, even if we discover that Honor did come to the house, there's no evidence that she did anything untoward. It's all supposition. And none of it proves that Ellie wasn't down in Suzannah's basement. There's still the DNA, remember. What we really need is something solid that casts doubt on Ellie Canning's story, not something that implicates someone else."

HONOR: DECEMBER 2018

The call came while she was at a fundraiser. One of Honor's clients, a former fashion model who'd just written her memoir, was the charity's patron. Once upon a time, Honor had loved this sort of event: the glittering crowd, the stink of power and, in some cases, corruption. It had given her a thrill to be included, even if only in a minor way, in this hyperprivileged world, this alternative aristocracy. She'd come alone. While once she would have dragged Dougal along, too, these days he rarely accompanied her. He'd never really been as enthusiastic—his connections to the rich and powerful were far more substantial, if less showy—and he would much prefer to stay home and have an early night. Just lately, though, Honor had begun to feel a similar sense of ennui. Over two decades some things had changed—the people, the clothes, the settings, even the menus—but the conversations had more or less stayed the same.

It was nine o'clock, and she'd been cornered by an author who'd recently received some extra attention owing to her controversial stance on stay-at-home mothers and was suddenly in high demand. She was wondering whether she should employ her own publicity agent— wouldn't she get more lucrative speaking gigs that way, increase her sales? Honor tried to stifle a yawn, was already dreading the lunch meeting she'd taken her phone out to schedule with the woman, when she discovered that she had more than twenty missed calls. All of them from Ellie.

She keyed in the novelist's contacts quickly, made a time, then smiled her apology and found a quiet place to make the call.

Ellie answered immediately. "Honor. Oh God, Honor. We're fucked. I'm fucked." She sounded drunk or high. Or both.

"What's going on?" Honor hoped that whatever Ellie had done, whatever she'd taken, wasn't going to involve a visit to hospital. She immediately thought about how she was going to contain the publicity. She went through her contacts in her head, the doctors who might be able to deal with such a situation, who owed her something and could be relied on to stay silent. She was annoyed: Ellie had had an interview with a popular but notoriously intimidating young YouTube journalist earlier in the evening. Normally Honor would accompany her on these occasions, but tonight she'd had this party. She'd left Ellie a Cabcharge with instructions to go straight back home after the interview, have an early night. Not only was it important that she maintain her squeaky-clean reputation, but she had a prerecorded Skype interview with CNN early the following morning—it would be only her third US appearance—and in the afternoon they were meeting with two production companies vying for documentary rights. Honor wanted the girl switched on and looking her best. As far as she could tell, the girl had been acquiescent; in fact, when Honor had left the apartment, Ellie and Dougal had been cheerfully arguing whether they should get takeaway or reheat the previous night's leftovers.

Now she could hear Ellie gasping in the background, as if trying not to cry. "Take some deep breaths, Ellie, and tell me what's going on."

"Okay." Her voice was still strangled, but she was speaking coherently. "I just did that interview. The one with that arsehole Andy Stiles. He wasn't—well, from the start it was clear he wasn't onside. And then . . . he showed a clip."

"A clip? A clip of what?"

Honor knew what she was going to hear even before the girl told her; oh, not the precise details, but their significance. Honor had always had a sixth sense about these things. Somehow she always knew when a client screwed up. When they'd done something career destroying, something that signaled the beginning of a dramatic downward trajectory. This was one of those moments—she could feel it.

Still, she did her best to reassure Ellie. That was her job. "This is what we're going to do. Firstly, *you're* not going to do anything, Ellie. You're going to go home and have dinner with Dougal. You're going to watch that crime show you wanted to watch, make yourself a cup of herbal tea, and go to bed. And tomorrow morning you're going to do the CNN interview as planned."

SUZANNAH: DECEMBER 2018

Mary and I made the trek up to the mailbox early in the morning to avoid our ever-diminishing press retinue, the excited dogs racing ahead of us and then back again, barking joyfully. Mary chased them for a bit but quickly ran out of energy and trudged behind, complaining about the distance, the heat.

The night before, Chip and I had waited until we were alone to discuss not the import of Chip's disclosure, but the substance. I had begun with the obvious question: Why hadn't he told me? And his answer was just as clichéd: he had been afraid.

"We'd been seeing each other, off and on, for a couple of years. It never meant anything to either of us. I didn't want a permanent relationship, and there's no way she would ever leave Dougal; her life with him is too easy. He adores her, and I think she actually loves him, in her own way. Neither of us wanted more. It was like . . . it was just an itch being scratched. And when I told her it was over, and about you, about the baby, it was nothing. Truly. She didn't even look upset. She basically just shrugged, for fuck's sake. She poured us both another drink and made a toast. She was pleased for me. For us."

"But what if it meant more to her than you realized? Maybe she'd thought the two of you . . . had a future. I mean, if I hadn't fallen pregnant?" I had to work hard to stay calm, to shake off the feeling that there was something he wasn't saying.

Chip seemed to sense my distress and took my hand. "You know there's nothing between me and Honor. And there'd been nothing, even before you told me about the baby. We hadn't really been together for months."

And I believed him, of course I did. There was no more reason for Chip to be lying now than there had been for him to be faithful five months earlier. I knew that his past shouldn't matter at all, that it was unreasonable of me to expect it. There was no place, no justification, for sore feelings on my part. Honor and Chip were history. I could tell myself that, but I still felt a sharp pang of jealousy. There was still the fact that Honor and Chip shared a history. That Honor knew him in ways that I didn't. And perhaps never could.

Mary had discovered her second wind and overtook me, making it to the mailbox first. She pulled out a handful of envelopes and ran back, the dogs at her heels. I shook myself out of my anxiety about Chip—right now there were bigger things to worry about, to focus on. Mary handed me her catch, panting loudly. There were a couple of utility bills, a catalog from an online pet shop for Mary, and a small envelope, addressed by hand. I gave Mary her missive from PetCo and considered the plain white envelope, sensing the nature of its contents, reluctant to open it.

I had been receiving anonymous letters ever since my arrest. The online commentary had been horrifying enough, but physical mail was worse. Not just the almost reflexive expressions of fleeting outrage, but actual letters—composed, addressed, stamped, posted—were so much more deliberate, effortful, and far more threatening. Most of these letters were so full of bile and rage and an almost visceral hatred that it was hard not to feel afraid, not so much for myself, although that was a part of it, but for a world that contained such a concentration of ugly feeling.

It wasn't until we were back in the house, the breakfast mess cleared away, Mary happily absorbed in her catalog, that I worked up the courage to tear the envelope open and pull out the single sheet of paper within. The message was typed and printed in a regular font, rather than the usual mad scrawl or the painstakingly retro newspaper cutouts that I'd come to expect.

The Canning girl is a liar. Check out Aphroditeblue.com.

Bizarrely, this was the first mail I'd received that had provided any-thing that was even remotely anti-Ellie, and even though I knew it was likely to be a dead end—and a sleazy one at that—I was desperate to check it out. But Mary had other ideas. I put the note in my pocket, then helped her choose springy new dog beds for Rip and Ned and, after some pitiful but persuasive begging, one for her, too.

I didn't get the opportunity to look at the site until late in the evening. Mary was in bed; Chip had tidied away the remains of dinner and was dismally flicking through the various TV stations looking for something to watch.

I opened up my laptop, pulled out the crumpled note, and keyed in the address.

The website contained nothing but images of young women, all pos-ing provocatively, in various stages of undress. The shots were strangely old-fashioned, slightly kitschy: an attempt to re-create a respectable nineteenth-century gentleman's idea of risqué, but with twenty-first-century raunch. Some girls were in lacy underwear—suspenders and corsets, with cigars suggestively placed; others, draped in sensitively revealing togas, held shimmering grapes between pouting lips. Clicking on any of the images took me to a gallery of stills featuring each model. It wasn't long before I found a picture I was already half expecting. I clicked on the image, which took me through to more.

Most of the images were too pixelated for me to be absolutely certain of the subject's identity; only one had the required clarity: a girl, somewhere in her late teens or early twenties, dressed only in lacy underpants, lounging invitingly on a velvet chaise. She was grinning at whoever was taking the photo, clearly enjoying herself. And just as clearly, I knew I was looking at Ellie Canning. Her expression might have been light-years away from the innocent, sunny smiles of her recent appearances, but it was brilliantly, wonderfully, indisputably her.

~

I was about to call out to Chip when my mobile pinged. It was a text from Hal. He'd sent a link to a YouTube interview between Ellie Canning and an English journalist. It had been up for less than a day, and already it'd had fifty thousand views.

Apparently her lawyers tried to stop them putting it up but failed, Hal wrote. I think this may be exactly what we need.

ABDUCTED: THE ELLIE CANNING STORY
A documentary by HeldHostage Productions © 2019

VOICE-OVER

In December 2018, an interview between Ellie Canning and YouTube talk-show host Andy Stiles, who is renowned for his aggressive take-no-prisoners interview style, went viral. Stiles's interviews are estimated to have a weekly audience of over six million.

[Cut to footage from *Andy Stiles Unplugged*]

STILES

So, Ellie, you've got to admit that you've become pretty famous pretty quickly, and for what I'd say are kinda spurious reasons.

CANNING

Oh. I'm not really sure what you mean. And I don't think it's, um . . . spurious. It's not like I ever planned any of this.

STILES

No. I'm sure you didn't. But you have to admit that you've become something of a national heroine to an awful lot of people out there—and a role model. "The face of a generation," I think someone put it.

CANNING

Yes—and it's overwhelming sometimes. I have to, I mean, I always try to do my best . . . to be, to make sure that I'm living up to . . . Actually, I'm sorry, but I'm not sure what your point is, what you're asking me.

STILES

Well, what I'm wondering is, do you ever wonder if any of this, ah, adulation is actually deserved? I mean, you were abducted, which was really terrible, and then you escaped—which is fantastic. Well done. I think everyone would be glad about that, yeah? But don't you think it's a weird kind of world when simply having something happen to you is enough to make you a celebrity? It's not like you've . . . solved third-world poverty or anything, is it?

CANNING

I, um—you know, I guess I do think it's a whole lot more than that. I think people are interested in the things I did before this all happened: my background, all that. There is a wider . . . social kind of question here, isn't there? And then there are the things I've done since. It might not be exactly saving the third world, as you put it, but I'm doing what good I can, whenever I'm asked.

STILES

So it's just some kind of runaway train, yeah? This whole media thing? And you're just riding it?

CANNING

I . . . well, you can look at it like that, I guess. But I don't know why you'd want to.

STILES

So, when you're talking about things you did before all this, you mean your backstory, right? Like coming from a really disadvantaged background—no dad, mum in rehab, foster parents. All that was hard, yeah? But you worked hard, getting in to good schools, university, college . . . You had it tough, but you managed to rise above it?

CANNING

I know I'm not unique, and there are other girls in similar situations. That's a big part of what I'm—

STILES

Sure, sure. But what I'm wondering is, what are we meant to make of other elements of your past? I mean, it hasn't all been hard work and no play for Ellie Canning, has it?

CANNING

No. For sure. I've had some fun times. Of course I have. Everyone has to have some fun, don't they?

STILES

So what I'm wondering is how these "fun times" fit in with the narrative we've been given.

[Stiles plays footage of a young woman having sex.

A close-up shows the girl is clearly Ellie.]

I mean, this is you, right?

CANNING

What? Where did you get this?

STILES

So is this you? You haven't answered the question.

CANNING

[Long pause] Okay. Yes. It's obviously me. I'm having sex. So what? Since when has sex been illegal? I was over sixteen.

STILES

It's not just a question of sex, actually. There's also the question of ti—

CANNING

Oh, come on. Are you trying to say that I somehow deserved what happened to me because I had sex? Isn't this just blatant slut shaming? What century is this?

STILES

Oh, come on. You can't keep playing the—

CANNING

I'm not answering any more of your bullshit questions, so you can turn that fucking camera off—

[Interview terminated.]

~

VOICE-OVER

Initially Canning and her legal team made efforts to have the Andy Stiles interview, along with the offending clip, blocked from YouTube, claiming that Canning's interview had been filmed without permission. While these efforts were ultimately unsuccessful, Stiles's attempt to smear her backfired. Canning's fiery response to Stiles's slut shaming went viral, and Canning's popularity soared.

Her subsequent comments regarding the sex tape, made during an interview with US talk-show host Antonia Saltis, brought her an international audience, and by the time of the committal hearing in January 2019, Canning had become a global sensation.

PART THREE

SUZANNAH: JANUARY 2019

The committal hearing was held in Enfield Wash. I recalled visiting a courthouse at some point during my childhood, on a school excursion, perhaps, but I'd never been inside a court that was in progress, let alone one that was charged with deciding my fate. I arrived early, but even so, the court was already packed. I'd expected the media to be out in force—despite the fact that as the victim, Ellie herself wouldn't be attending—but I was surprised by the presence of so many onlookers. Most were unknown to me, other than a few media people and a handful of my fellow teachers—all of whom were as careful to avoid making eye contact as I was—and one or two parents. Although I wasn't going to be questioned, the court was intimidating, and the prospect of coming face-to-face with Honor was terrifying. I scanned the crowd quickly when we entered, but there was no sign of her.

Mary, Chip, and I sat just to the right of Hal and his junior counsel, Sylvia, and a young legal clerk whom nobody had thought to introduce. We had considered leaving Mary at home, worried she might be restless or loud or cause some sort of a commotion, but she was strangely subdued, perhaps overwhelmed by her surroundings and the solemn atmosphere.

When the judge (who was straight out of central casting: bewigged, portly, glowering) finally arrived, Mary moved as close to me as she could, clutching my hand tightly.

Without Ellie, there were actually very few prosecution witnesses. The young farmer who'd found Ellie was called first. He answered the prosecution's questions nervously but straightforwardly. Next up, a doctor and pathologist gave evidence on Ellie's physical state and the blood samples taken in the hospital. Then Sally O'Halloran took the stand. The prosecution team, led by an elegant woman in her late thirties, had nothing new to ask her; Sally's answers to their questions tripped easily off her tongue, never deviating from what I'd read in her statement. But when Hal stood to begin his cross-examination, the poor woman looked suddenly terrified. Hal was careful to make his initial questions gentle, innocuous—asking her where she lived, how long she'd worked at the Franchise, whether she liked her job. His next question seemed to throw her.

"Can I ask you, Miss O'Halloran, whether a Mr. Albert Fielding is one of your . . . er . . . one of the residents at the home?"

She gave the prosecution lawyers an anxious look. "Mr. Fielding. I, ah. I think so? Yes."

"And are you aware that he is Honor Fielding's father?"

"Yes. That's right. Yes, he is."

"So I take it you know Ms. Fielding, then?"

"I . . . er. Yes. I knew her a bit at school. And I see her occasionally when she comes in to see her father."

"So you would recognize her if she happened to visit Suzannah Wells's home. You'd know who she was?"

"I guess. I mean, of course."

"And did she?"

The woman blinked. "Did she what?"

"Did Ms. Fielding ever call in when you were there?"

"I, ah. I don't remember her—"

"We actually have a statement here from Mary Squires, Miss O'Halloran. She says that she remembers Honor Fielding visiting the house while you were there."

The prosecution's counsel interjected, "Objection, Your Honor. Miss Squires is hardly a reliable witness. If she was, we'd be prosecuting her, too."

"The prosecution seems to have allowed Miss Squires's testimony where it suited them, Your Honor. They've brought in medical experts to have her statement included in the brief—"

"Yes, yes. That's fair enough. But perhaps you could get to the point, Mr. Gascoyne?"

"Miss O'Halloran, if you could answer my question. Do you remember Ms. Fielding visiting Ms. Wells's residence while you were there?"

"Oh. I . . . I don't . . ."

She paused, looked imploringly at the prosecuting counsel, who responded with a not terribly encouraging smile.

"You must answer the question, Miss O'Halloran." The judge spoke sharply. "And remember, you must answer truthfully at all times."

"Well, maybe she did call in once."

"Can you remember when that was?"

She frowned, concentrating fiercely. "It was a Monday, I know that, because she came when I was watching my serial."

"Can you remember which Monday?"

"Not really."

"Was it in winter?"

"It must of been. I remember thinking her feet must've been freezing. She was wearing sandals, and there was still frost outside."

"Can you recall the month?"

"Frost was late this year. Not till the last week of July. I know because of my roses," she added helpfully.

"So after the July school holidays, then?"

"It must of been."

"And before news of Miss Canning's escape."

"I guess."

"And can you recall the purpose of Ms. Fielding's visit?"

"I don't really know. I think she . . . Yes, she said that there was something she needed to pick up. She was borrowing a dress, maybe? She thought it was in the laundry."

"And did she go into the laundry?"

"I suppose so."

"You didn't accompany her?"

"No. I was . . . busy. And she said not to worry, she knew what she was doing."

"So you didn't actually *see* where she went?"

"No. But she told me she was going to the laundry."

"Do you know how to access the laundry from inside the house?"

"I've never had any reason to go there, but I know it's downstairs."

"Yes, it's downstairs. You can get to it from outside the house, too, but it's generally accessed through the door in the hallway—that very one you say you were told not to open in case Mary fell down the stairs. The same one that you say you heard strange noises emanating from."

"Oh."

"Oh, indeed. So, as far as you know, Ms. Fielding went downstairs to retrieve an item from the laundry."

"Yes."

"And she didn't have any trouble opening the hallway door?"

"Not that she said. No. You'd have to ask her, though, to be sure."

"But you've stated that the door to the downstairs rooms was always kept locked—that you were expressly told never to use it."

"Maybe . . . maybe Honor had a key?"

"This visit—if you're correct about the day—must have been during the time that Ellie Canning was allegedly being held downstairs."

"Oh, but . . . I'm not sure."

"Did you happen to see the item of clothing that Honor Fielding retrieved from the laundry when she left? What it was that she borrowed?"

"No, I didn't."

"Miss Squires has suggested that the visit had something to do with Ms. Wells's birthday. Some sort of surprise, apparently."

"I don't know anything about that."

"And you didn't think you should mention the visit to Suzannah Wells when she arrived home? Just to let her know what had gone on that day. Wouldn't that be the standard thing to do in such a situation?"

"I must—well, we're always in a bit of a rush in the afternoon. I guess, I guess I just . . . forgot all about it."

"And you didn't think to 'remember' it later, when all this happened, like you 'remembered' the noises?"

"I don't see what difference it makes. That girl could of still been down there. Maybe Honor just didn't see her . . ."

"And didn't hear anything, either, apparently. These shouts that you say you heard coming from the basement rooms. Did you hear them when Honor Fielding was visiting, when she went downstairs to the laundry?"

"I don't know, exactly. I mean, it's not like I heard them all the time. Maybe it was when she was . . . asleep, or unconscious or whatever."

"Perhaps it was. I just have a few more questions, if you don't mind. Now, Miss O'Halloran, if you can cast your mind back a little further, to a few days before Ms. Fielding's trip downstairs to the laundry."

This was something new. I looked at Chip inquiringly, but he shrugged, whispered, "No idea. I know Hal got an investigator to do some hunting around. He must have found something else."

Sally took her time, frowning. "A few days before? I'm not sure. It's a long time ago now."

"It is, isn't it? But I'll see if I can narrow it down for you. This time we have an exact date: July 27. It was a Friday. On that evening Ms. Fielding visited your home."

"Oh. Maybe."

"No maybes. She did. We have a witness, one of your neighbors, who says she saw Honor pull up outside your home and go inside. The witness was surprised, because she didn't realize you and Honor were friends."

"We're not."

"But she visited your home?"

"I . . . yes. She did."

"Would you be able to tell us why?"

"I . . ." Sally looked about wildly, her growing desperation evident.

The prosecution's counsel stood. "Objection. The witness doesn't need to answer that question, Your Honor. It has no bearing on the case."

The magistrate gave Sally a long, thoughtful look. "Actually, I think I'd like to hear this. Miss O'Halloran, please answer Mr. Gascoyne's question. Why did Ms. Fielding visit you at home?"

"She . . . wanted to talk to me."

"Can you tell us what she wanted to talk to you about?" Hal asked the question casually enough, but there was an edge of excitement in his voice.

"No."

"No?"

"I can't remember."

"You can't or you won't? Is that because Ms. Fielding wanted you to do something unlawful?"

"Objection!"

"You may ignore that, Miss O'Halloran. Mr. Gascoyne, the witness has told you that she can't remember. Have you anything further to ask?"

"No more questions, Your Honor. Thank you, Miss O'Halloran. You've been a great help."

Sally got to her feet, then stood, unmoving, as if dazed. The usher spoke to her quietly, then led her gently from the box. She exited the court quickly, her head down, careful not to make eye contact with anyone.

Chip turned and glared as she passed us, but I looked straight ahead. Hal turned around in his seat and nodded before turning back to call the defense team's first and only witness, David Lee. The prosecution team was struggling to hide their alarm, shuffling through papers, passing notes. "We haven't been advised of this witness."

The magistrate looked up briefly. "Apparently the witness has only just been located. No matter—you'll get your cross-examination, Ms. Battisti."

Lee was somewhere in his midthirties and exceptionally good-looking. His shirt, untucked, was rolled halfway up well-defined forearms, displaying intricately tattooed sleeves. The judge looked alert for the first time all day, clearly intrigued by the way things were progressing.

Hal stood up. "Mr. Lee, you describe yourself as an 'artrepreneur.' Can you tell us what that means?" He gave the man an encouraging smile.

Lee didn't smile back. "I'm a photographer and filmmaker."

"How would you describe your work?"

"Objection. I fail to see how this is relevant." The prosecuting counsel looked flustered.

The magistrate gave her a small smile. "No. But I suspect you're going to find out. Objection overruled." He turned his attention to Hal. "This had better be good."

Hal gave a curt nod and turned back to Lee.

"Mr. Lee, can you tell us a little about your work? Your subjects, your audience, that sort of thing."

Lee cleared his throat. "Well, it's a bit more than just art—I like to think that I'm actually providing a social service. I'm all about helping women explore their potential. I get them comfortable with their bodies, then take them out of their comfort zones when it comes to connecting with others. It's a serious project."

"Your website features pictures of half-naked women, Mr. Lee. Some might call it soft porn."

Lee looked disdainful. "I suppose they might, but they're looking at it from a typical heteronormative perspective. It's not about cheap thrills; it's about empowering women."

"I guess it's all a matter of perspective, as you say. Regardless, the pictures are reasonably tame, aren't they?"

"We do the occasional full frontal, but it's always tasteful."

"And you just . . . sell these photographs through your website? Forgive me if I'm being a little cynical here, but these images don't really seem like they'd cater to contemporary tastes."

The man shrugged. "I have a pretty select clientele. They're after something different. Arty. A bit retro."

"And you're a filmmaker as well? There's no mention of films on your website. Why is that?"

Lee looked uncomfortable. "They're only available to special members. Subscribers."

"Are the films as retro as your photographs?"

"They're not always retro. They're for women who want to explore their limits, their power, take it further."

"And by taking it further, do you mean you film them having sex?"

"If that's what they choose to do." Lee ignored the muffled laughter and stared straight ahead, his expression stony.

"How do you produce your films, Mr. Lee? How do you, for instance, find the 'talent' to act in them? Do you use an agency?"

"Not really, no. Usually . . . it's a case of people finding me. They're seeking the experience. But occasionally it's just a . . . random meeting in a bar or whatever."

"And when you film them, do these girls give their consent?"

"Well, it's pretty obvious what's going on, with the cameras and everything. I've never met a girl who isn't turned on by a camera. They all want to be stars. And I pay them."

"What about your male leads, Mr. Lee? Where do you, er, source them?"

Lee took a moment to answer. "Most of the time it's me."

"You mean you're actively having sex while filming?"

"Yeah, sometimes it's hard. But I know these girls—they trust me. We have a connection." There was more muffled laughter, some awkward shuffling in the seats.

Hal took his time, playing the crowd. "Do the girls you work with know that you're selling the footage?"

"Of course. Most of them anyway, yeah."

"And they don't mind?"

"No." He glared defensively. "As I said, they get paid."

"I'd like you to look at some photographs." Hal's clerk handed Lee a thin pile of printed sheets. "Can you confirm that these images have been taken from your site?"

The man shuffled through the papers. "Yes."

"They haven't been doctored in any way?"

"No. They look right."

"And the date stamps at the bottom of each image—these are the dates that the pictures were taken?"

The man looked at the pages closely. "If that's what's on the site, yeah. There's no reason to change them."

"Would you mind telling us the range of the dates?"

The prosecutor objected, "Your Honor. I don't see the relevance of this question."

The magistrate gave a grim smile. "I think I'm beginning to, Ms. Battisti. Carry on, Mr. Gascoyne."

"If you wouldn't mind telling us the date of the earliest photograph and the date of the latest, Mr. Lee."

Lee went through the sheets carefully. "Okay. The first one is dated July 7. And the . . . um . . . final one is July 25."

"And are there images that were taken between these dates, too?"

The man shuffled through the papers again. "There's probably some from almost every day."

"I take it you remember the woman who is the subject of these photographs, Mr. Lee?"

"I do."

"What name did you know her by?"

"She told me her name was Olivia."

"And have you seen her elsewhere, before or since?"

"She's that girl, the one who says she was kidnapped. Ellie Canning."

There was a communal intake of breath, and the entire assembly seemed to shift forward in their seats, eager to hear more.

"Are you sure?"

"I'm dead certain. She told me she wanted shots for her portfolio—and ended up staying at my place for three weeks. We did a fair bit of . . . filming. Had a lot of fun. She didn't give me a forwarding address, so I put her pictures up. I assumed she'd be in touch. Actually, I was sorry when she went; she has talent. I think I could have taken her a long way." He looked regretful. "I could really have pushed through those boundaries."

HONOR: JANUARY 2019

Honor sat in the gallery, where she could get a decent view of everyone but still go virtually unnoticed herself. She wasn't there to be seen—not yet anyway. She had a simple statement ready to make on Ellie's behalf, once this show was done and dusted, but right now she was happy to blend into the background. She tried and failed to suppress a pang when she saw Chip and Suzannah take their seats, with a frail and uncharacteristically scared-looking Mary between them. Despite the very obvious stress of her situation, the now heavily pregnant Suzannah looked radiant—her skin clear, her eyes bright, her dark hair thicker than Honor recalled.

Honor had prepared herself for what she imagined would be a boring and unnecessary rehash of the prosecution's evidence. She'd felt a vague sense of unease when the defense insisted on the hearing, but Ellie's lawyers had reassured them that it was just a way for the defense to gain time and there was nothing to worry about. They might cross-examine, but they had submitted no new evidence, called no new witnesses. On her advice, Ellie, who wasn't required at the hearing, had taken a flight to an exclusive Fijian resort with Jamie and was no doubt lying back in her private spa right now, enjoying a cocktail and whatever else was on offer.

The initial proceedings had been exactly what Honor had anticipated—the witnesses introduced nothing new in their testimony, and the defense cross-examination had been perfunctory. Even Hal's questions regarding the possibility of the DNA evidence being planted had lacked energy. And Sally O'Halloran had scrubbed up surprisingly well for her appearance. Her hair had been colored and styled, and the suit she was wearing, though an appalling mauve color, looked almost stylish. She answered the prosecution's questions calmly and clearly and made a far better impression than Honor had expected, her description of the noises she'd heard from the basement somehow managing to be both understated and chilling. It was only when the defense began their cross-examination of Sally, and Honor intercepted an expectant look between Chip and Suzannah, that she began to worry that something was about to go badly wrong. By the time David Lee made his surprise appearance, it was clear that the whole house of cards was about to collapse.

She'd had to resist the urge to run then, to make her escape swiftly and out of the public eye, had forced herself to sit through the magistrate's sternly worded decision. It was not his job to stitch together the facts of the matter, he said, only to decide whether Suzannah Wells had a case to answer. Which, as Miss Canning appeared to have been otherwise engaged at the time in question, she most certainly did not. What had really occurred was something for others to discover, though he had no doubt that it involved criminal conspiracy and collusion. It was a grave matter—quite apart from the very real reputational and psychological damage suffered by the defendant, it had wasted valuable police and judicial time, which was not a matter that should ever be taken lightly. He would most certainly be making a recommendation to the DPP that the matter be investigated.

The case was dismissed, the defendant discharged.

Honor left the court with the crowd, hoping she would go unnoticed, but her ruse didn't work. The scandal-hungry media scrum surrounded her just as she reached the bottom step of the courthouse, thwarting her escape. For once they were not on her side, not her friends. It was almost the first time in her career that she didn't have a response at the ready, that she hadn't prepared for a worst-case scenario. She should have seen the danger when the footage first appeared, but she'd managed to smooth things over with Andy Stiles, had been confident that that little problem had been permanently put to rest. Honor could always be relied upon to bury the bodies; it was how she'd made her reputation. But this time the hole hadn't been quite deep enough. She'd miscalculated and exposed not only the client but herself.

There was nothing to do but brazen it out. Honor made it clear that she wasn't in the least fazed by the clamoring press, gave a sigh that was full of repressed impatience, raised a disdainful eyebrow.

"This has been a clear miscarriage of justice, based on insinuations rather than facts." Her voice was clear, certain. "Ellie will release a statement about Mr. Lee's allegations shortly, and we will be talking to the DPP. I have no doubt that my client was abducted and held by Suzannah Wells. We *will* get to the bottom of these absurd claims, and my client will be vindicated."

"But what about Sally O'Halloran's testimony, Honor? Is it true that you visited Suzannah's home just before Ellie appeared?"

"Did you visit Sally O'Halloran?"

Honor gave a cool smile. "Both of these women were known to me before Ellie Canning appeared, and both of these visits were entirely unconnected to the case."

"Why did you go down into the basement, Honor?"

She allowed herself a hard laugh. "I think Miss O'Halloran might have been a little confused about that."

The defense team had exited the court, followed by Suzannah, Chip, and Mary, and she was saved from any more scrutiny. As Honor watched the crowd surge back up the steps, Suzannah looked across at her, and the two women made eye contact. Honor turned away quickly, but she had seen the burning anger in the other woman's face. And the questions.

HONOR: JULY 2018

It's not like she'd planned any of it. The girl had approached her outside the office when Honor left in the late afternoon. She had been annoyed at first, thinking she was being hit up for drug money, that the girl was a junkie. Because that's what she looked like at first glance: underfed, half-dressed, her hair in need of a wash.

"You're Honor Fielding, aren't you?" The girl's middle-class accent was jarringly at odds with her appearance.

"Yes, but how . . . ?"

"You made a speech at the Abbey school last year. I'm a student there. Ellie. We had a conversation. You gave me your card—told me to give you a call when I'd finished school." She gave a sickly smile. "Well, I've finished."

Honor recalled the conversation, the girl's confidence, her bold admission. "My God. I remember you. What's happened?"

"I need your help," the girl said, her desperation apparent now. "I really need your help."

The girl's plight had moved Honor unaccountably, and she had made a split-second decision—for once not thinking about motives or possible consequences—and led her to her parked car. She had driven straight to her apartment, the girl slumped beside her in a drugged stupor. She had roused her gently, guided her to the elevator, gone straight up to the penthouse. Dougal was away on a golfing trip, and Honor had planned a lazy night in, a meal of cheese, crackers, and enough wine to blot out her recent humiliation. Instead, she'd ministered to the poor, silly girl—prepared coffee, sat her before the fire, fed her a bowl of reheated minestrone and hot buttered sourdough. She'd poured her a drink, cold white wine, a generous glass. Then let her tell her story.

ELLIE: JULY 2018

Ellie had been cautiously optimistic about the latest plan for a mother-daughter reunion. Her mother had just been released from a stint in rehab and had written to tell Ellie that she'd been out and clean for three months. She'd been set up in a nice flat in Surry Hills, and she wanted to see Ellie. The letter had been followed by a phone call, and her mother had sounded good, better than Ellie could remember. They'd even had a proper conversation, her mum asking her how she was doing at school, listening to her replies. When Ellie told her she had to visit Sydney for the interview at St. Anne's College, her mother had pressed her to visit, suggesting she stay for the holidays.

"I haven't seen you for so long, darlin'," she'd said huskily.

When Ellie had explained that she'd need to study for her trial exams, her mother had pressed even harder. Her place was quiet, she'd said, and she had work at a local café during the day, so she wouldn't bother Ellie. She could study in the flat or go to the library, even, and then the two of them could spend the evenings together. She wasn't much of a cook, it was true, but there was always takeaway, and how fun to curl up on the lounge together at night, watching *The Bachelor* and eating corn chips. The plan appealed—there was no particular joy for Ellie in her current foster home—and the wheels were set in motion. Her mother's story had checked out; her living conditions had been deemed appropriate by the powers that be. Ellie would turn eighteen during the holidays, and after that the department's responsibility was negligible.

Ellie had caught the train up from school, arrived early on the Friday evening, and caught the bus to her mother's flat. From the outside, the flats had seemed respectable enough—an old redbrick block of six, on a tree-lined street. Her mother's place was at the top, and Ellie had tramped slowly up the two flights of stairs, her heavy backpack jolting, and paused, slightly out of breath, when she reached the dim foyer. Before she could knock, her mother's door opened, and a woman came crashing out, red-faced, angry, lugging a flat-screen television. She'd taken no notice of Ellie, pushed past her, still yelling obscenities as she blundered down the stairs.

Her mother followed, dressed in pajama bottoms, an old T-shirt, and socks, an unlit cigarette in one hand, a bottle in the other. She paused momentarily when she saw Ellie, grinned, and gave her a wink before screaming down the stairwell, "Bitch. You're a bitch, Stacey." She'd broken off in a coughing fit and taken a swig from the bottle, then turned to her daughter, who was waiting patiently for her attention, resigned and barely surprised. "G'day, my baby. I forgot you were coming tonight. But good timing, eh? Give us twenty bucks and I'll go get us a feed."

Her mother took the twenty dollars, which Ellie had handed over reluctantly, and stamped down the stairs. Ellie went inside and waited, although her first instinct had been to run. The flat was freezing, filthy, and almost completely bare—the only item of furniture a grimy suede couch in the middle of the lounge room. It was hard to imagine how the department had deemed it suitable for Ellie, although she supposed that the absence of furniture might have been a recent development.

Her mother returned half an hour later, but she brought no food, and there was no possibility of any sort of conversation. Within minutes her mother was dead to the world, curled on the worn carpet. Ellie covered her with a dirty leopard-print fleece she found covering the window in the bedroom, then locked and chained the front door, jamming a chair under the doorknob for good measure. She cleared a space on the couch and sat down. Took a swig from her mother's bottle and considered her options.

There were, of course, girls in her year she could appeal to for a bed for the night—or even for the entire break, if it came to that. The four who had traveled up in the train with her—Annabel, Grace, Eliza, and Sophie—all lived close by in the eastern suburbs. They were her friends, she supposed, as much as any of the Abbey girls could be considered friends, but the thought of having to disclose anything at all about her circumstances, the disaster that was her family life, made her feel physically ill. Being on a scholarship was only just acceptable—being a foster child with a junkie mother was something she didn't need to share. She could imagine the patronizing concern of the parents, the barely hidden disdain of her well-bred peers.

Clearly, there was no possibility of Ellie spending the holidays as planned now that the fantasy of mother-daughter bonding had dissolved. Ellie had the college interview early the next morning, so she was stuck there overnight, but she didn't have to go to sleep just yet. There was nothing to do here—no TV, no internet, just the ragged snoring of her slack-jawed, waste-of-space mother. The night was young, and so was Ellie. She was in the big city, and she was hungry and thirsty—and not just for food.

For as long as she could remember, Ellie had been hungry. When she was a small child, the hunger had often been literal. But as she grew older, even though she'd been given everything she needed in a material sense, that feeling of emptiness remained a constant. By the time she was fourteen, what she hungered for had changed: Ellie didn't want bedtime stories and birthday parties anymore—she wanted booze, boys, drugs, freedom. Not necessarily in that order.

When her Manning High English teacher had told her that the Abbey was offering senior scholarships to bright girls from disadvantaged backgrounds and suggested she apply, Ellie suddenly realized that she was hungry again. Perhaps this could be her way out. Her way up. Perhaps this would satisfy that gnawing pain.

And so it had. For a time, anyway.

But the hunger had gradually returned. And now, after three years of hard slog and considerable success—her academics were first-rate, her behavior impeccable, her reputation stainless—Ellie didn't want any of it. She was over the constant effort, the pretense of virtue, the wank. She was sick of having to work so hard for everything when the other girls had it so easy. They didn't even have to try, most of them: the good life was theirs for the taking, regardless of their efforts, their talents, their intelligence. The school motto was *Laborare ut procul*: work hard, go far. What bullshit when they would all go far regardless.

And Ellie knew—because who didn't?—that there were other options available to smart, good-looking girls like her. There were other ways to get on in the world, other ways of making it. Other ways of satisfying her hunger.

There'd been a speaker at the school at last year's valedictory. She was some hotshot media person . . . what was her title? Celebrity manager? Agent? She'd started out as a country-town newspaper journalist. She spoke about her varied career, and then, as all their visitors inevitably did, about the great potential, the amazing lives they were heading into, the immense privilege they enjoyed, the duty they had to work hard, do good, go far. *Laborare ut* fucking *procul*. The world, she'd said, was their oyster, and they would be its pearls.

Her speech had been lame, but it was the woman's actual job description that had made Ellie sit up and take notice. She made people famous, made people rich. In her introduction, the head had included a list of these people—most of them famous for their sporting prowess, their acting, their beauty, while others were high-profile victims or occasionally criminals. All of them, it seemed to Ellie, had managed to succeed without the years of drudgery and sacrifice she was facing.

After the speech, she'd been introduced to the woman as one of the school's brightest sparks—"so much potential," "we're very excited about her future." Ellie and the woman, who had some weird old-fashioned name—Faith, Hope, Chastity—had stood chatting awkwardly for a few minutes. Ellie had mouthed all the usual crap about her hopes and dreams, the bright, shiny future that lay ahead of her, that gleaming oyster world. The woman had smiled at her vaguely, murmured the expected things, too: *So very lucky, such an opportunity. Make sure you don't waste it.*

Ellie had taken a deep breath. "To tell you the truth, what I'd really like is to be rich and famous," she'd said softly, giving the woman her sweetest smile. "Although I'm not sure how, exactly. Not yet, anyway."

The woman had snapped to attention at that, given her a calculating look. Laughed. She'd dug in her handbag, handed Ellie a business card.

"Give me a call when you finish school," she'd said. "And I'll see what I can do to help."

~

Now, at her mother's, Ellie changed into her tightest jeans, her highest heels. She outlined her eyes, darkened her lips, straightened her hair. She looked not only older but different. Her eyes in the mirror looked back at her harshly, her gaze cool and hard and blank. The innocent schoolgirl was gone; in her place stood someone else entirely.

She walked into the first pub she encountered. It was dim, seedy, and full of half-drunk middle-aged men more interested in the football that was playing on enormous screens than the company. No one had turned to look at her as she walked up to the bar, and the barmaid barely glanced at her ID when she asked for a vodka. She sat at the bar, downed the drink thirstily, ordered another. There was a man sitting alone across from her. Unlike the other clientele, he wasn't watching the screens but had his phone out, was busily texting. He was far more attractive than all the other men in the bar: Asian, with a full head of hair, a taut jaw, good skin, looked fit, well heeled. He wasn't that old, either, only in his early thirties, she thought.

When the man noticed her looking at him and gave an expectant, knowing smile, her hunger sharpened, clarified. She squared her shoulders, took a deep breath, and walked toward him.

From then it had moved quickly. One drink, then two, and then a third, seated at a table at the back of the bar now, a conversation about nothing much. He told her bits and pieces about what he did, who he was. His name was David, he said, he lived in the city, took photographs in his spare time. It was only a hobby really, portraits mostly. She had no idea whether he was telling her the truth, but it didn't matter. Everything she told him was a lie anyway. She said she was twenty-three, that her name was Olivia, that she was studying medicine. That she'd moved here from the Gold Coast and modeled to support herself.

"A medical student, eh? Smart as well as beautiful." His drink went down quickly. He wiped his hand across his mouth and bared beautiful white teeth. "Why don't we head back to my studio," he suggested, the smile never wavering. "Maybe I can add a few things to your portfolio."

It was tempting. Ellie thought hard, did some quick calculations. She could have fun, but she needn't burn all her bridges—she had to go to that interview. One night at her mother's wouldn't be that hard.

"Not tonight."

"Tomorrow then?"

"Why not?"

The next morning she got up early, donned the modest A-line skirt, sensibly low-heeled boots, and black cashmere sweater she'd purchased for such occasions. She pulled her hair back into a low ponytail, applied her makeup sparingly. Her mother was semiconscious when she emerged from the bathroom. Ellie dropped another twenty on her lap, blew her a kiss, grabbed her bag, and left.

The interview was a success. She was given a tour of the college first—taken to see the accommodation, the dining hall, the common rooms, and the grounds—and had been disappointed by the meanness of the bedrooms, the down-at-heel shabbiness of it all. A faint whiff of hospital—bland food and disinfectant—overlaid with a slightly musty smell permeated everything. From the little she saw of them, the students were a dreary bunch—all nerdy-looking, earnest, even tamer than the Abbey girls.

According to her guides, St. Anne's had a reputation for producing the best scholars—professors, surgeons, scientists, politicians, women who ended up devising public policy, sitting on boards. Quiet trailblazers rather than celebrities. Still, it was her best bet if she wanted to go to university; none of the other colleges offered financial support that was quite as generous. And it was better than the alternative—some grubby share house with a bunch of public-school losers and the drudgery of weekend work in hospitality to pay the bills.

The interview panel was surprisingly tough, and there was no way to gauge their attitude toward her, but Mrs. Whittaker, a college alumna and head of the charitable board that provided the scholarships, shook her hand warmly.

"I can't say too much, Ellie," she said. "But I'm confident we'll be seeing you here next year. You're exactly the sort of girl our program was set up for. To be honest, your school recommendation sounded too good to be true, but now that we've met you—well, it's clear you're everything they say you are. And more." She patted her hand. "Now, back to school and get those silly examinations out of the way, and we'll be seeing you back here in the new year."

Ellie gave a shy smile, and her thank-you had been full of gush and enthusiasm, but she almost ran out of the gates at the end of the long gravel driveway, she was so relieved to escape the fusty earnestness of the place.

It wasn't until she climbed onto the crammed bus heading back to the city that she could breathe again, even though she had to stand, pushed up hard against a seat, a dirty old woman glaring and muttering in the corner, a couple of doped-out kids giggling, the middle-aged man behind her moving closer than was strictly necessary.

This was a scene she could deal with, a world she could understand.

Ellie had missed that train home after the interview at St. Anne's. But the missing had been deliberate. There'd been no coffee at the café, no meeting with the friendly middle-aged kidnapper. Instead, she'd made a quick phone call, changed back into her jeans in the toilets at Central, made up her face, let down her hair, and done her best to look as unlike her scholarship-girl self as possible. It wasn't all that hard; perhaps that self was never real to begin with.

And the man she was going to meet offered a world that, right now, felt more real than St. Anne's or the Abbey ever could.

HONOR: JULY 2018

Initially, Honor had tried to persuade her to go back to school. "It's not like you've burned your bridges," she said. "You can tell them you've had a difficult time with your mother, that you couldn't get any work done." She even offered to call them on her behalf. To drive her down there. "And you're a smart girl," she added. "A couple of weeks of not studying?" She clicked her fingers. "So what?"

But the girl was adamant. It's not that she couldn't go back; she wouldn't. She didn't want the college place, didn't even want to go to university. It was all bullshit, anyway. Who had she been kidding? She had no idea what she wanted, but she knew it wasn't going to be found in the hallowed halls of academia, the dull dorms of St. Anne's.

"So what do you think you're going to do, exactly?" Honor was half-exasperated, half-admiring.

The girl shrugged. "I dunno. I'll get a job, find a place to live. I just need to rethink."

Honor suggested she get in touch with her guardians or the school, at the very least—just to let them know, stop them raising the alarm. Hadn't the new term begun? The girl shook her head. Her school had an extra week off. They wouldn't be worried, not yet. Her foster parents wouldn't have a clue—they hadn't been expecting her back before school anyway. And even once term began, it would be a couple of days before the school got worried enough to contact her foster parents. And they'd have to check that she hadn't run off with her mother—something she'd done once or twice when she was younger.

And tracking *her* down could take some time. Anyway, she'd turned eighteen, so officially she was no one's responsibility. The girl explained all this completely dispassionately, without any self-pity: it's just how it was, how it had always been.

The elements of tragedy weren't lost on Honor; she was moved, almost against her will. She told Ellie that she could stay the night in her apartment—there was a spare room, and her husband was away for a few days. If she got a good night's sleep, perhaps her head would be clearer and things would look different. She might change her mind.

"Life's much harder than you think, Ellie," she said quietly. "And for a girl like you, with no family, no connections, it's even more difficult."

She wasn't sure what her own motives were, exactly. This sort of spontaneous kindness was certainly out of character. Perhaps there was an element of empathetic recognition—she'd been feeling raw for the last week or so, had been cast back into the memory of her own adolescent unhappiness by Chip's revelation.

Honor sent the girl for a shower and, while she was in the bathroom, googled her name, suddenly anxious that a search might be already underway. The girl was so young, so vulnerable, and it seemed extraordinary to her that no one had noticed her absence. But there was nothing. The only web reference to her was in the school's newsletter, naming her a member of the year's "leadership team." There was a photo of her receiving a prefect's badge, perfectly demure in her old-fashioned kilt, her hair pulled back into a bun, face scrubbed.

Ellie wandered back into the room, wrapped in a towel. Honor closed the tab, and the browser opened on an old "Whatever happened to" article about Suzannah Wells that she'd been obsessively reading the previous day. A publicity picture of the bikini-clad starlet was juxtaposed with a candid shot, taken five years or so after the series ended.

"Hey," the girl said, peering over her shoulder. "I know her."

"Really? I'd have thought you were a bit young to have watched that rubbish."

"No, not the show, the woman. I mean, I've never actually met her, but I know who she is. She used to live in Manning—she taught drama at the private school there. I used to see her around the place. Do you know her?"

"A little. She lives in the town where I grew up. Enfield Wash."

"Is she your friend?"

"My friend?" Honor shrugged. "Not really."

The girl was still looking at the photograph. "Is she still a teacher?"

"She is. Why?"

"She was involved in some scandal at the school and had to leave. Everyone was talking about it just before I went to the Abbey."

Honor's journalist antenna was up and quivering now. "What sort of a scandal?"

"I dunno exactly. There were all sorts of rumors. I think some girl there accused her of touching her or something. It was probably bullshit, but the parents made the school get rid of her. The girl was expelled anyway. She ended up a big fat loser." She gave a desolate little laugh. "Like me, really."

The girl wrapped her thin arms around her body. Her face was pinched, her eyes huge and darkly shadowed. She looked about twelve.

"What the fuck am I going to do? I really don't want to go back to school, but there'd be no point anyway. The trial exams start on Monday, and I haven't done anything. There were assignments, too. And I need crazy high marks to get into St. Anne's."

"Maybe it's not that bad. Aren't there extenuating circumstances? Maybe you can say that you . . ."

"What?" The girl snorted. "What the fuck can I say? That I forgot to study? Maybe I suddenly got amnesia but I didn't know it? Oh, I know—maybe I could say I was knocked unconscious for the entire break. That I was kidnapped."

And there it was: the seeds of a plot.

HONOR: JULY 2018

The story came together remarkably quickly. It was bizarre, almost unprecedented, but its very improbability made it seem even more authentic. Who could make this shit up? Once upon a time, they'd have needed a knight in shining armor to make it properly satisfying. At the very least, there'd have been a sweetly handsome young prince eager to wake the heroine from her slumber to administer true love's kiss. But women, and girls, too, had moved way beyond that. And the story didn't need it. It already had all the best elements of a fairy tale—the poor girl made good, the single tragic mistake, the imprisonment in the tower, the brave and brilliant escape—without all the complications that true love inevitably brought. Honor might have designed the basic structure, but the girl was a natural confabulator, coming up with plot twists and diversions that would never have occurred to her. In another life, with a different kind of background, maybe Ellie would have been a novelist, a playwright.

Under different circumstances, perhaps Honor would have been disturbed by Ellie's enthusiasm, her willingness, her lack of compunction when it came to destroying the life of an innocent stranger. But the beautiful logic of revenge only accentuated the perfect synchronicity of Ellie's arrival at this particular moment. Honor had nothing but admiration for the girl's singularity of focus, the way she'd thrown herself into it, as if it were a school assessment, a major work for one of her final subjects. There were definite similarities, she supposed: the whole thing could be viewed as a radical performance piece, or some avant-garde installation, with real-life consequences.

And any guilt Honor might have felt on the girl's behalf was easily dispensed with. There was no question of manipulation. Honor had been up front about what the girl was likely to achieve in the way of fame and fortune once the story hit the media. Ellie wasn't doing it for Honor—she was doing it for herself.

When the girl asked what was at stake for Honor, she told her the truth—or as much of the truth as she understood herself.

The girl nodded sagely. "I knew there had to be a man involved somehow. When it's revenge, there always is."

Usually it was Honor's job to fan the flames of a fire that had already been lit, to add some fuel, work hard to control the conflagration. But this time it was different—she got to build the pyre *and* strike the match. This time it was her fire.

Honor had come up with the big-picture stuff, the concept, but the girl was more methodical, smarter about the details, working out who was where when and knowing how to make sure every possible loophole was closed. She wrote down all the days, all the times. She could see all the places where things might go wrong, where there were gaps in the plot, so to speak, and worked out ways to fill them.

It was her idea that Honor visit the house, to take photographs of the room, of the staircase, of the layout of the yard, of the house from the outside and inside, of details that would be impossible to know otherwise. Her idea that she removed some things and planted others.

Ellie had read accounts of other victims' time in incarceration. Of course her imprisonment wouldn't be anywhere near as long or as dramatic as that girl in Germany, the trio in Cleveland, Elizabeth Smart. But every word she said would need to sound real, feel authentic.

She was well aware that however genuine-seeming, her story wouldn't be accepted as tragic, or even all that terrifying: she'd have lost only weeks and not years of her life. There was no way her story would be as explosive as those other girls'. Oh, there was the hideous craziness of the situation—the middle-aged woman kidnapper, the mad old lady. And then there was the girl's own backstory—her difficult past, her heroic transformation, the near ruin of all that hard work. Her escape. "They're going to like that, aren't they?" The girl giggled. "The fact that I managed to get out, that I'm resourceful. I'm literally girl power in action, aren't I?" She'd looked so pleased with herself that Honor wondered if she was actually beginning to believe her own fabrication.

But it was still not enough. They needed another angle. Something big. Bigger than big. Something to get the public sharing and tweeting in outrage.

"What if we say that they were raping me? That would be gross, wouldn't it? Women raping a young girl? People would love that."

Honor considered it, but only for a moment. Displaying the appropriate level of trauma might be difficult for Ellie—who wanted badly to get on with the rest of her life—to sustain. And perhaps it was too grotesque to be media-friendly in the long term.

"Or what if I suggest that the bloke's involved? That could work. The other two would look like victims, too, and I could be singlehandedly kicking the patriarchy's ass. That way the story would be more . . . relevant, don't you think? And it'd be nice for you, too."

Her idea was good. It was so tempting, so zeitgeisty in these #MeToo days, but it was dangerous enough as it was—making him central would only complicate things. And perhaps implicate Honor. She was going to inflict pain on him—it just wouldn't be direct.

In the end it was Honor who came up with it—the accusation that would provide both motivation and sensation and, with an ironic twist, an impossibly elegant coup de grâce, which would make her revenge all the more satisfying. All the sweeter.

It was easier than Honor had ever imagined. So much of it depended only on Ellie's word—and who was going to question her seriously when there was all the DNA evidence to substantiate what she said? No one ever argued against that shit these days. And even if they tried, there was too much—clothes, bodily fluids, hair. It was irrefutable. And then there were Ellie's own memories of her time in captivity, the details that were surely unknowable otherwise.

It was too much, too compelling, and there wasn't even a hair-breadth of doubt. No one would be speculating about whether the whole thing was a setup—not even the flat-earthers on the net. No one seemed to be talking conspiracy, inventing ways in which Ellie could have set the whole thing up. Because why would she? It had been established, and confirmed by Suzannah herself, that she'd never even met Suzannah before. There was no question of revenge, of spite, of payback for past injustices.

Getting the nurse onside was an unexpected bonus. Sally O'Halloran had been at school with Honor, who remembered her as weak, the type of girl who collapsed into defensive, whiny tears when challenged. A coward, easily persuaded.

Honor hadn't been expected at the nursing home, had arrived unannounced and earlier than usual—she had other plans for the afternoon, the evening. There'd been no one at reception, so she'd headed straight to her father's room without bothering to sign in.

The door to her father's bedroom was ajar, and she'd pushed it open farther without a sound. There was a nurse in the room, but she hadn't noticed Honor, had her back to the door, her attention on her patient, who was lying on his bed. Honor couldn't see her face, but she'd recognized Sally O'Halloran's graying bob, her narrow shoulders. She'd recognized, too, the frozen horror of her father's expression.

You filthy old bastard. Sally had hissed the words, but Honor had no trouble making them out. *You dirty old man. What did I say to you yesterday? That if I had to clean up your disgusting mess one more time I'd be rubbing your face in it. I ought to make you eat it. You've got a bell, you stupid prick. Why don't you try ringing it next time?*

Honor's first instinct had been to intervene, to shout at the woman, to report her, see that she was dismissed, deregistered. Arrested. But Honor rarely operated purely on instinct. She knew that even the worst moments could be turned around, put to good use.

She took her phone out of her bag, clicked the video function on, zoomed in. She watched the woman hold the shit-laden sheet close to her father's petrified face, listened to her taunts and threats, heard her father's desperate moans, witnessed his fear.

She backed away, quietly pulling the door closed. She felt vaguely guilty. Perhaps she should have intervened, saved the old man this indignity, but she knew the feeling would pass eventually. Honor had long recognized the importance of holding her fire, biding her time; she understood the way past misdemeanors could provide future advantage.

SUZANNAH: JANUARY 2019

There was no way to avoid the crowd as we exited the courthouse. Hal made a brief statement to the media, emphasizing my innocence, the elaborate nature of the hoax, the cruelty of the perpetrators, the amorality of elements of the press. He was confident there would be an investigation into the crime committed against me. It was clear that there were several persons of interest, including the so-called victim, but at this point the most important thing was that I would be able to resume my interrupted life and career, enjoy my pregnancy, try to forget all about this nightmare.

Chip, Mary, and I stood beside him, blinking into the flashing bulbs.

Questions were shouted, but Hal shook his head. "That's all I'm going to say for now. My client will make an official statement in the next day or two, but for the moment that's it."

I heard the buzz of their voices as we pushed through the crowd. Chip had one arm around my shoulders; his other hand gripped Mary's elbow.

Suzannah, have you got anything to say? Suzannah, how does it feel? Suzannah, are you going to sue? What's next, Suzannah? How do you feel, Miss Squires? Mary, have you got anything to say?

Mary wrenched her arm out of Hal's grip and stepped forward dramatically. She glared out into the crowd, raised an imperious hand to silence them.

"If they'd listened to me in the beginning, we'd never have had to put up with any of this shit."

"What do you mean, Mary? What did you tell them?"

"I told them that little bitch *had* my Chanel pajamas, but I never said she *stole* them. That was the other one. They weren't listening properly, were they?"

The crowd laughed.

Mary kept going, encouraged. "And I always knew that little bitch was lying."

I grabbed her arm, hissed, "Oh God, Mary, can you just not?"

"How did you know that, love?"

I knew what was coming next, but short of throttling her, there was nothing I could do.

"The way she . . ." Mary's mischievous smile faltered. "The way . . ." She stared out at the crowd, her face blank, gaze unfocused. She looked exhausted suddenly, and very, very old. She moved close to Chip, clutched his hand.

"Can we please go home now?" Mary's voice was tremulous, small. "I'm tired."

I had glimpsed Honor as we walked out of the court and could just make her out now, trying to push her way through the onlookers gathered at the bottom of the courthouse steps. I was free; my life and my reputation had been restored. I should have been happy to get out of there, start afresh, move on, forget. But there was still so much I didn't know, that I needed to know, if my—our—life was ever going to return to something resembling normalcy. While Chip and Hal helped a slow and uncertain Mary to negotiate the stairs, I hurried past them, ignoring Chip's surprised words of caution, as well as the avid curiosity of the crowd, then rushed along the footpath, propelled as much by a desire for information as by rage.

"Honor."

She paused, turned slowly, her reluctance evident. "Suzannah."

"Why? Why the fuck, Honor?"

There was the sound of feet pounding.

"Oh Christ." Chip was behind me, his hand on my shoulder. "You don't need this right now, Suze." His voice was low, urgent. "We can do this some other time, some other way."

"She only wants to know why. I think that's reasonable after what she's been through." Honor's voice was icy.

"What you've put her through, you crazy bitch. What you've put us both through."

Her eyes widened. "What I've put *you* through?" She laughed, shook her head sorrowfully. "I take it you haven't told her, have you, Chip?"

HONOR: OCTOBER 1986

His reaction to her news wasn't as she'd imagined it.

The pregnancy was a disaster, on every level. What else could it be? No sane person could think it was anything but a disaster. Honor wasn't even eighteen yet; he was only just. They both had their whole lives ahead of them. She'd been prepared for him to be shocked. Panicked. Had expected a degree of fear, even.

But she'd imagined, too, a degree of concern for her, thought he'd ask how she felt at the very least. And she'd imagined some acceptance of the mutuality of the whole thing—they'd done this together; now they would sort it out together. She wasn't expecting contrition, exactly, but something like it. Surely they were in this sick-making boat together, even if they were both about to scuttle it and swim back to shore.

Oh, she hadn't imagined fanfares or marriage proposals, declarations of undying love. She wasn't stupid. (And she didn't want that anyway—she was going somewhere; she was going to be someone.) But she hadn't imagined this blank disavowal of responsibility, of complicity either. And she could never have imagined him saying what he'd said—his eyes hard, voice cold. He'd looked right through her as if they were strangers, as if what they'd done, what they'd been, had meant nothing to him.

"Why the fuck," he'd asked, "aren't you on the pill?"

He hadn't even bothered to wait for her response. "You can't keep it," he'd said. "I don't want a kid. Fuck. Fuck. Fuck. This is bullshit."

They weren't in the same boat at all. They weren't even sailing on the same ocean.

"And, anyway, how do I know it's mine?"

At that she'd vomited on his shoes. And just for a moment, she'd felt better.

SUZANNAH: JANUARY 2019

"What haven't you told me, Chip? What's all this got to do with you?" He tried to pull me closer, but I stepped away.

He looked at me for a long moment, his expression unreadable. "Honor got pregnant. When we were going out. She had . . ." He faltered, started over. "She had an abortion."

Honor laughed again, but this time it sounded more like a cry.

"I was . . . we were just kids, Suze. There was nothing else we could do." His eyes met Honor's. "I couldn't know, could I? I couldn't know what was going to happen."

HONOR: 2006

Wasn't this the way the universe worked? It was some sort of law, surely. Murphy's Law? Sod's Law? The law of *if I can fuck you over twice, three times, four, even, I will.* There was some immutable natural law that meant it was always going to happen, that it was always going to be exactly like this, and against such forces, Honor never stood a chance.

There had been no grief when she'd aborted that baby. Maybe a pang for a future she could glimpse from the corner of her eye, just a chimera: one where she and Chip raised the child together, where she was welcomed with open arms into the Gascoyne clan, where Honor became one of them, his mother melting into a soggy pile of grandmotherly gratitude when introduced to their baby boy (and this baby would be male, natch; people from those families always had their boys first: hale, hearty, full of that born-to-rule vim and vigor). It had been a ridiculous fantasy when she actually thought about it. The reality was that his parents would have been quietly horrified. They weren't snobs, not exactly—his mother was matronly, decent; his father genial, boozy, a little too fond of women—but they wouldn't have wanted their boy's future curtailed, constrained in such a way.

So that fantasy didn't really have traction, even if Chip himself hadn't been so resolute. And there was no complementary fantasy about being a single mother. She'd never fooled herself about that. Her own family wouldn't have welcomed a baby. Not without a father. Oh, they would have supported her, there was no doubt about that. But to see the disappointment in her parents' eyes—it didn't bear thinking about. Honor had a bright and glorious future ahead of her, her smarts a ticket out and up.

There was only one solution. At the time, it had meant relief from the constant sickness, the headache, the anxiety. There were no real regrets. Not then.

The regrets came later. When she was in her late thirties, and that clock she'd dismissed had begun to tick progressively louder, had chimed the hours, the halves, the quarters. She'd suddenly begun peering into prams, looking enviously at women with swollen bellies, begun thinking that there would be something nice about taking time off, time out, devoting herself to someone who wasn't after fame and fortune, who wanted nothing and everything from her, who might even return something more tangible than 15 percent. And of course there was Dougal. He had felt the same way—had wanted kids from the start, had been waiting more and more impatiently for her to agree. He was old-school to the core, and back then she'd loved that about him, too, his unapologetic conventionality. He was *homo suburbiensis* in the flesh, and the thought of finding herself barefoot and pregnant had become ever more appealing.

Honor had waited a full year before checking, that was what everyone advised. It was always going to take a while, after all that time on the pill; just relax and let it happen naturally, they'd said. She had waited, done her best to relax, but there'd been nothing, not even a scare. Every month she was as regular as clockwork. Ticktock. So after a year, she'd visited the doctor. He was married to a high-profile model she'd agented years before, who'd since left and had her own little brood—twin girls and a boy—in her midforties. Honor had been encouraged by her success. Her husband obviously knew what he was doing.

But her faith hadn't changed his blunt diagnosis: she would never have children. She'd told him about the pregnancy, of course, and the abortion. Had there been any complications after the procedure? She'd thought back. She could remember that the aftermath had been much worse than she'd expected, than she'd been told to expect. She'd had some pain, heavy bleeding—but how much was too much? She remembered that she had felt unwell—her whole body aching, her temperature high—for a week or so after, that she had stayed in bed, had told her mother that it was nothing, just a bad cold, that she didn't need to see a doctor. How could she tell anyone? At the time the potential shame of discovery had seemed far worse than any possible future ramifications. And in a way, she had welcomed the illness; it felt right—a physical manifestation of her barely acknowledged grief over Chip's desertion. But by the end of that week, not only was she three kilos lighter, it was as if the sadness had burned away.

The doctor's nod was solemn, perhaps slightly judgmental. *That could be it. It's not uncommon. Weren't you warned? You should have seen a doctor immediately.* "But maybe," he'd added, as if to lessen the blow, "maybe that early pregnancy wouldn't have gone to term anyway. Perhaps there was damage even then." It was difficult to tell when the damage occurred, or why. And there was no point worrying, really. Her insides were a mess; she would never have a baby. She should consider a hysterectomy to avoid possible complications down the track. Her eggs were fine, he'd told her, looking determinedly cheerful. Such a pity.

She'd done as he'd suggested and agreed to have the lot out. Dougal had cried when Honor broke the news, but she didn't tell him that once upon a time she'd been capable. How could she hit him with that?

But she told Chip, by God she did. It was years later, just after they'd begun their affair. She'd watched with something close to pleasure as he lowered his eyes, shamed by his younger self's behavior, his young man's hardness, his obliviousness.

"Jesus, Honor," he'd said, "I was a little shit. But it would have been impossible then, wouldn't it?"

Looking back, she had thought maybe not, that maybe there were ways they could have done it, ways they could have made it work, that there was a whole alternative life they could have been living had they decided to keep that child. Who knew whether what either of them had now was better? Who could ever know? But at least he, too, had been denied the pleasures of parenthood. At least the universe had granted her that.

And then it hadn't.

HONOR: JANUARY 2019

Honor drove a few blocks from the court, well away from the slowly dispersing crowd. She pulled over and parked under a tree, tried to regulate her breathing, calm her mind. She needed to call Dougal. Ellie would have to be told, too—her exposure had been more damaging than Honor's—but for the moment she was safe at her media-free resort. Honor needed to talk to Dougal first to see if he could see some way out—for both of them. His advice had been invaluable over the years, whenever her clients' fuckups had proved too much even for her; he was knowledgeable when it came to legal ramifications and the myriad ways around them. And he had the contacts, would know who could help her make it all go away. Even if he wasn't all that keen on helping Ellie, there was no way he would refuse to support Honor.

She wasn't looking forward to telling him about the questions surrounding her own behavior but was certain he would believe her version of the story. She had already worked out how to frame it: she would admit to visiting Suzannah's but claim they were mistaken about the dates. And her visit to Sally O'Halloran, that could be easily explained, too. Honor had had some concerns about her father's treatment—wasn't it natural that she would visit an old classmate, get her private opinion of the nursing home? The idea that this proved collusion or conspiracy was ludicrous.

She made the call, keeping her voice low, as if she were at risk of being overheard. Dougal's voice was similarly subdued. He'd heard the news, he said, had been waiting for her call.

"I couldn't phone straightaway," she said. "The media were every-where. It was insane. You can imagine."

"I think I can."

She got straight to the point. "You do know that it was all just rub-bish?" She was surprised by her own sudden breathlessness.

"About you visiting Suzannah's? And talking to the nurse?"

"Yes, that, of course. You know I didn't have anything to do with it. But I'm talking about Ellie, too. That witness, David Lee—he's lying, it's been fixed somehow. They must have—"

"Honor—"

"Surely there's something we can—"

"Honor." His voice was stern. "David Lee was telling the truth. Everything Ellie Canning said was a lie. From beginning to end. She was never in that house. I know it."

She felt cold suddenly.

"And you know it, too."

She ignored his final assertion. "What do you mean, you know it?"

"Because I was the one who told the defense about David Lee."

"What?"

"He was trying to contact you. You'd gone out somewhere and left your phone at home, and I picked it up. He told me he was ringing to tell you he had information about Ellie Canning."

"Why would he call me? Why not the police?"

"Perhaps he was ringing to blackmail you. I don't know. I don't care, to be honest. But I wanted that information, so I paid him for it. He told me that she'd been with him—sent me the photos, the footage."

"And you sent it to Andy Stiles?" It was impossible to disguise her fear.

"I did it for you. I thought Ellie was trouble. I was trying to protect you." He paused. "But it turns out you didn't need protecting. When I heard what went on in court today, it all suddenly fell into place. You buying the property up the road from Gascoyne's. All those visits back to see your father, pretending to be the dutiful daughter. Encouraging me to stay home, saying you needed the peace and quiet, that you wanted time alone. My God. I don't know how I managed to be so blind. You and Chip—childhood sweethearts!—how you must have laughed."

"Dougal, I—"

"It must have almost killed you when he chose Suzannah. After all that effort."

"I don't know what you're talking about." Even she could tell that her words lacked conviction.

"Of course you do." He laughed, but there was no joy in the sound. "You know exactly what I'm talking about, Honor. You always have. It's a talent. I used to admire it, that ability you have to listen properly, to work people out, spot their weaknesses, and exploit them." His voice was full of a deep, dark sorrow. "I just never imagined you'd need to exploit mine."

SUZANNAH: JANUARY 2019

Chip pulled up in front of the house.

"I'm just going to go home and check on a few things. I'll be back as soon as I can."

He helped Mary out, and we both stood by the idling car and watched her climb up the veranda steps. She gripped the railing, dragging each foot onto each stair slowly and painfully.

"Actually," I said, "I might wander over when she's asleep. I feel like a walk."

"A walk? Now? In this heat? Are you sure that's a good idea?" He paused, looked at me worriedly. "And don't you think we need to talk?"

I laughed. "Oh God. No. Not today. I just can't." I gave him a reassuring smile. "And anyway, it's history."

"It might be history, but it almost—"

I cut him off. "Honestly, Chip. Can't we just forget it for now? I'd rather talk about the future. Actually, I'd rather talk about the price of mutton."

"Fine." I could hear his relief. "As a matter of fact, there have been some interesting developments in the sheep industry. We'll have plenty to discuss."

I laughed. "How about I just wander over when it cools down? I need to get out. It feels like I've barely moved since this all began. I'll come over through the paddock, and we can walk back over together."

He frowned. "I don't know that you should really be out in the dark alone."

"It won't be that dark. What if I bring the dogs?"

That almost satisfied him. "Bring a torch. And your phone." He ran his hand down the firm curve of my belly. "And walk slowly."

"I don't really have much choice about that, do I?"

"Probably not." He kissed me lightly and slid back into the car.

I poked my head through the open window. "And can you put a bottle of something in the fridge? We need to do something to celebrate."

Mary was surprisingly compliant. She barely ate her toasted cheese sandwich, which was pretty much the only dinner I could concoct with our dwindling supplies—a loaf of frozen bread, cheese, butter, some wrinkled apples.

We'd ordered new pajamas online, and they'd just arrived the day before. They were short-sleeved cotton pajamas, not quite the same as her lovely silk "Chanel" pair, but at least the colors were similar, and she was eager to put them on and go to bed, happily forgoing her bath and the nightly game of Trouble. Instead, she listened to a few chapters of the abridged version of *Heidi* we seemed to have been reading forever. We were up to the part where Heidi put on all her clothes to travel down to the city with her aunt.

Mary laughed. "I did that once, you know."

"Did what?"

"Once when I was coming back from LA, I couldn't afford to pay for my extra luggage, so I wore half of my outfits under this big coat. I was so huge, I could barely squeeze into my seat. And it was bloody uncomfortable. But I was coming back for good."

"You were?" This was a story I'd never heard.

"Yeah. It was just after me and Jonno split up. I'd had enough. I thought I'd come back to Australia. I was going to go back to Sydney, try and make a go of it with you. See if I could actually do the mother thing, you know, settle down, make some sort of family."

"So what happened?"

She didn't respond. I could see her eyes drifting, losing focus.

"So why didn't you come back, Mary?" I prodded. "You flew to Sydney, and you were coming back for good?"

"I . . . oh, it was just the usual."

"What do you mean?"

"I met someone at the airport. This guy I used to know. He offered me some blow." She shrugged. "Anyway, I didn't make it home that time." She patted my hand. "But I'm here now, aren't I? We're together." She wriggled down in the bed and gave a deep, satisfied sigh.

"We are." I closed the book, pulled the blankets up under her chin, and tucked her in. Her eyelids were fluttering.

I turned out the lamp. Kissed her forehead. "Night, Mary."

"Night, kiddo."

She closed her eyes and turned on her side away from me. As I started down the hallway, I could just make out her quiet singing.

I soon will be in New Orleans, and then I'll look around, and when I find Suzannah, I'll fall upon the ground.

But if I do not find her, then I will surely die,

And when I'm dead and buried, oh, Suzannah, don't you cry.

HONOR: JANUARY 2019

She had called his number over and over, left message after message, but there had been no response. She had sent dozens of texts, desperate missives, rambling and incoherent. She had abased herself in every way possible, begged forgiveness, promised the world. Nothing.

When a message finally lit up her screen, it wasn't even Dougal, but an unknown number.

> Just heard them bitchs have got away with it. J & D are goin for
> a drive up Wash rd tonite. Cheryl

Honor read the message twice. She thought about calling back. Thought about calling the police.

Revenge: they say it's best served cold, but who knows when it's digestible?

SUZANNAH: JANUARY 2019

I waited until Mary was asleep, then called the dogs, who were both immediately eager for adventure, despite the late hour. They rushed ahead of me when they realized we were heading for their home, barking excitedly, dashing off to snuffle in the bushes before running back to check on me. It was dark now, darker than I'd expected, the only light from a small sliver of moon and my flickering phone torch. I trod cautiously, not wanting to trip or stumble, the new house a brightly lit beacon at the end of the rough path. I paused for a moment as I approached. Chip was facing the kitchen window, a glass of wine in his hand, gazing out into the dark. I waved my little light a few times to reassure him, the dogs rushing forward noisily. He returned my wave and walked toward the veranda door. I heard his even footsteps across the timber floor and then faster as he walked down the driveway to meet me.

The dogs reached him first, raced around him, yapping. He clicked his fingers, and they immediately ceased their antics. Although they sat obediently, their pleasure in seeing him was still evident in the swishing of their long, elegant tails, their hopeful panting.

"I hope you don't expect that sort of behavior from your women."

He clicked his fingers again, feigning disappointment when I refused to obey. "You probably shouldn't be sitting out here in your condition anyway. You could . . . well, I'm sure it's not good."

"So what should I be doing?"

I knew what I should be doing at this point, what anyone sensible, anyone else in my position (but who has ever been in this particular position?) would suggest: that we should debrief, decide on next steps, ways forward. But right then I didn't want to be sensible; I didn't want to think.

"Oh, I dunno exactly"—he held out his hand—"but I'm thinking it involves a medicinal glass of wine, some soft music, and er . . . putting your feet up."

I took his hand, let him pull me toward him.

~

I dreamed I was standing beside my grandfather at a barbecue, holding a platter he was loading with badly burned sausages. Suddenly my grandmother was there beside me, pulling the heavy platter from my fingers. "Where's your mother?" she asked, and her voice was filled with the familiar disappointment-tinged exasperation. "This is Mary's job, not yours." The acrid smoke from the burning timber stung my eyes, and Nan's form blurred as my eyes filled.

I woke up, my eyes still watering, a tickling at the back of my throat. Chip was fast asleep beside me, pushed up against the cushions, snoring gently. The french doors were wide open to catch any night breeze, and there was a smell of burning in the air, a slight haze. Even from my position on the lounge, I could see a faint orange glow coming from the direction of my house. I nudged Chip and, when there was no response, pushed him hard. By the time he was up and dialing triple zero on his home phone, I was heading for the path, with Rip and Ned racing ahead of me, barking up a storm.

The house was ablaze. It was terrifying—the sight, the smell, the sound, the heat. It was a scene I'd seen countless times in films, on the news, but the reality didn't compare. The flames already seemed to be everywhere but somehow kept expanding, like some monstrous devouring beast that had broken its shackles and was intent on making its escape—licking under doors, bursting through windows, running along the guttering and onto the roof. I edged toward the bottom of the veranda steps, moving as close as was bearable, and screamed out desperately, but I couldn't even hear my own words over the roar. There was nothing I, or anyone, could do. If Mary was still inside, there was no way in—and no way out either.

I staggered back on legs that were barely working, unable to do anything other than watch, helpless, as the beast consumed everything in its path.

There was a momentary lull in the angry roar, and I heard, but only just, the shrill barking of the dogs. In all the terror, I had forgotten them completely, but there they were, safe, at the end of the breezeway, barking and scratching frenziedly at the laundry door. I was across the yard and had wrenched open the door before I'd even managed to process what I was doing. And there inside was Mary, sitting cross-legged on the cement floor, the washing basket upended, its contents in a pile before her. She'd changed out of her pajamas and despite the heat was wearing a pair of flannelette pajama bottoms belonging to Chip and an old T-shirt. The dogs rushed at her, licking her face, barking exuberantly. She pushed them away and looked up at me, her expression sorrowful.

"I wanted my old Chanel pajamas. That pair you bought me weren't right—they were scratchy. I thought maybe you'd put my old ones in the laundry basket, but they're not here."

~

"Nice pj's, Mary," Chip said later. Mary was lying on a stretcher while a paramedic checked her oxygen levels. "But don't think you're keeping them."

She gave a luxuriant stretch. "I've decided I'm only wearing night-dresses from now on. I remember my mum always said it was important to let your lady parts get some fresh air at night. There's not much airing going on with these things." She flicked the elastic waistband. "You should probably be more careful of your parts, Mr. Chips. You don't want to damage them, do you?"

The paramedic attending her looked appalled, but Chip laughed. "Last time I looked my, er . . . parts were doing fine, Mary. Anyway, how are you? No scratches?" He turned to the paramedic. "Is she okay?"

He nodded. "She's been very lucky."

We all looked over at the house. The flames were finally under control, but the homestead was beyond salvaging. Mary and I were homeless, but we were both alive.

I knew there was probably no point, but I asked anyway. "What I don't understand is why you stayed, Mary. Why didn't you get out of the house? The doors aren't locked. You could have just walked out through the laundry."

"It was the dark," she said. "I looked out that window, and I saw how dark it was, and I didn't want to go out there on my own. I was scared I'd get lost. But I knew you'd come." She paused for a moment, added wistfully, "To be honest, I was hoping it'd be Chip."

There was no answer to that.

ABDUCTED: THE ELLIE CANNING STORY

A documentary by HeldHostage Productions © 2019

VOICE-OVER

Only a few hours after Suzannah Wells's sensational committal trial, Canning, holidaying at an exclusive resort in the Pacific, was interviewed by her then boyfriend, Jamie Hemara. During the interview, which was livestreamed on the 180Degrees YouTube channel, Canning claimed that the accusations against Wells had been fabricated by Honor Fielding, and that her own participation had been secured under duress, when she was in a state of mental confusion and fragility.

[Cut to footage from 180Degrees interview]

CANNING

I'd spent almost three weeks as a virtual sex slave, drugged out of my brain—and I know that there are people who will say that I asked for it, but I really didn't understand what I was letting myself in for. I'm not saying I went with David Lee against my will or anything—but the whole setup was just way out of my experience. I was a total wreck for months afterward. I was having flashbacks and panic attacks—all that was real. At the time I was so glad to be out of that place and so grateful to Honor, who'd given me somewhere to stay—that I felt as if she'd actually saved me. I think I would have done practically anything she wanted me to do. I'm not trying to make excuses—what I did was, like, totally wrong—but I was super easy to manipulate. So when Honor told me that Suzannah had once imprisoned a girl and gotten away with it, I really believed she deserved it. I'd heard the rumors about that girl in Manning, so it actually seemed legit. I now know it was stupid and wrong, and I really can't apologize enough for what I put Suzannah and her family through . . . But once the story became public, it was so big, and so overwhelming. It was like I was stuck in this nightmare and it just kept getting worse—there was absolutely no one I could talk to, tell the truth to. I was stuck in this terrible tangle of lies . . .

VOICE-OVER

In early February 2019, both Honor Fielding and Ellie Canning were arrested for perverting the course of justice. Canning, who agreed to act as a witness for the prosecution in return for criminal indemnity, was released without being charged. Honor Fielding was released on bail. A trial date has yet to be set.

Fielding, who continues to maintain her innocence, launched a civil suit against Canning in April 2019.

David Lee, the self-styled soft-porn "artrepreneur" who testified for the defense at the committal hearing, is currently under investigation by the Fair Work Commission, following recommendations by the presiding magistrate.

Ellie Canning remains a popular figure in Australia and internationally. In spite of Wells's exoneration and Canning's own admission of guilt, a recent online poll found that 48 percent of people continue to believe Ellie Canning was abducted by Wells. Paris-based cosmetics giant L'Andon has honored its contract with Canning, despite pressure from critics, and its Escape line is already an industry top seller.

Canning is a regular guest on a variety of talk shows, including ABC's *Q&A* and *The Project*, and has appeared on *I'm a Celebrity, Get Me Out of Here* and *Dancing with the Stars*. She also pens a popular "iGen" advice column for the *Guardian* and is writing a self-described "ficto-memoir," which is due to be published in all territories in late 2019.

Canning has spent the last six months attending drama lessons at the esteemed Finch Institute in Sydney. She has been cast as the lead in an upcoming HBO drama based on the life of Violet Charlesworth and will shortly be relocating to Los Angeles. Canning plans to establish a scholarship for disadvantaged girls at her former boarding school.

According to online sources, Honor Fielding's marriage to millionaire financier Dougal Corrigan has ended, despite his initial public declaration of faith in his wife's innocence. Their Sydney penthouse was sold for an undisclosed sum. Fielding, who resigned as CEO of Honor Talent and relocated to Byron Bay, is also said to be writing a memoir.

~

Suzannah Wells and Chip Gascoyne were married in February 2019, and their son was born in early March. Wells has declined to take legal action against either Canning or Fielding, despite pressure from the NSW director of public prosecutions. She has consistently refused to speak to the press about her ordeal. Mary Squires, who continues to live with the couple, has been featured in a Channel Ten documentary on dementia and has recently appeared in several advertisements for Ben & Jerry's choc-mint ice cream.

Despite intense speculation, no credible motive for the false accusations has ever been established.

AUTHOR NOTE

An Accusation is a contemporary take on the Canning Affair—an eighteenth-century criminal case that enthralled a nation, including some of the great legal and literary minds of the era, and one that still remains unsolved. Josephine Tey transposed the drama to postwar England in her novel *The Franchise Affair*, and my own (somewhat fanciful) twenty-first-century transportation owes much to her wonderfully wry, understated rendering of this "ridiculous and contemptible" tale. If you've never read it, you should.

ACKNOWLEDGMENTS

As ever, thanks are due to many.

To my agent Alexis Hurley for, well, so many things: faith, energy, excellent advice, encouragement, patience, and perspicacity, for starters.

To my publishers and editors, Alicia Clancy, Mary Rennie, Dianne Blacklock, Nicola Robinson, Laura Barrett, and Sara Brady, who miraculously pulled all the disparate, sometimes invisible, and occasionally nonexistent, threads together.

To the brilliant people at Lake Union and HarperCollins Australia who've worked so hard behind the scenes to get this book—and me!—out into the world in the best possible shape: Alice Wood, Pam Dunne, Darren Holt, Kellie Osborne, Steve Schul, Danielle Marshall, Nicole Burns-Ascue, Rosanna Brockley, Laywan Kwan, Gabe Dumpit, and Jacqueline Smith.

To my film agent Addison Duffy: for reading my first draft—and then wanting to read it again.

To my writing family: Rebecca James, Susan Francis, and Shari Kocher, who read and reread and reassured me that it could be done. And occasionally told me how.

To my early readers, friends, and family, who offered much-needed advice and encouragement: Mark Battisti, Marie Battisti, Marcia Huber, Jenny James, and Prue Macfarlane.

To Jeffrey Braithwaite, Kristiana Ludlow, and the rest of the CHRIS team at AIHI, for giving me much-needed time—and something else to think about.

To my family: Darren, Sam, Cat, Abi, Darcy, Nell, and Will. You know what for.

ABOUT THE AUTHOR

Photo © 2013 EMG Photography

Wendy James is the author of eight novels, including the bestseller *The Golden Child*, *The Mistake*, and *The Lost Girls*. Her debut novel, *Out of the Silence*, won the 2006 Ned Kelly Award for best first crime novel and was short-listed for Australia's prestigious Nita May Dobbie Award for women's writing. *The Golden Child* was short-listed for the 2017 Ned Kelly Award for crime fiction. Wendy has a PhD from the University of New England and works as an editor, teacher, and researcher. She lives in the coastal city of Newcastle with her husband and two of their four children.